Unlawful Kingdom

A Legion Archer
Book #6

J. Clifton Slater

A Legion Archer series and the associated books are the creations of J. Clifton Slater. Any use of *Unlawful Kingdom*, in part or in whole, requires express written consent. This is a work of fiction. Any resemblance to persons living or dead is purely coincidental. All rights reserved.

Weaving stories around history requires planning and a commitment to the process. In the daily writing, my thoughts bounce from antiquity to dialogue to the movement of characters. The person who keeps the story on the right path is Hollis Jones. *Unlawful Kingdom* emerged from piles of research notes and sheets of ideas to become a novel because Hollis Jones was on the job. For her steady hand and red pen, I am grateful.

And, my sincerest 'thanks' goes to you. My readers are the reason I can spend my days doing research and writing stories. Rendering a hand salute to you for being there for me. Ready, two!

If you have comments, contact me:
www.GalacticCouncilRealm@gmail.com

To follow my progress on upcoming books, read blogs on ancient topics, or to sign up for my monthly Author Report, go to my website:
www.JCliftonSlater.com

Unlawful Kingdom

Act 1

The storm of success that followed the capture of New Carthage delivered a windfall of goods, coins, and allies. It also brought envy. In the aftermath of the victory, waves of jealousy crept up to the soles of the young General's boots. Yet, the detractors stopped short of touching him. That would come later, after the accolades faded and the forces opposed to Cornelius Scipio had a chance to gather evidence against him.

Meanwhile, Cornelius solidified his position through negotiations and threats, sent precious metals to Rome, and hardened the Republic's positions along the northern coast of Iberia. Promises made and promises kept, the actions satisfied the Senators who voted to elevate him to Prorogatio of Iberia. With the home front secured, Cornelius turned his attention to the Carthaginian and tribal menace. Only then did the black shroud of betrayal get cast, and the shrill voices of his accusers begin a choir of condemnation.

With its culture of war and warriors, fertile land, and rich deposits of ore, the Iberian Peninsula was on the brink of becoming a new power in the Mediterranean. The region had sustained the operations of Hannibal Barca for over nine years and entertained a serious expansion of the Carthaginian society. In light of the power gathered by taking New Carthage, an allegation arose in the Senate of Rome. His enemies feared the Republic was in danger from a King Scipio and his Unlawful Kingdom?

Welcome to 209 B.C.

Chapter 1 – Behavior, Capacity, True Freedom

Cornelius Scipio sat alone in a chamber. A predawn breeze caused candle flames to dance and the light to flicker over his troubled face.

When the Prorogatio of Iberia installed his headquarters on Temple Hill, the clerics of the Healing God enthusiastically catered to his every wish. Especially in the aftermath of the massacre of New Carthage residents, they feared displeasing the young Roman General.

"I dread the daylight," Cornelius announced.

His voice bounced off the walls and ceiling. Out of the candlelight, Sidia Decimia stood silently by the darkened doorway. The bodyguard assumed Scipio spoke to the God Asclepius.

"I said," Cornelius insisted, "I fear the coming daylight."

Realizing he was being addressed, Sidia offered.

"You've seen the mines at Mazarrón, sir. Counted the captured ships-of-war and merchant vessels, twice, and shuffled the sailors and oarsmen," he listed. "Scrutinized the city's bolt throwers, and onagers, from their base beams to their counter stanchions and every fiber in the torsion cables. Plus, you've overseen the execution of Carthaginian prisoners, and for some reason, allowed the release of spearmen from Iberian tribes. After all that, General, what could possibly give you apprehension?"

"Following every battle, Hannibal Barca frees any captured man not from Rome," Cornelius informed Sidia. "Many return to their tribes and encourage their chiefs to become allies with the Carthaginian. I need that layer of support."

"The spearmen, sir, are your problem with daylight?"

"No, Sidia. My worry concerns the last uncounted cache from our campaign."

Cornelius approached the door. To Sidia, he appeared as a dark silhouette. Even when the shadow stopped a couple of feet away, the bodyguard remained stationary.

"New Carthage's treasury?" Sidia guessed.

"Senior Magistrate Silanus completed an accounting of the treasury yesterday. We know to the last bronze coin what's there," Cornelius responded. "Coins aren't the issue. At daylight, Centurions will begin parading the hostages held by the Carthaginians before me."

"Will you free them like you did the tribal spearmen?"

"And there is the reason I fear daylight. I don't know," Cornelius admitted. "I've been imagining myself in the Lyceum, sitting on a bench, surrounded by Plato, Aristotle, and Socrates."

"You're very clever, sir," Sidia pointed out. "With you in the company of those Greek philosophers, I assume it's a lively discussion."

"Not as lively as you might think," Cornelius told him. "I was searching for an answer. But as they often do in their lessons, the Greeks give examples and leave the solutions up to the individual."

"What solutions did you find, sir?"

"Plato taught that human behavior flows from desire, emotion, and knowledge. While Aristotle believed the enslaved naturally lacked the capacity to deliberate, and thus for their own good, they must remain slaves. And

Socrates advised that all human life is like slavery, and true freedom exists only in death."

"Behavior, capacity, or true freedom," Sidia pondered. "Is there a solution in that, sir?"

"Only if I'm wise enough to apply the correct teachings to the right hostage," Cornelius replied. He blew the air from his lungs, inhaled, and ordered. "Optio Decimia, open the doors. Let's see what the day holds for me."

***

Cornelius marched from the tranquil chamber into the temple. Immediately, the Tribunes, Centurions, and Velites stopped, and froze in place. From a myriad of voices and the clicks of combat sandals echoing around the temple, the space fell silent.

"I want measured, hushed, and respectful tones," Cornelius instructed. He pointed to the center of the temple and the massive statue of Asclepius and his snakes. "During these hearings, we will have decorum. As is befitting the home of the God of Healing."

Typically, military tribunals lacked the sophistication of civilian trials. Partly because the military court didn't allow a rowdy crowd of citizens to voice their opinion after each decision. Hence, without an audience or the need for lengthy legal arguments, the presiding officer had the ability to quickly dispose of cases. Unless the judge, like Cornelius, needed to weigh the results carefully and evaluate the advantages and drawbacks for each of his verdicts.

Cornelius marched to a raised chair at a table where a pair of clerks waited. He picked up a glass of wine from the table and lifted it in salute. Before he took a taste, Sidia Decimia stepped up behind him.

"Sir, I'd prefer you drink from this glass," the bodyguard suggested. He filled a second glass from a wineskin and handed it to Cornelius.

"Do you think someone would try and poison me in the temple of healing?" Cornelius inquired.

"Of course not, sir," Sidia assured him. "Definitely not in the temple of healing with exotic tonics on every shelf."

Behind his back, the bodyguard handed off the full glass. A servant would dump the suspect wine on the dirt outside the temple. Not because it was a known danger, but out of caution to protect the Prorogatio of Iberia.

**

Colonel Lucius Marcius entered the temple and marched to Cornelius.

"Good morning, sir," the Battle Commander greeted him.

"Take a seat Colonel and we'll see how good it is."

After sliding onto a chair beside General Scipio, Marcius accepted a glass of wine from a servant.

"God Asclepius, we thank you for lending your counsel to these proceedings," Cornelius exclaimed before taking a sip. A moment later, he directed. "First Centurion Turibas, bring forward the first hostage."

"Wings Legion, General Scipio," Turibas bellowed while snapping off a salute.

Any duty where Centuries preformed near their General was prestigious and a source of pride. The exuberance of Wings' First Centurion testified to the fact. Wings hadn't lost enough men in the taking of New Carthage that the Velites might seek revenge on the hostages. This made Wings Legion the natural choice to handle the important captives. Proud of the assignment, and with two Centuries station in and around the temple, his yell could simply be a recognition of the duty. Or, Turibas screaming his Legion's name in the presence of Marcius, the Colonel of Bolt Legion, might be a little Legion against Legion razzing.

The reason didn't matter to General Scipio. He did need to enforce civility in the temple and cut short the proceedings by reducing the ceremonial speech.

"If we formerly acknowledge my rank and your Legion for the retrieval of every hostage, we'll spend half the day issuing sentiments to my authority," Cornelius warned. "And while my admiration for Wings of Nortus Legion is second to none, let this be the last time it's spoken of today. Wings Legion."

"Sir, Wings Legion," Turibas replied before marching to a doorway on the far side of the temple.

***

From behind the line of columns supporting the roof of the temple, a Tribune of Artillery ran Cornelius' words through his mind. On the second run through, he twisted them into phrases that served his purpose.

"Instead of placing his headquarters on Citadel Hill, Cornelius Scipio selected the Temple of Asclepius to show his authority came from a God. And while sitting on a throne, he insisted that everyone show an emotional and sentimental response to his royal authority, rather than embracing the titles bestowed on him by the Senate of Rome. Further, Cornelius Scipio insulted a Legion of Rome by ordering the attendees to let this be the last time the Legion would be spoken of."

A junior staff officer marched from the exterior porch of the temple to the location of the spy.

"Tribune Furia, we've positioned the onager on the upper terrace," he reported. "The Centurion said to get your approval before we hauled the stones up the hill."

Justus Furia looked down on the Junior Tribune.

"An excellent idea," Justus agreed. "You never want to burden your Legionaries with extraneous tasks. It's bad for morale. Let's go check the launch position."

The tall Tribune strolled from the temple with the Junior Tribune rushing to keep up.

***

In the temple, First Centurion Turibas shoved a hostage into motion. The man moved in hesitant steps as if preparing to spin around and fight his guard.

When the pair approached Cornelius Scipio and Lucius Marcius, the captive began strutting forward. Sidia moved up to protect Cornelius. The bodyguard held a Legion dagger at hip level as a warning to the hostage to stay away from the General.

"Sirs, may I present to you Biurdiki of the Turdules Tribe," the First Centurion announced.

When he noticed Sidia's blade, Turibas gripped the hostage's shoulder and pulled him back. A silent challenge flashed between the bodyguard and the hostage.

Trying to ease the tension, Marcius noted, "The tribesman's face shows signs of struggle."

"No doubt he is a son of Mars, sir," Turibas reported. "And he tries to prove it at every opportunity. Because of his status, our Velites have shown an amazing amount of restraint in dealing with him."

7

"I am Biurdiki," the hostage stated. "Brother to the King of the Turdules. You can't hold me. No invader can."

Marcius bent to Cornelius and whispered in his ear, "The Turdules are from south central Iberia. They have silver, copper, and iron mines at Pozo Rico, fertile land in the low country, and sheep pastures on the slopes of Guadalcanal."

"That sounds like an ally I could use," Cornelius remarked.

"No, sir. The Turdules have armor and steel weapons. And they know how to use them," Marcius advised. "Seven different tribes surrounded their land. To protect their resources, the Turdules learn to fight from a young age."

"We are the best warriors in Iberia," Biurdiki bragged. "We fear no enemy and serve no master beyond the people of Turdules."

"If you're such a good fighter," Cornelius inquired, "why were you a prisoner of the Carthaginians?"

"Mazarrón," Biurdiki spit the word out like a curse. "They have a seaport and can export their inferior metals by ship. Hasdrubal Gisco demanded we stop raiding the mines at Mazarrón. To ensure my brother stopped the raids, Gisco demanded a safeguard. Me. But now, I will go home, and triple the raids."

Cornelius dipped his head and put his fingertips to his temples. It appeared as if he was listening to someone. Finally, he nodded and looked up to see Jace Kasia enter the temple.

"Senior Tribune Kasia. How goes the preparations?" Cornelius asked the staff officer from Wings Legion.

"Sir, we're setting the last onagers on the hillside," Jace answered. "If the Carthaginians come, and try to cross the north bay, we'll drown them with rocks from the sky."

"Very good," Cornelius commented. Then he pointed to the tribesman. "This is Biurdiki, a powerful and deadly warrior. And for reasons too long to list, other than his brother is a King, I must give him true freedom. Any ideas?"

"Generally, sir, I'm not the one you want for a diplomatic mission," Jace proposed. "But in this case, I'll be happy to oblige."

Jace strolled to a pair of light infantrymen from his Legion.

"I need your shields and one of your spears for the tribesman," he instructed.

"Sir, if he has a spear, shouldn't you have one as well?"

"It's a diplomatic mission," Jace reminded the Legionary. Drawing his skinning knife, he directed. "Give him the war gear."

***

While Biurdiki received a spear and a shield, Jace strapped the other shield to his left arm. When he finished, he raised his right hand and waved at the tribesman.

"Through the generosity of General Scipio, you are free to leave," Jace explained. "Unfortunately, there are Velites blocking every exit, except the one behind me."

Biurdiki shifted his grip on the shaft and stepped towards Jace.

"Then I'll go over your dead body, Latian," he threatened.

From the very first step, the tribesman quickly pushed off the floor, breaking into a sprint. The tip of his spear rammed dead center into Jace's shield. Well aimed and solid, the force should have driven Jace back and unbalanced him.

***

The strike might have taken an average shield bearer off his feet. But the Cretan Archer learned personal combat in a small circle, against a stronger and more experienced opponent.

"Your advantage," Zarek Mikolas said to the boy sprawled on the ground.

"What advantage?" Jace cried. *"If it's not the tip knocking me down, it's the shaft, or the butt end. How is that an advantage for me."*

"As I started to say. Your advantage, when a foe attacks with full force, is you know where he'll go next. Your job, then, is to put your weapon where he doesn't expect it."

"A lot of good that does me when I'm on my back."

"For now, that's true," Zarek agreed. *"But look where I am. My legs, my arms, my head and neck extension, and the twist of my hips. What do you see?"*

Jace Kasia blinked to clear the tears of frustration and studied the unstable stance. The overextension of his teacher's arms, the awkward placement of his feet, and hips that had expended all their power, were obvious if one took notice. In short, the all-out assault by his teacher left Zarek Mikolas vulnerable to a counterattack.

***

Jace rolled to his left, causing the spear to glance off the shield. Spinning in a full circle, the Cretan Archer extended his right hand. The short blade of the skinning knife reached the overextended tribesman and slit the side of his neck.

Momentum carried Biurdiki two more steps before the brother of the King of Turdules dropped to his knees.

"Socrates said true freedom is death," Cornelius proclaimed. "Carry the word to the people of Turdules that the warrior known as Biurdiki died in combat, a free man."

Jace signaled three infantrymen to remove the body. As they lifted the corpse, two Priests of Asclepius raced over to wash away the pool of blood.

"Hold," Cornelius ordered. "Leave the evidence of my decision for the other hostages."

Using their shields, light infantrymen crowded the priests away from the wet spot. During the brief confrontation, First Centurion Turibas appeared with a woman and two children.

"No. No," a clerk groaned.

"Is there a problem?" Cornelius questioned. He scanned the mother and her children. "That woman, who is she?"

The clerk shifted uncomfortably at the same time the woman noticed the blood on the temple floor. She tightened her lips, displaying tension.

"Ama is the wife of War Chief Mandonius of the Ilergetes Tribe. And the children are Budarica and Betina, daughters of King Indibilis," the clerk introduced the hostages. "Mandonius is Indibilis' brother. The woman and children weren't supposed to be presented yet."

The glass slipped from Cornelius' hand, rolled off the edge of the table, and shattered on the floor.

"Indibilis and Mandonius of the Ilergetes Tribe," he breathed out. "The war leaders who murdered my father."

A half a step behind the woman, the First Centurion assumed the glass was an accident and didn't hear the clerk or Cornelius. He started to announce, "Governor Scipio, may I present…"

But Turibas was interrupted by Ama's scream of terror at the mention of the Scipio name. Mandonius, her husband, had often boasted of attacking the Legions and killing General Publius Scipio. And now, facing another member of the Latian clan, Ama expected a quick death or worse.

Chapter 2 – Find Their Value

Hugging the children, the wife of Mandonius dropped to her knees, exposed her neck, and waited for the blade to sever her head from her body.

"Get up, wife of Mandonius," Cornelius urged.

While holding the children against her breasts, she stood.

"My man took your father, Scipio," Ama challenged Cornelius. "Why would you not take the life of his wife?"

At the casual use of his General's name, Turibas made a fist and raised his arm to strike the woman. He almost did, but Cornelius recovered from the jolt of her words before Turibas delivered the punch.

"Still your arm, First Centurion," Cornelius ordered. He stepped away from the chair, and while walking around the table, added. "If we punished everyone for telling the truth, in a perfect world, there would be long lines at the punishment post."

"Yes, sir. I guess," Turibas stated, not sure of the General's meaning.

Cornelius marched to the row of columns and vanished through the supports.

"Colonel, what do we do now?" Turibas asked Marcius.

"We wait for our General, First Centurion. It's all we can do."

***

From the top of the temple steps, Cornelius gave a cursory glance at the homes and the businesses on the northern side of New Carthage. They stretched for blocks from the bottom of Temple Hill to the defensive wall. Beyond the wall, fishing boats navigated the bay.

On the road circling the Temple of Asclepius, Velites loaded the body of Biurdiki into an empty cart. Jace Kasia stood beside the cart talking with a tall staff officer.

Cornelius thought he recognized the man, but his mind was elsewhere.

"Senior Tribune Kasia, a moment," Cornelius called across to Jace.

After a few words to the staff officer, Jace pointed to a spot east of the city. Then he jogged across the road, and up the steps to Cornelius.

"We'll burn the body outside the walls, sir," Jace described, providing an excuse for why he delayed in responding. "The residents have been complaining about all the funeral fires, the stink, and the smoke."

Cornelius glanced at the hills to the east. Next, he rotated his head until he again faced the north bay. People assumed many things about Scipio's measured pauses before reacting. Some claimed he consulted with Gods, while others, close to him, figured he talked with ancient scholars, like the poet Quintus Ennius.

But Jace knew the reason for the delay rested in Cornelius fighting the image of a brash and careless young man. By working through each situation and selecting the appropriate words, Scipio came across as a man wiser than his years.

While Cornelius thought, Jace watched the cart roll away.

"I have a dilemma," Cornelius finally admitted, "and I need your help."

"If it's diplomatic, I may not be the best man for the job."

"I have no diplomats who can walk into Ilergetes territory and tell me what's in the hearts of a King and a War Chief."

"Sir, I'm an archer not a seer."

"Perhaps I haven't explained this well enough," Cornelius conceded. "Let me try again. I'm holding the wife of Mandonius and the children of Indibilis. If the Ilergetes don't hold them in high regard, they're worth little to me. And I won't waste my time offering them as trade."

After a moment of contemplation, Jace inquired, "Not even for a ransom?"

"No quantity of coins will repay me for the loss of my father. If, however, I can make a pact with the Ilergetes and keep them off our shields, the trade will be worth more than all the silver in Iberia."

"You want me to find their value?" Jace guessed.

"Sending an armed delegation would only get good men killed," Cornelius remarked. In a flash of understanding, he attempted to amend the comment. "Jace, I meant a detachment would be attacked. While a single man of your talents might, well…"

"Get dead, but not start a war?" Jace finished the thought. "Not to worry, General Scipio. Cretan Archers only have one question."

Cornelius stared at Jace waiting for the question. After a moment, he realized no query was coming.

"What's the going rate for a Cretan Archer?"

"I like the sound of Colonel Kasia, Battle Commander for Wings of Nortus Legion."

"Junius Silanus and Bolt Legion are rowing for Tarraco tomorrow," Cornelius told Jace. "That'll cut down on your overland travel. And when you come back with the information, I'll gladly pay the price."

"If you'll excuse me, General Scipio," Jace begged off, "I need to settle Wings Legion into their duties and buy some tools."

"Tools?" Cornelius inquired.

"My mentor taught me, if you want to blend in," Jace explained, "you must have a reason to be where you're exploring."

***

Lucius Marcius, First Centurion Turibas, the daughters Budarica and Betina, Ama, the clerks, priests, and Velites drifted mentally. While duty or spears held them in the temple, their minds pondered problems as vast as the future, or as mundane as what to have for lunch.

"That's settled," Cornelius boomed when he strutted from between the columns. "Turibas. Assign a squad to escort the woman and the girls to a villa. Be sure they're kept safe. After that, bring out the next case."

When Cornelius reached his seat, Marcius noted, "You seem to be in a better mood, sir. It's like a weight has been lifted from your shoulders."

"Only temporarily, Colonel. Clerk, who's next?"

"General Scipio, the next hostage is Isceradin," the clerk read after consulting a list, "from the Carpetani Tribe."

"Carpetani territory is in the center of Iberia," Marcius informed General Scipio. "Because they're inland, the Carpetani aren't plagued by invasions from the sea. But the acreage they claim does attract marauders. It requires them to maintain a massive army to guard their borders. And there, sir, lies a contradiction. Their capital, Madrid, is a seat of culture. Almost every Carpetani can read and write."

"That is interesting," Cornelius spoke as a man crossed the temple floor. Dressed in woolen pants, with no shirt, the man had a length of silk draped over his shoulders and upper chest.

In fluid strides, he easily outpaced the First Centurion in his armor.

"Sirs. From the Carpetani Tribe," Turibas called out. Even if his body was behind, his voice at least raced ahead of the hostage, "may I present sculptor Isceradin."

"Sculptor, painter, designer of pleasing, tantalizing, religious, or if you wish troubling mosaics," Isceradin exclaimed. "Call me what you will. But know in my heart, that I am an artist."

"Tell me artist Isceradin, why are you in New Carthage?" Cornelius asked.

"The sunrise over the sea. A bird on the wing. Clouds that play children's games in the sky. Why would an artist be anywhere?"

"I meant, why did the Carthaginians take you from your people?"

"I'm not sure of the details. But it had something to do with my brother, the tribe's King, not dealing with Latians," Isceradin giggled and indicated Cornelius. "And yet, here I am, dealing with a Latian."

"First Centurion, have a squad escort Isceradin back to his studio. He'll be staying with us. Clerk, prepare a missive to the King of the Carpetani Tribe. For the safety of his brother, he must not deal with the Carthaginians. And have him send a delegation to me. We'll work out the details," Cornelius directed. Then to Marcius in hushed tones, he said. "Aristotle would approve. For truly, if a man lacked the capacity to deliberate, for his own good, he must remain a slave."

With silk streaming in his wake, the artist strutted ahead of the Legion squad as they left the temple.

***

"Clerk, what drama is in store for me next?" Cornelius requested.

"Sir, Oretani, a mountain tribesmen from the Vascones."

A female voice easily carried from the holding room. Through the open doorway, it crossed the temple to the

Legion officers. While the tone cut through the air, the words were garbled by the door and the distance.

"The altitude at Vascones must be soothing," Marcius observed, "for the voice of that tribesman is as alluring as the aroma from a spice shop."

Pitched low, as if carrying passion on every breath, the voice spoke again. This time clearly.

"My friends and I are but visitors to New Carthage," she protested. "Who is in charge of this debacle?"

"General Scipio is the Prorogatio of Iberia. But ma'am, you'll have to wait your turn," Turibas told her in his command voice.

Men feared to cross the First Centurion of Wings Legion. His martial skills were tested and proven in battle. His directions never ignored. Yet, when a shoulder and an arm appeared from behind the door and a soft hand caressed his face, the fierce combat officer melted.

While the small hand remained cupped to his stern jaw line, a lithe, long-haired beauty slipped from the room. Behind her, two more young women emerged. Finally, a fourth, the owner of the restraining hand came fully around the door. She allowed her fingers to lightly brush Turibas' lips as she passed by.

"First Centurion. Who do we have here?" Marcius shouted.

Overcome by the surprise attack of femininity, Turibas was unable to reply.

"I am Aurunica, daughter of Karisker, an important landowner of the Bastetani Tribe," the beauty stated as she glided over the temple floor. "Why are my friends and I being detained?"

"That's a good question," Cornelius replied. "Why are you a hostage?"

"So now daughters of this land are hostages," Aurunica shot back. "Are we not allies now that you control New Carthage? Or should I call it New Scipio?"

"You can call it anything you like. But you've yet to answer my question."

"We are simple, country girls. Unfortunately, on our trip to the big city, your army climbed the walls like spiders and began devouring people in the streets," Aurunica responded. "Fearing for our lives, we took shelter in the closest compound. That, as it turned out, was Hasdrubal Gisco's home for his guests."

Mesmerized by her voice and self-assurance, Cornelius listened, nodding at her every word.

"So, you aren't a Carthaginian hostage?" he asked.

"Of course not," she assured him. "And we are weary of the city and would like to return home to our village."

***

During Aurunica's description of the error, the temple hushed. Priests, clerks, officers, and Velites were captivated by her voice. Everyone except Sidia Decimia. When you've felt the presence of a Goddess in hot stream and dangerous vapors, you become immune to physical lures.

While everyone watched Aurunica, Sidia shifted his focus around the temple. Seeing nothing threatening, he began studying the other three women. All appeared to be a little younger than the speaker. And each was attractive in her own way.

One of the women noticed his eyes on her. She allowed a sly grin to grace her lips. Then she mouthed a couple of words and raised an eyebrow.

Sidia shook his head to let her know he didn't understand. In response, she marched around the table, walked up to the Hirpini, and touched his brass armlet.

"Your name?" she whispered as if they were alone in the temple.

"Sidia Decimia. Optio Sidia Decimia."

"My name is Sucra," she purred. "We've been locked up for days and it seems we'll be so again. But oh, I am dying for a new dinner companion. And better conversation."

Before Sidia had a chance to ask her what she meant, Cornelius spoke up.

"Optio Decimia. If you've finished interrogating the young lady, perhaps she can join her companions," he teased. "They are leaving."

"Yes, sir," Sidia acknowledged.

Sucra tugged on Sidia's arm, and he leaned over.

"Come have dinner with me tonight," she invited.

Without waiting for a reply, Sucra scurried to catch up with Aurunica and the other women.

Cornelius stretched and asked, "Isn't there a mountain tribesmen stashed somewhere?"

Stoned faced, to hide his embarrassment at being outmatched by a woman, First Centurion Turibas marched for the door to the holding room.

***

"I am Oretani, Captain of the Vascones," the tribesman announced. "My situation here assured that my command blocked the high passes and prevented Latians and their allies from crossing the mountains."

"And if I free you?" Cornelius inquired.

"Logically, the trail through the Pyrenees would be closed to Carthaginians and their allies," Oretani replied. "And opened for you and your command."

Cornelius didn't respond to the tribesman. Instead, he addressed Lucius Marcius.

"Colonel, take Captain Oretani with you to Tarraco," Cornelius directed. "Along the way, write up a letter of agreement stating that if the Oretani fail to uphold their end, I will march on their territory and annihilate their people."

After voicing the threat, Cornelius stared into the eyes of the Oretani Captain, and inquired, "Do you have any doubt?"

"None, General," Oretani uttered.

After a squad of light infantrymen left with the Vascones tribesman, Marcius asked, "You took him at his word. Was that wise?"

"Plato taught that human behavior flows from desire, emotion, and knowledge," Cornelius replied. "Oretani displayed all three. Further challenging him would have been like beating an obedient horse. It would only serve to decrease his commitment."

"General, I have to prepare Bolt Legion for the trip to Tarraco," Marcius requested. "Do you mind if I abandon you for the rest of the hostage evaluations?"

"I'm sure the clerks can fill me in on which territory is under consideration. You're dismissed."

Marcius left and the interviews continued. But, by midafternoon, Cornelius grew bored. He informed the priests and clerks that they would resume the processing of hostages in the morning.

"Optio Decimia, I'm going to my villa to meet with officers from Trumpet of Aeneas Legion," Cornelius told his bodyguard. "Why don't you take some downtime. Go see if you can find a diversion?"

"Thank you, sir. I do have an activity in mind."

Chapter 3 – Four Perfect Statuettes

Following a visit to a tonsor's shop for a shave, haircut, and nail trim, Sidia visited the baths. Then, freshly scrubbed and dressed in a clean tunic, the NCO strolled to one of the villas assigned to the hostages. A guard met him at the gateway.

"Optio Decimia, this is a closed compound," the Legionary said while blocking his way.

"I'm not visiting. I'm here to escort a hostage to dinner," Sidia informed the guard. "Her name is Sucra."

"Please stay here."

The infantryman marched to a side entrance of the house and spoke with someone through the doorway. Back at the gate, he reported, "The Bastetani woman will be along shortly."

Sidia stepped away from the wall and lifted his face to the sun. Winter in New Carthage reminded him of late spring at home in the Apennine mountains. Warm with a cool breeze, except the air in the mountains smelled of pine and cedar. While along the coast of Iberia, salt and fish tinted the air.

After a few moments of sunning, he glanced eastward across the city. From street level, he could see the solid block walls on Citadel Hill and the tall columns on Temple Hill. Most officers and Legionaries didn't know why General Scipio had chosen the unfortified location for his headquarters. But Sidia understood. In order for Cornelius Scipio to rule Iberia, the General needed to appear to the populace as a civilian governor. Not as a military commander sequestered in a fortress on Citadel Hill.

"Sidia Decimia, you came," Sucra said with glee in her voice. She stood in the gateway of the compound beaming at him. "I wasn't sure if you could pull yourself away from your important duties."

Sidia crossed to the gateway and offered his arm.

"Just as I wasn't sure you were serious about going to dinner. I'm surprised you're willing to pull yourself away from your friends."

"Oh, they aren't my friends," Sucra tossed out.

Her phrase "not my friends" might be a simple opinion based on being forced to live with three other women for weeks. Or, it might hold a secret.

Because Sidia was a fixture behind General Scipio and blended into the background, people forgot the bodyguard was present. Sometimes they spoke plainly and often made remarks contradictory to their public statements. His cousin, Jace Kasia, had coached Sidia to not react to inflammatory or suspicious remarks. Rather he should listen, and probe if possible, and then report them to Cornelius. Following Jace's advice, Sidia didn't respond to Sucra's comment.

The bridesmaid linked one arm in his and reached over to rest the other on his upper arm and the brass armlet. As they began walking, an older woman appeared from the house and followed.

"We have a shadow," Sidia suggested.

"She's my chaperone," Sucra laughed. "You'll buy her dinner, won't you?"

"Where are the three of us eating?" Sidia inquired.

***

The third-floor terrace of the restaurant overlooked south bay. Fishing boats rowed in with their catch, and a few merchant vessels appeared, having reached Cartagena Bay after a day of sailing. Far out at the harbor's inlet, four Roman quinqueremes floated on the tide. The five-bankers were there in case pirates or Carthaginian ships-of-war attempted a raid from the sea.

Sidia and Sucra were seated at a table near the edge of the balcony. The chaperone selected a table near the exit stairs as if to prevent the pair from escaping.

"She's very accommodating," Sidia observed, meaning the older woman gave them space to converse in private. "Has she been with your family long. Oh, excuse me. Perhaps she's your grandmother."

"My Amona is fifty miles northwest of here," Sucra replied. "And I wish I was with her."

"Too many days in the big city," Sidia offered. "I know when I left my father's farm, I was intimidated by the crowds and high walls of Benevento."

"Ortillo has walls. Not as big as Jarales nor this grand. And not near as many miles long," Sucra reminisced while indicating the defensive walls of New Carthage. "But on market days, when the farmers come to town, the streets get packed. I usually stay in my room and avoid them."

"I thought you were from the same village as Aurunica," Sidia questioned.

"She's from Jarales and the other two are from cities farther west."

The proprietor brought a platter, interrupting her response. Sliced lamb, with a mixture of boiled broad beans, lentils, and peas, and a clay container of berry and honey jam filled the platter. Sucra divided portions into three bowls. After handing one to Sidia, she carried the other to her chaperone.

"How did you end up in New Carthage?" Sidia inquired when she returned.

Using a piece of flatbread, he focused on scooping up a too large helping of the vegetables and meat. His fumbling with the overloaded piece, drew a laugh from Sucra.

"If she's not your Grandmother, who is…" the bread dipped halfway to Sidia's mouth. In a cascade of lamb and vegetables, the food toppled to the table with only a tiny part landing in the bowl.

Sucra giggled and attempted to hide it by placing a hand in front of her mouth.

"Oh, this is so much better than meals with Aurunica, her servants, and the girls," she declared. Then she thought about the comment before saying. "I hope I haven't offended you by laughing."

"You have a lovely laugh," Sidia complimented her. "As I started to ask, before my flatbread rebelled, who is the chaperone?"

"She's one of Aurunica's ten servants."

"For a shopping trip," Sidia questioned, "she brought ten servants and three friends?"

"Goddess Coventina bless us," she cried. "Mother of abundance and fertility, my side hurts."

Sidia scooped up a smaller portion and ate while Sucra composed herself.

"We aren't here shopping," Sucra revealed after a moment. "The girls and I were selected as Aurunica's handmaids."

"Selected?"

"Chief Karisker held a banquet for all the young women in our region," Sucra told him. "Do you think a party of four perfect statuettes happened by accident?"

"I had no reason to believe it wasn't a gift from Philyra, the Goddess of beauty," Sidia admitted.

Sucra's face scrunched up with humor.

"Thank you," she uttered. "But sometimes Goddesses need help to create perfection."

"Why not have Aurunica's friends accompany her to the wedding."

"When you marry a Prince, everything must be uniformly pretty."

Despite Jace's advice to probe and not display emotion, Sidia's lower jaw dropped.

"Aurunica is marrying a Prince? Which one? Who?"

"It shouldn't matter to you Latians," Sucra divulged. "Aurunica sent to her father for a ransom. She'll pay your General and we'll be leaving tomorrow afternoon."

Realizing he needed to change the subject and not seem too interested, Sidia denied the label. "I am not Latin. I'm Hirpini from the Apennines. My people are independent mountain dwellers and not part of the Republic."

"Yet, you guard a Roman General."

"Truth be told, I hate farming," Sidia explained. "Being an Optio in the Legions is a steady job. And securing a position as General Scipio's bodyguard is a good assignment."

"Your General, what kind of man is he?" Sucra asked.

The question might have been part of the normal flow of the conversation. Or, based on Sucra's meticulously stacking vegetables on a piece of flatbread and her intense focus on the task, it was the reason she asked him to dinner.

"What kind of man is General Scipio?" Sidia repeated as if he'd never considered the question. After a moment, he replied. "Cornelius Scipio is a studious man who keeps faith with the gods. He sacrifices, prays, and consults with them daily. He desires peaceful and profitable situations. And paramount to creating the proper conditions, he'll negotiate and uphold his part of any bargain."

"Your General sounds like a fair and just man," Sucra observed.

"He is that," Sidia confirmed. Then he delivered the warning in as nice a manner as possible. "He is fair and just. But when attacked, or a tribe breaks a treaty, or people lie to him, General Scipio will, without remorse, depopulate a region as retribution."

The stark admittance that Scipio would murder an entire community if angered, showed in the widening of Sucra's eyes.

"Plus, the General is an excellent strategist," Sidia added to see what effect it had on her.

"How so?" Sucra inquired.

"Scipio captured New Carthage in two days," Sidia reminded the bridesmaid.

A quick glance between Sucra and the chaperone brought the old woman to the edge of the table.

"It's getting late, and I must get back before dark," Sucra apologized. "Thank you for the dinner and the conversation."

After Sucra and her shadow left, Sidia stretched out his legs, and raised a hand over his head.

"Proprietor, I have thinking to do. Bring me a pitcher of your best red."

Sidia Decimia sipped and watched the inner and outer bay darken. But while his body remained idle, his mind went over every word of the conversation with Sucra.

***

Appearing like priestesses coming to a dawn ceremony, Aurunica, followed by Sucra and the other two bridesmaids filed into the Temple of Asclepius.

"General Scipio, I was surprised at your summons," Aurunica admitted. "But it was judicious. My father, Karisker, wants me home. You see, my mother has taken ill, and I must be there to care for her. After selling a team of horses and combining it with a stash of coins from last year's harvest, he managed to raise a ransom. With it, he hopes to purchase my release."

As it had the day before, her low voice carried promises with each syllable and hinted at secrets a man, even if he didn't understand the need, might want to explore.

Unimpressed by the dramatic announcement, Cornelius advised, "Make that the first and last time."

"Forgive me General, I'm confused," Aurunica purred. "What have I said to warrant such a rebuke?"

Knowing Sidia had warned her, through Sucra, not to lie, Cornelius ignored the future bride and addressed Turibas.

"First Centurion," he instructed. "Form the heavy infantry of Wings Legion and prepare to march for Jarales."

Turibas, typically alert and ready to comply with any order, hesitated. Wings of Nortus had Velites, skirmishers, artillery men, and squadrons of cavalry. But Wings Legion had no Legionaries, other than the veterans of First Century. Certainly not enough heavy infantrymen to call them a Legion or to be a military threat. Then the truth dawned on him.

"A question, General Scipio," the First Centurion requested. "Do we take our second Maniple? They are a blood thirsty lot, sir, and don't always leave survivors to sell as slaves."

Cornelius lifted his head and peered at the center of the temple as if communicating with the statue of Asclepius. While he concentrated on the God of Healing, everyone in the temple fell silent and waited. The quiet interval proved too much for Aurunica.

"General Scipio, I lied," she confessed. "My mother's not sick. But my father is sending a ransom for my release."

His eyes drifted down to look at her in an indirect manner. A heartbeat later, Cornelius' head dipped, and stared directly at the bride-to-be.

"Who is the lucky man?"

"I don't know what you're…" Cornelius held up a fist then extended two fingers. With the other hand, he pointed at the second finger and shook his head, no. Moving away from the falsehood she was about to deliver, Aurunica offered. "I am the fiancée of Allucius, Prince of the Celtiberi Tribe."

As if a hot poker had been driven up his spine, Cornelius Scipio hopped off the chair. He landed beside his seat, then doubled over as if punched in the gut. Sidia wrapped a supporting arm around his waist and hovered over his General. With his face as red as the tip of a hot iron, Cornelius stammered, "Get them out of my sight. Take them back to the villa."

Velites stomped forward, forming a barrier between the General and the wedding party.

"I don't understand," Aurunica pleaded. "I told the truth."

"First Centurion, make sure none of the infantrymen assigned to guard the women were in my uncle's Legions," Cornelius ordered.

"Yes, sir," Turibas assured him.

Recovering a little from the shock, Cornelius stood erect.

As his head appeared behind the shields, Aurunica tried a different tactic, "I have coins coming to pay for my release."

"A Legion patrol intercepted the carriage from your father before daylight," Cornelius told her.

"Sidia, why this treatment?" Sucra shouted as the women neared the exit to the temple. "I thought he was just and kind unless attacked, or a tribe broke a treaty, or people lied to him."

"I must have forgotten one other item," Sidia replied.

"Forgotten what?" Sucra called from the edge of the temple.

"For people subject to revenge, there is no compassion."

Before the guards escorting the wedding party reached the steps of the temple, Cornelius grabbed Sidia's arm. Towing the bodyguard, Scipio headed for the chamber he used for meditation.

***

In the dark, Sidia extended an arm, restricting Cornelius' movements and creating a barrier against an assassin's attack. Before long, wicks flickered to life as priests rushed around lighting the beeswax candles. Only when he could see objects in the muted light did Sidia drop his arm.

"I'm sorry, sir, about the rude and rough treatment," the bodyguard offered.

With the candles lit and their job of appeasement completed, the priests fled the chamber.

"Optio Decimia, if only you could guard my heart from the pain, and block the knives stabbing into my gut," Cornelius sighed. "Then I might separate my emotions into usable parts. A logical mind to see beyond revenge. A clear vision of justice unclouded by vengeance. An ability to draw on ancient wisdom. And the foresight to embrace the Gods. But no path lays unshrouded by the blood of my uncle caused by the desertion of the Celtiberi heavy infantry."

"Sir, you handled the situation with the Ama woman well enough," Sidia proposed.

"No, I didn't," Cornelius admitted. "I sent Jace to the Ilergetes under the guise of finding out if the King and War Chief cared about the hostages. But even as I set the plot in motion, I imagined the joy of crucifying Mandonius and Indibilis. And then sacrificing Ama and the girls in the name of my father. I'm afraid I hid behind Jace Kasia to avoid committing to an action."

"Perhaps, General, the Gods put a Cretan Archer at your disposal for that exact reason," Sidia suggested. "And seeing as Aurunica is Bastetani, this situation is easier."

While scanning the chamber, candlelight reflected in Cornelius' shifting eyes. Finally, he looked at Sidia and announced.

"Unlike the Ilergetes, we can assume Prince Allucius cares for Aurunica," he proposed. "And a delegation from the Bastetani tribe can deliver the bride and a message from me."

"What will the message say, General?"

"I'm going to kill you and your cowardly infantry," Cornelius growled.

"General Scipio, you are the Prorogatio of Iberia, the supreme commander of Roman forces in the region, and a Governor charged with making Iberia profitable," Sidia reminded him. "Whatever strategy you use is the correct one. As for revenge, leave the killing to men trained for it."

"Men like Jace Kasia," Cornelius guessed.

"Yes sir, if that's the solution you truly require."

Act 2

Chapter 4 – Priest of Evil

Fat drops of rain hammered into the puddle of water. With each impact, miniature fountains popped into the air. As the fountains collapsed, they sent out ripples. Each ripple collided with a neighboring ring, causing the surface of the pool to surge over its tiny banks.

The puddle, broadly viewed, represented the wet landscape on either side of the wagon track. And, as if mirroring the damp earth, the sky above hung low, gray, and heavy with moisture.

A sandal splashed down into the puddle. Destroying the rhythm of the rain, the footwear sent most of the collected water out in a single stomp. The man in the sandal didn't notice the result of his action. It wouldn't be the last time, over the next few days, he brought ruin to the natural order of things.

***

"We'll find shelter soon," the man promised the draft animal at his side.

The mule didn't respond. Since daybreak, the beast had kept its face turned from the human. Out of indignity from being taken out of a dry stable, or being made to walk quickly in a downpour, or from the wet harness tugging against the mule's shoulders and chest, the beast of burden blamed the human for all its misery.

Behind the mule, the wheels of a peddler's wagon bumped through the empty puddle. Only after the wagon passed did the water flow back into the hole in the road.

The wheels rolled, the hooves carried the mule and wagon forward, and the sandals continued to splash along the road. It felt as if the world had vanished, leaving only the muted colors of a rainy day, and damp clothing as a reminder that civilization once existed.

And although there was nothing civilized about the discovery, the man, the mule, and the wagon would soon find they were not alone.

***

Tucked under overlapping and leaking oiled skins, three unemployed soldiers waited out the rain. No one had traveled the route all morning, putting the destitute men in a foul mood.

"Sakar, you have better eyesight than me," Cio suggested. "Is that a mirage, or our next meal coming down the road?"

The one known as Sakar sat up, then rolled to his knees. The top of his head bumped the roof of the rain tarps, spilling water down into the shelter.

Cold water drenched the clothing of a third man and he complained, "That wasn't bright."

Sakar's knife cleared its scabbard.

"There's only a single peddler," Sakar warned. "We don't need you for this operation."

The complainer used two fingers to move the tip of the blade away from his nose.

"The cold water shocked me, that's all. And I mouthed off, sorry."

"Don't let it happen again."

By then, the wagon, the mule, and the tradesman emerged clearly out of the sheets of rain. The three soldiers stared with greedy eyes. Their hearts hard, bellies empty, and consciences unrepentant. Yet, although the three soldiers watched, they didn't see. To a man, they missed the footwear that suggested the tradesman wasn't easy prey.

The sandals had thick soles to protect the feet in rough terrain and were secured for running and long marches with wide leg straps. Not favored by Republic Legionaries nor Greek Hoplites, the footwear came from the heavy infantrymen of the Mogente tribe. In reality, the source was less important than the tradesman who chose to wear combat sandals on the open road.

***

"Well friend, this is your lucky day," Cio announced as he stepped out from under a dripping tree branch.

Sakar and the third soldier flanked Cio, each holding an old spear with a rusty iron head. In lock step, the three marched to the center of the roadway, pivoted smartly, and blocked the wagon trail. The two with spears, leveled their shafts at the traveler.

"Lucky, because you have a chance to live," Sakar explained. "You just leave your wagon and the mule. We'll take them off your hands."

Adding to the implied threat, Cio drew a short sword.

"Doesn't that sound better than the alternative," he suggested while pointing at the tradesman's chest with the steel tip.

There was little doubt the soldiers were prepared to fight. The question hanging in the heavy rain, did the tradesman want to resist? A moment later, the three received an answer.

The tradesman patted the side of the mule's muzzle then went to the rear of the wagon. Before running away, he pulled a bundle and a long case from the back. A few heartbeats later, the tradesman vanished in the rain.

"That went well," Sakar observed.

"If we knew robbery was this easy," the third soldier mentioned. "We could have done this anytime instead of joining the company and fighting for Mago the Carthaginian."

"Maybe too easy," Cio said. Sheathing his sword, he instructed. "Get the mule and walk the wagon to our camp."

"Hurry up, I'm hungry," Sakar added.

***

Late in the day, the rain stopped. Staggering and stumbling from the wine he consumed, Sakar built a cookfire. Shortly afterward, he squatted unsteadily and turned the spit. Soon the aroma of pork cooking over the flames filled the air. And from the misery of being hungry and damp, the three soldiers dried and brightened as they inhaled the roasting meat.

"What's his trade?" Cio asked the third soldier.

"Who?"

"The tradesman we took the wagon and mule from," Cio snapped.

"Him? How would I know?"

"You were in his wagon," Cio said in frustration. "You know, when you pulled out the wineskins and the salted pork."

"I didn't look," he admitted. "There were a lot of containers and long leather straps. Oh, and pieces of curved wood. From the aroma, I'd say maple."

"That doesn't tell me much," Cio insisted. "Sakar. Any idea what a tradesman would do with carved pieces of maple?"

"Not a clue…"

Zip-Thwack!

Sakar rolled away from the cookfire. Not in a display of acrobatic skills, although the tuck and tumble resembled one. What spoiled the controlled roll was the arrow shaft protruding from the bottom and the top of his thigh muscle. After the summersault, amid screams of agony, he came to rest curled up around the injured and incapacitated thigh.

At the sudden movement of Sakar, Cio reacted. As would any experienced soldier, he jumped for his shield.

Zip-Thwack!

The arrowhead cut through the muscles of one butt cheek. Quivering as Cio trembled in pain, the shaft rocked with each shiver. To ease the hurt, the soldier lay still while panting.

Unlike Cio who went for his shield, the third soldier scurried behind a tree trunk. From there, he crawled away and vanished in the bushes.

***

Jace Kasia hopped down from the saddle between two branches, collected his bundle and the empty bow case. Holding a notched arrow on the bowstring, he glided through the forest to the camp of the robbers.

"That looks painful," he mentioned to Cio while taking the man's sword and knife.

"Yes, curse you, it is," Cio admitted between groans.

At Sakar, Jace took the knife and kicked the spear away from the soldier.

"I have some good news, and some bad, and some worse," Jace announced to the two wounded men.

"What's the good," Cio inquired.

"You aren't going to die," Jace replied.

"What's the bad?" Sakar demanded.

"I'm only going to treat you with vinegar," Jace remarked.

He squatted beside the fire and cut away a piece of cooked pork.

"If you treat our wounds and we aren't going to die," Cio questioned, "what's the worst that can happen?"

"You're well trained and relatively fit," Jace told him between bites. "And I don't care to fight you. So, we'll travel to Lleida, together."

"What's so bad about that?" Sakar challenged.

"I'm leaving the arrows in place," Jace informed them. "On one hand, you'll hurt. On the other, you won't be in any condition to attack me."

As the two robbers whined and complained, Jace removed the harness from the mule and rubbed the creature down before hobbling it near a patch of tall grass. Once the mule was settled, he tied cloths around the exposed ends of the arrows and doused them with vinegar. The complaining stopped as the two unemployed soldiers cried out in agony.

Before dark, Jace gave the wounded men several slices of meat and sips of water as a sign of goodwill.

"Tell me," he inquired as he fed Cio, "do you know Indibilis and Mandonius."

"Sure, King Indibilis and War Chief Mandonius invite me to all their holiday celebrations. But I have to turn them down due to my busy social schedule."

"That's great," Jace said thinking this was the easiest contract he'd ever been given. "Tell me, does…"

He realized something was wrong when Sakar began laughing until the pain in his leg turned the chuckling into moans.

"What's so funny?" Jace asked.

"Cio has the same social schedule as me," Sakar managed to get out between groans. "Which is none. Other than fighting for Mandonius, having our spoils taxed by him, and then being discharged by the War Chief when we got home, we know him as well as we know you."

"I understand," Jace stated while placing another piece of pork in Cio's mouth.

***

In the light of a new day, the plain of Lleida extended far into the distance on both sides of the road. Although the region consisted of grass or farmland, trees along tributaries flowing to the Segre River prevented Jace from taking in the full vastness of the land. And while birds chirped and whistled from trees along the wagon track, he couldn't enjoy the songs. Because every bump brought howls from the men in the wagon.

"Correct me if I'm wrong," Jace called back to them. "But you interfered in my life and not the other way around. And now you're reaping the reward."

"How is this a reward?" Sakar asked.

"You're alive for now," Jace answered.

"For now?" Cio inquired. Muffled by the blanket under his face, and the restriction of speaking while attempting to hold his butt still, the soldier's voice came out feeble and didn't travel far.

Jace ignored the question and continued walking the mule, his prisoners, and the wagon towards the city of Lleida.

Several miles from the camp, Jace noted a compound set back from the road. Cultivated fields spread out behind a house and outbuildings enclosed in a defensive wall. Figuring to get information about the Ilergetes brothers, Jace slowed as he approached the turnoff. Before he guided the mule onto the side road, three riders galloped from the compound.

If they had been dressed as farm workers, or wearing finer clothing, Jace would have waited. But they weren't and he didn't.

Rushing to the opposite side of the wagon, and out of sight from the riders, Jace pulled a quiver and the case with his war bow from the wagon.

***

The three heavy cavalrymen raced their mounts around the wagon with lances leveled. Once they completed the turn, the trio reined in.

"I have to say," Jace exclaimed from the wagon bed, "I've had warmer welcomes."

A steed and a lance were formidable weapons. But a war bow held by a man standing on a raised platform and off to the side of the lances, more than equaled the horse muscle and steel tips on three wooden shafts.

"You're on our Lord's land," one alleged.

In turn, Jace aimed a single notched arrow at the riders.

"And you're standing on my section of the roadway," he responded. "I guess we have a disagreement. Let's settle this right now. Who wants to die first?"

Zip-Thwack!

The arrow flashed from the bow to the side of a rider.

"You missed," one of the cavalrymen growled.

"Did I?" Jace questioned.

Red liquid flowed down the side of a horse and dripped to the surface of the dirt road.

"Are you alright?" another rider asked.

The cavalryman with the damp horse reached down, pulled the arrow from a sack, and lifted it to his mouth. After licking the arrowhead, he protested, "That was good cherry wine. Made with aged Jerte Picota Cherries."

"And now it's a puddle on the roadway," Jace pointed out. "How about I continue my journey. And you return to your Lord and say you chased me off. Or we can fight."

At the word fight, Jace reached into his quiver and extracted five arrows. In the blink of an eye, he notched one arrow and positioned the other four between his fingers.

To the cavalrymen, the spread feathers of the fletching appeared to be the ruffled feathers of a bird-of-prey.

"You're an archer," a cavalryman gushed.

Jace wanted to say something about people who state the obvious. But from the looks on their faces, he had impressed them.

"If your flashy handling of a bow and a handful of arrows creates indecision in your enemy," Zarek Mikolas had coached, *"don't open your mouth and spoil the illusion."*

Breaking with his training, Jace attempted to enhance the declaration.

"A Cretan Archer," Jace confirmed to the riders.

"What's that?" two inquired.

"On the island of Crete, we are given bows while still in the crib."

"Why?" the third rider demanded. "Why give a baby a bow?"

"Let's just say I'm a master of the bow, and leave it at that," Jace offered.

Cio moaned and a cavalryman nudged his horse to the rear of the wagon.

Seeing the two soldiers, he inquired, "Are you also a collector of the dead?"

"If I didn't have this arrow in my leg," Sakar threatened, "I'd drag you off that horse and show you who is dead."

At the outburst from a man with an arrowhead near his hip, and the shaft threading under the skin of his thigh, and another man lying face down with an arrow through one butt cheek, the cavalryman yanked the reins of his horse.

"Get away," he warned the other two riders. "The archer is a magician. His arrows capture men and makes them into slaves."

The three trotted off the main road, turned their mounts, and blocked the trail to the compound.

"Priest of Evil, leave us be," they prayed. "Go away, Wizard."

Deciding not to argue the validity of the accusation, Jace hopped down. He strolled to the mule and pulled on the bridle. He, the beast, and the wagon proceeded along the main trail.

"Not very cordial, were they?" he asked the mule.

Unlike the mule's response during the rainstorm, the pack animal bumped Jace's shoulder with his head.

Behind them, one of the cavalrymen noticed the exchange and asked, "Do you suppose the mule was once a soldier before the Wizard captured him?"

The three riders shivered at the thought of being hit by a cursed arrow and becoming a mindless slave.

Chapter 5 – A Change of Reason

Farther away, with the hostile compound hidden by trees, Jace halted the mule. He walked to the rear of the wagon and stared down at the robbers.

"I've been in Ilergetes territory for three days and two nights," he mentioned to Sakar and Cio. "And, I've had my life threatened twice. What is it with your tribe?"

"Our lands are owned by Lords and worked or guarded by friends of the Lords," Cio told him. Then he added with pride in his voice. "That leaves the rest of us to be soldiers."

Softly, Sakar volunteered, "And between wars, we survive by being thieves and robbers."

Without speaking to the injured men, Jace soaked their bandages with vinegar. Once back at the front, he started the mule moving forward. As he kept pace with the animal, Jace adjusted the plan.

His disguise as a humble but excellent bow maker wouldn't work in the near lawless territory. He'd need to be more high profile to get the attention of King Indibilis and War Chief Mandonius. High enough to complete the mission, but not so much that it got him killed.

***

Late in the afternoon, the roofs of wooden buildings appeared on the horizon. As Jace drew closer, broken shingles and collapsed thatched roofs on a few of the buildings became clear. He stopped the mule and went to his prisoners.

"Gentlemen, this is where you get off," Jace informed them. "You have two choices."

"What choices?" Sakar asked.

"I can leave you here with the arrows embedded," Jace explained. He pressed down on the flesh over the shaft on Sakar's thigh. The big thief jumped from the pain. "It would take a brave man to remove an arrow by himself. Although, I've seen it done. Or, if you remain peaceful, I'll take them out."

"Why can't we go into Lleida with you?" Cio questioned.

"I had planned to turn you over to the local authorities. Hopefully for a reward," Jace replied, hiding the part about gaining some fame. "But, as you've explained, a local Lord won't care that you robbed an innocent tradesman."

"An innocent tradesman," Sakar sneered. "There's nothing harmless about your black heart. And how did we rob you? You're the one guiding the mule and we're injured."

"And there is another reason I don't want you riding with me," Jace pointed out. "Choose a quick pain now. Or a mile of pain as you hobble to reach a doctor?"

"Take it out," Cio told him.

Jace put a hand on Sakar's shoulder and forced the soldier to roll over on his side.

"Remain facing away from me," Jace warned. "If you roll towards me, I'll cut the arrow shaft out, and leave you on the side of the road to die."

After Sakar nodded his understanding, Jace scored lines around Cio's arrow just beneath the fletching. Once he had a deep enough groove, Jace snapped the shaft.

"Bite down on this," Jace ordered. He forced a thick piece of leather between Cio's teeth.

Growling, the soldier tried to protest. That's when Jace jerked the shaft through and out of one gluteus maximus muscle. The growl of irritation became a muffled howl of pain.

"Looks good," Jace declared as he inspected the tissue and blood covered arrow shaft.

Cio spit out the leather piece and announced, "It's disgusting."

Sakar shifted his head, eyed the shaft, and asked, "What's good about that?"

"No sign of the rot," Jace answered. "Your turn."

After seeing the reaction of his companion, Sakar admitted, "I don't know about this."

"How do you feel Cio?" Jace inquired.

"It's like the time the barber pulled a rotten tooth," he described. "It hurt right up until he pulled it."

Jace held the leather piece in front of Sakar's mouth and raised his eyebrows in a questioning manner.

"Fine but make it quick," Sakar proclaimed. He lay back, bit down on the leather, and closed his eyes. "Do it."

Below the arrowhead, Jace cut lines around the shaft. Then he snapped the top of the arrow off.

"Sakar, I want to apologize," he mumbled.

"Huh?" the soldier questioned.

"For this," Jace said.

Low on the man's thigh, Jace cut a two-inch slice above the shaft. Then he rested the knife hand on the leg to steady it. By continuously twisting and pulling, Jace drew the arrow through the muscle and tissue along the length of Sakar's thigh.

Sakar responded to the sensation of having the muscles in his leg being extracted along with the arrow shaft. He bolted up to a sitting position. But he didn't attack Jace. Rather, the soldier probed his thigh to be sure it was still intact. His breath came in short sharp gasps, and tears rolled down his cheeks.

"You cut me," he managed to say between breaths.

"I can sew a clean cut easier than ripped skin," Jace informed him.

***

As the sun touched the horizon, Jace helped Cio and Sakar off the wagon bed.

"Don't do anything to rip the stitches," he instructed. Then in a magnanimous gesture, Jace dumped the two old spears and two of the three shields on the ground. While walking away, he advised. "Keep the wounds damp with vinegar and you'll be healed in a week."

"Then I'll find you and kill you," Sakar challenged.

Jace walked back and approached the soldier.

"The next time, Sakar," Jace suggested while poking the man's chest with his finger, "I'll put the arrow right here, in your heart."

Jace Kasia strolled to the mule, took hold of the bridle, and tugged the animal forward. Behind him, Cio and Sakar slung the shields on their backs. Using the spear shafts as walking sticks, they limped after the retreating wagon.

***

Lleida was a divided city. On the east side of the Segre River, the apartments and shops were constructed of old lumber, mostly patched with rough boards placed over rotten walls. On the west side of the river, the appearance was quite the opposite. The villas and businesses had stone foundations with rock walls. But the river and the building materials weren't the only signs of separation.

"Get in line," the ferryman ordered.

Jace angled the mule off the muddy track, making sure the wagon cleared the path from the river to a dirt road. Behind him, on the streets of east Lleida, men dressed in tattered clothing or threadbare robes. Even the facades of the shops seemed to droop. Mostly from age, but also from a lack of quality goods and paying customers.

If he hadn't interacted with the cavalrymen from the compound and the robbers, Jace might have stayed on the east bank of Lleida. But knowing the ways of the tribe, he figured the west side held more promise.

Ahead of Jace, a farmer with a cart of vegetables waited for the ferry to return. Then a nicely appointed carriage with a matched set of horses passed him and stopped besides the farmer's cart.

"Don't be jealous," Jace whispered to the mule. "The horses aren't that pretty."

The mules bumped Jace's shoulder.

"Alright, maybe they are," he teased. Then Jace had an idea and hinted at it. "Do you think they can swim?"

Waving his arms, the ferryman ran to the driver of the carriage.

"You're blocking the roadway," he shouted.

"The Lord Indíbil does not wait for tradesmen or farmers," the driver replied.

"But you're blocking the exit from the ferry," the ferryman protested before the driver interrupted him.

While the two argued, Jace studied the Segre. Based on marked stakes in the river, the water near the banks wasn't very deep. But, from the movement of reeds caught on the poles, the current was swift. Swift enough to wash a tradesman's wagon downstream, taking a mule and a reckless driver down river with it. Even if he was third in line and might not cross until morning, Jace decided to wait.

After a promise of being next on the ferry, the carriage driver gave in and backed the horses away from the edge of the river. The move left a gap to allow the wagon on the ferry to squeeze around the carriage when it landed. But while it cleared the path, the move placed the wheels of the carriage beside Jace's wagon.

Trapped between the wheels of the carriage, the trees on the bank, and the farmers cart, Jace told the mule, "I guess we're spending the night here.

Out in the middle of the river, four ferrymen pulled on a rope cable while walking the length of the flat-bottomed boat. When one reached the front of the ferry, he'd rush to the rear, grab the cable, and began pulling and walking again. The movement and rotations of the four men powered the ferry and its cargo across the river.

The splashes of water along the bank, the rhythm of the ferrymen, and the long day lulled Jace into a relaxed state. Unguarded, he didn't pay attention at first.

From a block away, a voice rang out, "That's him."

In a rough town, full of unemployed soldiers, a raised voice meant nothing.

"That's him," the voice shouted, "the man who killed Cio and Sakar."

***

Jace wouldn't have recognized the man if he passed him on the street. But from the accusations, he knew it was the robber who fled Cio and Sakar's camp.

"Conceal your numbers and erase your tracks," Zarek Mikolas had lectured. "No one can righteously charge you with an action if they don't have an eyewitness."

The Master Archer had ruthlessly killed the five marauders who robbed and cut Uncle Dryas.

"Never start a fight you don't intend to finish," Zarek instructed.

Leaning against the cart, Jace looked down at the blood on his hands.

"I didn't expect," the twelve-year-old stammered.

"It's never easy," the archer acknowledged. "But in the end, it was their lives or ours. Would you have a different outcome?"

"No. This had to be done. I knew that after sewing up Uncle Dryas' ear," Jace admitted. "Should we dig graves and offer prayers for the dead?"

"Whenever possible, cover your tracks and erase all the evidence of your campsite. The goal is to leave as little a trace of our activities as possible. For a File of archers on an assignment, it helps hide how many bowmen are present, and their direction of march. For us, burning the cabin and the bodies, like collecting the arrows, hinders anyone coming after us."

"Someone might come after us?" Jace asked.

"We just murdered five soldiers of Rhodes," Zarek remarked as he tied the straps on his quiver. "Surely they have friends, relatives, comrades, and commanders."

"Master Mikolas, forgive my leniency at letting the third robber get away," Jace whispered to the memory of his mentor.

He ran to the wagon and retrieved his war bow and a quiver of arrows. Taking a position behind the carriage, Jace notched an arrow and gripped four more between his fingers. Then he began to pick targets.

A few raging ones at the front would slow the mob. Next, he'd drop a couple of the loudest ones to stop them from urging the crowd forward. After that, he'd wound a few rioters to dissuade the more timid.

"Thank you, stranger," the carriage driver said as he stepped up beside Jace. "I was afraid this would happen."

Confused by the comment, Jace glanced sideways. The driver of the carriage held a small shield and a short sword. Braced for combat, the teamster faced the mob.

"It's the least I can do," Jace uttered as if he understood the situation.

"Get him," someone deeper in the crowd bellowed.

Two big men raced ahead. Considering their shabby clothing, it came as a surprise when they drew steel swords from scabbards.

Zip-Thwack!

Having learned his lesson, Jace's arrow split ribs and pierced the first man's heart. From a sprint to his knees, to the ground, to dead, took no more time than Jace needed to notch another arrow.

Zip-Thwack!

The next arrow cut through the second man's throat. A shaft jutting from a neck gave the men behind him pause. They slowed. But rioters on the side missed the warning of the gore.

Two charged into the carriage driver. He bashed one rioter to the ground with his shield and parried the other's sword.

Zip-Thwack!

The rioter on the ground ceased to be a threat.

"Hold," a voice from behind the mob ordered.

In most cases, a single word would not break the momentum of a mob. But the voice cut through the mania as sure as a bolt of lightning cut the night sky.

"Hold or die," the voice said again.

Jace peered over the heads of the crowd to see five cavalrymen. Their lances leveled at the backs of the mob and their steeds snorting from anticipation.

"About time," the driver spit out. Then he faced Jace. "What's your name, tradesman?"

"Jace Kasia, Cretan Archer and bow maker," he answered.

"When you get to the west side, find me at the Indíbil compound. Ask for Belos. A guard will find me."

The driver marched to the carriage and spoke to the occupant before climbing to the driver's bench.

***

"But Captain, he killed Cio and Sakar," the third robber protested.

The mounted officer nudged his horse into the crowd.

"That's not possible," the cavalry officer replied. "On the way in, we passed Cio and Sakar on the road. And this mob wasn't after retaliation. To me it appears to be an attempt to rob and assault a Lord of the Ilergetes people."

After being stopped and having the hidden motivation for the riot revealed, nefarious men began drifting away. And, with the news that Cio and Sakar lived, the rest dispersed. All that remained were the dead and no one seemed interested in removing them.

"Put your bow and the arrows away," the Captain ordered as he rode by Jace.

"Yes, sir."

***

The five riders sat behind the carriage as the ferry touched the stones on the bank. Shortly after the arriving wagon left the flatboat, the carriage rolled onto the ferry. Then the ferryman approached Jace.

"Lord Indíbil wants you to cross next."

"What about the farmer and the cavalry?" Jace inquired.

"Don't know," the man admitted, "and don't care. The Lord wants you across next. And that's all that matters."

Although grateful for the chance to be away from any revenge by Sakar and Cio, Jace worried. Officers of calvary weren't accustomed to being shoved aside for tradesmen.

"Captain?" he inquired.

"You did a service for Lord Indíbil," the cavalry officer stated. "He wants you across and that's all that matters."

Chapter 6 – In the Hunt

Jace parked the wagon beside the landing on the west bank and unpacked for the night. To the delight of the ferrymen, on their last trip across the Segre River, they found a cookfire glowing on the shoreline.

"I'm new in town, and for days, I've been alone on the road," Jace explained. "And there's so much meat and wine, I need help eating it. Do you mind?"

Hungry from walking and pulling the boat back and forth across the river, the ferrymen dropped down by the fire. One by one, they cut pieces off the pork shoulder and sat devouring the meat.

"What are you doing in Lleida?" a ferryman inquired.

"There's little demand for a solo archer," Jace told him. "And only slightly more for a craftsman of hunting bows. But if I put them together, I can earn a living."

"How's that work?" another asked.

"I sell a bow then instruct the new owner in the proper use of the weapon," Jace described. "Maybe even take him hunting so he gets the bow hunting experience."

"And you earn a living doing that?"

"I'm not rich but I support myself," Jace replied. "But there are things about Lleida and your people that I don't understand."

"In that case, my friend," a ferryman assured him, "you have the right dinner companions."

Another ferryman took a stream from a wineskin.

"Our passengers don't notice us when they travel across the river," he informed Jace. "They forget we're close enough to hear their private conversations. And they talk openly."

"My cousin is a bodyguard for a high-ranking man," Jace offered.

"Then you know important people often ignore the help. What do you want to know about Lleida and our nobles?"

***

Before daylight, Jace waded into the river and washed. Back at the wagon, he put on a clean woolen shirt and pants. Then with the mule harnessed, he headed into town to look around.

A lone man strolling by shops before they opened might be suspicious. But as a tradesman with a wagon, Jace received no scrutiny from guards patrolling the streets.

Once he was familiar with the roads and alleyways, Jace stopped one of the patrols.

"Can you direct me to the Indíbil compound?" he inquired.

"It's to the west of town," the NCO answered. "Just look for the stone works. You'll find the compound next door."

Jace knew the location from the ferrymen. But it never hurt to be able to say a Corporal of the Guard gave him directions.

**

A reason the crowd on the east side of the river switched, from attacking Jace for murder to targeting Lord Indíbil, came into view after the last residential building. Scrawny men hauled large stones, gaunt stonemasons chipped out shapes, and underfed porters carried the shaped stones to piles. Their misery told the story. Cruelty in the name of profit wasn't rare. But using neighbors and fellow tribesmen in such a foul way was unusual. It appeared Lord Indíbil made enemies with the way he treated his employees. The mob, then, had used the attack on Jace as an excuse to try for revenge.

A mounted guard trotted from the entrance of the stone works.

"What are you doing here?" the rider demanded.

Jace glanced back at the last building of the city, then at the misery in the stone works.

"Taking my mule for a morning stroll," Jace told him.

"You're what?"

"I said…"

"I heard you," the guard roared. "Move along before I search your wagon for contraband."

"That's not advisable," Jace offered.

"Why is that?"

"Because the wagon is full of weapons," Jace stated.

"Yo," the guard shouted to a group of mounted men, "trouble. He has weapons."

In response, two riders galloped from the stone works. In moments, the three circled Jace, threatening him with the steel tips of their lances.

"What's the problem?" one asked.

"This one says he has a wagonful of weapons."

"What are you doing here?" one of the newly arrived guards questioned.

"Taking my mule for a morning stroll," Jace repeated.

"Let me rephrase and be careful how you answer. Where are you going?"

"To the Indíbil Compound to see Belos," Jace replied.

The tension between the three guards broke with the explanation. They walked their horses away from the vendor.

"Move along," the first mounted guard advised.

"Thank you," Jace acknowledged.

But the shout, the targeting of a tradesman, and bits of the loud conversation reached the guards at the gate to the Indíbil compound.

Jace jerked the bridle. The mule and wagon began moving towards a gathering of men-at-arms. They clustered around the gate to the compound as if preparing to defend it against an army. Consequently, while the guards from the stone works had been curious, Lord Indíbil's household guards appeared downright hostile.

***

"That's close enough," an officer instructed. "Why are you here? And what kind of weapons are you hauling in that wagon?"

"I'm glad you asked," Jace beamed. He walked the mule around until the rear of the wagon faced the gate.

"This, gentlemen, is the finest weapon in the hunt or on the battlefield."

Jace reached into the bed of the wagon. In response, the guards snapped their shields up and formed a shield wall. When Jace stepped back holding a bow and a quiver, their spears dropped to the top of the shields. While the guards stood braced against an attack, Jace pulled an arrow from the quiver. He paced off a hundred feet to the side and stabbed the arrowhead into the turf. Then he pulled a silver coin from a pouch. After displaying the small object to the alert guards, Jace rested the coin in the notch of the arrow.

"Say this is the heart of a deer or a foe," he announced while strutting back to the wagon.

"It's kind of small for a heart," a household guard challenged. "More like an eyeball."

"Alright, we'll go with that," Jace exclaimed. "Say this is the eyeball of a deer or a foe. And you need to end its life."

"I don't understand," another of the household guards stated. "Nobody aims for an eye."

"No one, my friend, aims for an eye," Jace concurred as he drew an arrow from the quiver. He whipped the arrow overhead, inserted it on the bowstring, spun to face the silver coin, and pulled.

Zip-Thwack!

All the guards stared at the empty notch of the arrow.

Without looking, where the tiny target had been, Jace finished, "because nobody has a superior weapon like a bow customed made by a Cretan craftsman."

"Where's the coin?" a guards inquired.

"It's there in the grass," Jace answered. "Go see for yourself. If you find the coin, you can keep it."

Three household guards jogged to the arrow and began searching the ground around the shaft.

"It's not here," one scoffed. "Probably a trick."

"An arrow from a Cretan bow travels fast and delivers power against an enemy," Jace informed them with a wave. "Try farther out."

The trio spread apart and moved away from the arrow while scanning the ground.

"I've found it, I think," one boasted. He held up a halfmoon of silver. "At least I think this is the coin."

"A trick," one of the guards declared as he inspected the bent coin. "You couldn't hit that dead center with an arrow."

"Would you care to put a few coins on it?" Jace asked.

The shield formation broke apart as the household guards dug into their purses for coins to bet. Soon, stacks for or against Jace spilled over from their height.

"And just so no one thinks I'm using a trick coin," Jace proposed, "I need someone to put up a new coin."

"I'll have this back and my share of the winnings," the guard officer claimed.

He rested a silver coin in the notch of the arrow. But, while bent over, he twisted the shaft. When the officer rose to leave, more of the coin's edge then the silver face presented itself to Jace.

"Wait," a guard protested.

Before he finished, the officer snarled, "Shut your mouth."

Intimidated by his commander, the household guard walked away without mentioning that the twist made the target much smaller.

"This is the finest weapon in the hunt or on the battlefield," Jace repeated the claim. "You've shown your faith, or mistrust of the bow, with your coins. Now, let's test the accuracy."

Jace sorted and selected a wide bronze arrowhead with one blade made of thin, but sharp bronze. It topped a flexible shaft. Once satisfied with the missile, the archer dropped his foot back and lifted his arms.

While pulling the bowstring across his chest, the guard officer shouted. Nothing specific, just an outburst meant to unsettle the archer. And it worked.

The arrow left the bow at an upward angle. Almost floating, the shaft pushed through the air rather than cutting a straight path.

Moans came from the believers. And the nonbelievers started to laugh, knowing their bets were safe.

Then the arrowhead dipped, the shaft leveled, and the arrow bent around an invisible corner.

Zip-Thwack!

Two shiny pieces from the silver coin flipped away from the notch.

As with most cheaters, the ones attempting to change the odds were the most vile about losing.

"He cheats," the officer exploded. "Seize him. I'm confiscating his wagon. He can pay off his debt in the stone works."

Jace placed the bow behind his knee and bent the arms. Once the tension lifted, he unstrung the bow.

"You asked when I arrived," Jace emphasized, "why I was here. I'm here at the invitation of Belos. Would someone run and fetch him for me."

Belos stepped through the gate and declared, "No need, I'm already here."

In the presence of the Lord's bodyguard and driver, the guard officer shuffled to the rear of his detachment.

"Don't you people have better things to do?" Belos challenged.

The officer and the ones who bet against Jace quickly filed through the gates. After taking their winnings, the others marched away.

"Do you always bet with dangerous men?" Belos inquired.

"If I want to make a profit," Jace submitted. He scooped up the remaining coins. "I do have a question."

"After witnessing that thing with the arrow, I refuse to bet against you."

"I don't want to bet," Jace said while counting out a few coins. "I was going to ask what the taxes are in Ilergetes territory."

"Lord Indíbil will like that," Belos stated. "Bring your wagon into the courtyard. Then follow me."

***

Lord Indíbil carried the muscles of a younger man and the scars of an old bull. His appearance left little doubt that he earned his position in the tribe and the title of Lord in battle.

"For you, sir," Jace said while dropping a handful of coins into the rough palm of the Lord.

"Usually, when a man fights for me, it's my coins that are handed over," Indíbil noted.

"Paying taxes, sir, makes me an honest craftsman," Jace responded. "But I do have a request. If I'm allowed?"

Noticing the smell of soap coming off Jace, rather than sweat, Indíbil sniffed and smiled at the cleanliness. Jace caught the approval and silently thanked the ferrymen for the advice.

While jingling the coins in his hand, Indíbil asked, "What can I do for the man who saved my life?"

"I'm a bow maker and I'd like to meet King Indibilis," Jace explained. "If I can convince him to form a company of archers, I could be their Captain. And earn an officer's wealth."

Indíbil walked to a table and deposited the coins in a box. Then he faced Jace.

"My cousin is a fair ruler and a warrior of fame," Indíbil described. "But he is a poor politician. He's too busy to expand his army. Currently, he's trying to hold his coalition together and remain King of the Ilergetes."

"But he beat two Roman armies. Or is that a myth?" Jace questioned.

"We defeated them but then our Carthaginian Generals ran from a patched together Roman army," Indíbil complained. "Since then, a couple of young war chiefs have been challenging Indibilis."

"If he had archers on his side, he could easily defeat any challenger," Jace proposed.

"If he had his daughters back from New Carthage, he could marry them to the upstarts and end the challenges."

The answer to one of his questions came so quickly, Jace missed it.

"But the archers could, ah. Excuse me, Lord Indíbil?"

"I was young once and I understand an ambitious young man," Indíbil granted. "But you aren't Ilergetes, and the Kings' daughters are in New Carthage. So, get that idea out of your head."

Jace had no designs on the daughters of Indibilis or the throne. But now, he understood that Cornelius Scipio held captive two girls who were worth a kingdom. With half his mission completed, Jace had to think of a tactic to get near Mandonius, the King's brother.

"If King Indibilis is indisposed, perhaps his second in command could use my services," Jace proposed.

Indíbil's face darkened and his eyes flashed. A little of the old warrior flexed beneath the surface of the old man.

"You seem to know a lot about my Tribe's business," the Lord remarked. "Maybe too much."

"Please sir, I can explain," Jace begged. "Last night, I spent the evening with the ferrymen. They like to talk and I'm a good listener."

"The ferrymen? Gods, they are like village wives discussing the appearance of a two headed cow," Indíbil laughed. "They've never seen one. But, like the ferryman on the subject of what happens in a Lord's compound, they can talk about it from dawn to dusk."

Jace remained silent. He'd pushed as far as he could without getting accused of being a spy.

"Belos, get him fed and find him a safe place to sleep tonight," Indíbil instructed his bodyguard. "He needs to be up early."

"Early, sir?" Belos inquired.

"Yes. Before daybreak," Indíbil replied, "if he wants to join the caravan to Algerri."

"Sir, what's in Algerri?" Jace asked.

"My cousin, Mandonius, War Chief of the Ilergetes People."

***

In the light of a setting moon, Jace eased the mule and wagon into a space between shadowy wagons in a supply caravan formation.

"As much as I appreciate the safety," a tradesman complained, "I could make a lot more if I had the freedom to set my own route."

"No one is making you stay," another told him. "You can leave the caravan, anytime."

"Sure, I can. And, lose my purse, my horse, my merchandise, and my cart to highwaymen. No thanks."

Between the poverty of the tribe, the abundance of unemployed soldiers turning to robbery, the wealth of the Lords, and the power of the War Chiefs, Jace realized that a treaty with the Ilergetes wouldn't hold. He'd need to warn Cornelius about the unbalanced society and the danger of trusting King Indibilis.

A rider trotted alongside the wagons and carts and alerted the merchants.

"Get ready to move," he called out to the dark shapes. "Check your wheels, and the hooves of your animals. We don't stop for repairs or for treatment of the lame."

"We don't stop," the complainer grumbled. "If anything is lame, it's having to do business this way."

"What we need is a good war to thin out the rowdy ones," the other tradesman offered. "And a war would bring a lot of trade to the territory."

Jace remained quiet as he pondered the ramifications of the statements. Not only was the population suffering from the activities of unguided youths, but the working class had given up on controlling them. More fodder for his argument not to trust a treaty with the Ilergetes.

Act 3

Chapter 7 – What Are You Today

After traveling four days on a trip that Jace could have run in a day and a half, the muted mountains in the distance became a collection of ever-growing peaks on top of recognizable slopes. Closer in, the caravan traveled through foothills with herds of sheep grazing on the slopes.

"Good land for sheep," Jace remarked.

The younger brother of the trader with the wagon ahead of Jace pointed to the shepherds.

"In the places where we trade, you'd see, at most, a tender and a dog in a day. But here, the shepherds stay within sight of each other."

"Bandits," Jace guessed.

They strolled along with Jace's mule between them. Underfoot the soil had been pounded into powder by passing hooves and wagon wheels. To accommodate the soft layer, all the traders wore smooth soled sandals with enclosed sides. The shape was comfortable. And, as anyone who ever walked behind a herd of animals understood, the enclosed sandals kept merda out from between toes. Plus, they were easier to clean than thick soled footwear.

"I like your mule," the boy remarked. "It's gentle. Someday I hope to buy my own trading rig."

"My teacher always said, if you earn a profit on little deals," Jace offered, "soon you'll have the coins to take advantage of big endeavors."

"Big endeavors," the boy stated. "I like the sound of that."

***

Later that day, the caravan topped a hill, and they caught a view of a broad valley. Fields of grain bordered wagon trails, olive groves sprouted from flattened mounds, and close to streams, rows of almond trees fought with oaks and maples for the water. On the far side of the valley, hard packed streets and brick buildings covered the lower slopes. Behind the buildings and high above the valley, stone walls announced the presence of a fortified installation.

"The Fortress of Algerri," the youth informed Jace.

Remembering what the ferryman said, Jace whispered, "King Indibilis' source of power."

"What's that?" the boy inquired.

"I was just wondering how the village managed to protect the fields and groves," Jace lied. "I guess patrols from that fort would do it."

As if summoned by the remark, six riders cantered over a rise from the side of the trade convoy.

"Where's the bow maker?" one demanded.

"Here," Jace announced. "Is there a problem?"

"Get out of line and follow us," the cavalryman ordered.

In what could only be an insult, the riders cantered towards the head of the caravan, leaving Jace behind. The move might have been to show superiority over a tradesman, or maybe a joke aimed at a man walking beside a mule. But the mule was long legged, the craftsman's wagon lightly loaded, the axles well-greased, and the tradesman a Cretan Archer.

When the cavalrymen reached the caravan guards at the front, they reined in. All five bent a leg and casually slung it over the saddle. The caravan guards rode out of line and assumed the same posture. They would have a while to talk before the tradesman arrived.

"I'm here," Jace announced from behind the riders. He scanned the relaxed cavalrymen. "I've had days to get to know the guards. But if you want to catch up with them, I'll meet you at the fort."

After a gentle tug on a long line, Jace, the mule, and the wagon raced by the riders. Aggravated by the counter to their jest, and the challenge to their superiority, the mounted men snapped their reins, and kicked their horses into motion. But two urged their mounts forward before lowering the bent leg. They toppled backwards off their horses. The four still mounted glanced back in response to the shouts of their companions.

"Do we go back?" one asked.

"No. That tradesman has lynx in his blood," the leaders stated. "It'll look bad if he beats us to the fort."

"Even if we arrive short two of our patrol?"

During the conversation, the cavalrymen stopped the frantic motions needed to keep the horses galloping. The mounts slowed to a comfortable trot. But the distance from where the caravan emerged from the hills, through the town, and up to Fort Algerri was less than three and a half miles. And while the mounted escorts faltered on the trail, the longed legged mule and the Cretan Archer never wavered.

***

The winding path carried Jace and the mule through the town and up to an open gateway. Slowing, they entered the fort. A spearman met them in the courtyard.

"Who are you?" the sentry demanded.

"Jace Kasia. I believe I'm expected."

"Don't know anything about that," the sentry admitted. "Wait here."

Jace patted the mule's neck. Then a voice rang out from an elevated balcony.

"That's him. That's Tribune Kasia."

Looking to escape, Jace faced the gateway. But four cavalry mounts filled the portal, blocking the route. Next a file of spearmen came from a doorway and surrounded Jace.

"Are you sure?" another man on the second-floor patio asked in a bored voice. "He doesn't look very intimidating."

"War Chief Mandonius, at the fall of New Carthage, I watched him converse with General Scipio. The General and his Colonels all listened to him."

Mandonius handed a pouch of coins to the man who identified Jace.

"Tell my cousin that I appreciate the warning," Mandonius said. "Guards, bring the tradesman to my audience chamber."

At spear point, Jace was herded through a door, up a flight of steps, and into a large room.

***

While a physically imposing man, befitting a War Chief of the Ilergetes people, Mandonius appeared to be half asleep. It went beyond the bags under his eyes and the red where the whites of his eyes should be, the man slumped as if exhausted.

Jace strutted to the center of the chamber, braced, then nodded as if agreeing with something, before saying, "I see."

"See what?" Mandonius questioned.

"In training, I often felt sorry for myself because I'm an orphan," Jace answered. "At those times, my teacher took me on a hunt."

"You don't know what I have on my mind," Mandonius thundered.

"Overwhelmed is overwhelmed," Jace suggested. "Be they worries about your brother's hold on power. Attacks on your border, bandits threatening chaos, or worry about a far-off loved one. It's all the same to your heart. It hurts and you can't sleep."

"What are you getting at?" Mandonius asked.

"When a man draws a hunting bow and aims an arrow at the heart of a deer, his mind can't hold onto negative thoughts," Jace informed him. "Do this. Lock me up and hold me for ransom. But understand, I'm not worth more than a couple of donkeys. Or, put me in a fighting pit and watch your men die on my blade. Or, cut my neck and watch me bleed."

"Are you that ready to die?"

"No, War Chief, I don't want to die," Jace confessed. "What I want is to talk to the best version of you. Not a sleep deprived husk of a man."

At the insult to their War Chief, spearmen stepped away from the walls and leveled their shafts.

"Stay where you are," Mandonius ordered. "How do you know I'm sleep deprived?"

"Because I was once a stick," Jace explained. "Dull, misshapen, and pointless. And for nights on end, I stood awake with only owls for company."

"Why do I care about a stick?" Mandonius inquired.

"A stick if treated right becomes an arrow that flies true. When you hunt, you can only care about the hike, the stalk, and the arrow's flight," Jace told him. "And afterwards, you'll eat a belly full of fresh meat. Then, truly exhausted, you'll sleep for a day."

"You make hunting sound like a medicinal treatment or perhaps a religious ceremony."

"It's both a treatment and a ritual, War Chief," Jace told him. "Lock me in a storage room and send for me when you're feeling clear headed and rested."

Jace about faced and began to walk from the chamber. Caught off guard by his self-assurance, the spearmen remained against the walls of the room. He almost reached the doorway.

"I thought you were a Roman Tribune," Mandonius mentioned. "You don't sound like a military man."

"What is a man on any given day?" Jace proposed as he turned away from the doorway and his escape. "One day, he's a married man with a loving wife who is a worthy companion. The next he is called on to wage war. And the next to adjudicate between offended parties. And, on another, he's called on to soothe the feelings of a close relative. You say I don't sound like a Roman staff officer. Perhaps, War Chief, today I am not."

"We can lock him in a supply room until you decide his fate," a Captain offered.

A breeze blew up from the valley. On the current, the aroma of green leaves and freshly turned earth mixed with grain pollen. It blew over the town, and after climbing the slope, the gust reached the fort. Coming through a window, the wind blew the War Chief's robe, and the scents tickled his nose. After a giant gulp of air, Mandonius issued forth an enormous sneeze.

So powerful was the explosion of air from his lungs that it bent him over. He wobbled for a heartbeat, before standing erect. Tears rolled down his cheeks requiring him to blink away the moisture. And, as it turned out, the tears also washed the sleep from his eyes.

"Sir?" the Captain requested. "The prisoner?"

"You should. No wait. Maybe," Mandonius started and stopped as he realized his mind was as clear as if he'd spent a carefree day in the hills on a hunt. "Kasia is not a Roman name."

"It is not, sir," Jace said. "I'm a Greek from the Island of Crete."

"You talked of arrows," Mandonius remarked. "Crete is known for their archers."

"Earlier you asked what I am. Sir, I am a Cretan Archer, first and always," Jace boasted. "And in my wagon, I have hunting bows, and arrows straight and sturdy. All ready for a hunt."

Mandonius inhaled, his chest expanding as if he was a bull about to charge.

"You'll join me for dinner," the War Chief instructed. "And bring one of your bows and a quiver of arrows. I want to see if the tales of Cretan Archers are true."

"Hopefully, I won't disappoint you."

"What do we do with him?" the Captain asked.

"Lock him in a storage room for now, and post a guard," Mandonius answered. "Because the other thing

I've heard about Cretan Archers, they're trained to run long distances without rest."

***

Jace was thirsty. In a misguided gesture of hospitality, a spearman tossed a wineskin in with the prisoner. Although a nice idea, Cretan Archers didn't partake of strong drink. And so Jace Kasia was thirsty when the guards came for him.

They pulled the four boards that created a makeshift door from the storage space and called Jace into the corridor.

"I need to go to my wagon before the meal," he requested.

"Why?" a Captain asked. "We can collect anything you need."

"Do you know the difference between a hunting bow and a war bow?" Jace inquired. "Between a thick spine and a pole?"

"A pole?" the officer repeated.

"Take me to my wagon," Jace insisted. "The War Chief wants a demonstration of archery, and you don't want to disappoint him."

"You mean, you don't want to disappoint him."

"No, Captain. I mean exactly what I said," Jace corrected. "My archery skills have been tested since I was a small boy. If you bring the wrong equipment, I'll have you do the demonstration."

For a moment, the officer thought about his average and not entertaining skills with a bow and arrow.

"Take the archer to his wagon," he directed. "But watch for any tricks."

Three spearmen guided Jace down a corridor, up a short flight of steps, and along a rampart with a view of the valley. At another set of steps, they descended to the courtyard.

***

Jace's mule and wagon remained where he had left them. But the beast wasn't alone. Other wagons from the caravan were unloading supplies for the fort. One transport belonged to the two brothers.

After taking a long drink of water for himself, Jace watered and fed the mule.

"Sorry for the neglect," he said as the animal chewed the feed. "But you'll like the young trader."

Then he changed footwear. Off went the tradesman's soft sandals for the beaten soil of a caravan. And on went the thick soled combat sandals of the Mogente tribe.

"Yo, boy," he called before pulling two bow cases and two quivers of arrows from the wagon. "Give me a silver coin."

The boy jogged over from his brother's wagon. His face contorted in a puzzled expression, the young trader questioned, "A silver coin? I don't understand."

"One coin for one big endeavor," Jace replied.

Reaching into a mostly empty coin purse, the youth shuffled aside bronze coins until he located one shiny coin. He extracted it and placed the silver in Jace's outstretched palm.

"You've just purchased a mule and a wagon, plus bow making tools and supplies," Jace explained. "Now take the deal and go make a profit."

Dumfounded by the exchange, the youth led the mule and wagon to his brother. While the two traders held an animated conversation, Jace pointed to the steps.

"Let's go," he instructed the guards. "We don't want to keep the War Chief waiting."

***

Tables and chairs had been carried to a deck patio and placed in a semicircle pattern. All faced the valley, giving each attendee a panoramic view, while allowing them to see Mandonius. Of the six chairs on each side of the War Chief, all but two were occupied. One on the right end sat empty while the other vacant seat was on the War Chief's immediate left.

"Our Cretan Archer finally makes his appearance," Mandonius proclaimed from the center seat.

Jace reached the top of the steps and approached the banquet from the side of the patio.

"Am I late, sir?" he inquired.

"No," Mandonius told him. He indicated the chair on the far right. "We saved you a seat."

Jace crossed to the end of the seating and rested the bow cases and quivers against a short wall. Then, following his training, he leaned over and estimated the height to the lower level.

"I've stationed spearmen down there just in case you decide to leave the feast early," Mandonius warned.

Turning and putting his back to the wall, Jace smiled and suggested, "There's another empty seat. Perhaps archery following dinner, after your guest arrives."

The Captains and Lieutenants seated on both sides of the War Chief all looked down at the empty tabletop. It appeared as if they bowed their heads in prayer. But it wasn't a ritual or an honor, as Jace discovered when the War Chief snapped.

"The guest I reserved this seat for will not be joining us. As she hasn't for months of sleepless nights," Mandonius said in a threatening manner. "It's why I was so happy to get my hands on a Roman officer. If I can't touch my Ama, at least, I can wash my hands in the blood of a Roman."

For no good reason, Jace congratulated himself on the success of his assignment. Not on the completion of the mission, he would have to escape and make it back to the Legion at Tarraco for that. But he had uncovered the value of Scipio's hostages. The daughters were needed to secure a Kingdom, and the wife, Ama, controlled the Tribe's War Chief, and therefore the entire Ilergetes army.

"Can I assume the evening's entertainment is archery," Jace asked. "And not my disembowelment."

"You assume correctly," Mandonius promised. "That pleasure, I'm reserving for late tomorrow morning. That'll give me a long sleepless night to anticipate your death."

Jace reached for a bow case. As he touched the oiled skin, four spearmen rushed onto the patio.

"I have no interest in sacrificing my life," Jace remarked to Mandonius. "You are safe from my arrows. But I would ask that your strongest man step forward."

"Are you going to kill him?"

"No, sir," Jace said as he bent the war bow behind his knee. "I simply want him to draw the bowstring and release an arrow. If he can."

Chapter 8 – The Final Trick

An almost lifetime of training allowed Jace to stretch the bowstring, demonstrating the proper technique for bending the bow. After gently easing the tension, he offered the war bow and a thick-spined arrow to a husky Lieutenant.

"Over the defensive wall and a little uphill is a dead birch tree," Jace directed as he offered the war bow to the Lieutenant. "Find the wasp nest and put the arrow in it."

"I don't see a nest," the man admitted while stretching the big muscles of his chest and shoulders. "A dangling nest would be wasps. Hornet nests are inside the bark. And you can't see them."

"He's got you there, Archer," Mandonius informed Jace.

"Then put this arrow in the tree about ten feet up from the ground," Jace told the junior officer.

After another session of flexing his shoulders, the Lieutenant took the bow and notched the arrow. Holding the bowstring between the fingers of one hand and the belly of the bow with the other, he elevated his arms and put tenson on the bowstring. A heartbeat later, he lowered the bow in an attempt to draw the bowstring by pushing down on the bow. The string barely moved.

"Pulling a war bow requires practice and training," Jace said while taking the bow and the arrow from the officer.

"No one can effectively use that weapon," the junior officer complained.

Jace drew, aimed at the tree, and released.

Zip-Thwack!

Ten feet off the ground, the thick arrow split and peeled off a section of bark. A swarm of hornets emerged from the breach and from access holes. Soon a cloud of angry hornets buzzed around the birch tree.

"Excellent," Mandonius declared. "The placement proved the existence of a hornet's nest, and the heavy draw proved the Archer's proficiency with a war bow. What else, Tribune?"

The addition of his Legion association was a thinly veiled reminder that Jace was under a sentence of death. The War Chief had not forgotten, but neither had Jace.

Servants came from a doorway holding pots and platters. Each steamed with a prepared dish.

"Should we wait until after we eat?" Jace inquired.

"One more demonstration while they set the tables," the War Chief told him.

Jace selected a thick arrow and a thin one as he walked to the other side of the patio. As he crossed, platters were placed on the tables and pots set on stands. In a smooth pull and release, the Cretan Archer launched the thick arrow into the sky.

The guests craned their necks and watched its flight. Soaring upwards at first, but after a shallow climb, the arrow arched over. Gasps came from the officers when they realized the arrowhead was coming right at the tables.

Zip-Thwack!

A streak, quicker than a blink, crossed from Jace's bow and impacted the think arrow. From targeting the seated officers, the thin arrow drove the threatening one off to the side. They fell harmlessly over a section of wall, falling to the ground below the patio.

***

Dodging danger, even if there was little chance of being struck by the descending arrow, brought a roar of approval from the War Chief and his guests.

"Now we eat," Mandonius exclaimed. When Jace had taken his seat, the Chief explained. "See the valley below us. It's more than lush farmland. We are located on the northern edge of Ilergetes territory. From here we can ship food to every part of our homeland. And from the fort, I can stop an enemy attack at our borders. And if Lleida is attacked, I can march to my brother's aid."

"Meaning the Fort at Algerri is the seat of King Indibilis' power," Jace stated.

"And the truth is revealed," Mandonius announced.

"I don't understand," Jace admitted.

"You're a spy and your ability to gather information for Rome has been exposed."

"But you just told me about the importance of the fort."

"Drink Archer Kasia, eat Tribune Kasia," Mandonius directed. "Because tomorrow, you won't have the stomach for it."

The cruel joke, referencing Jace's fate, brought laughter from the officers.

With no thought to the poverty and suffering of most of the tribe, Mandonius and his commanders ate and drank with relish. Jace isolated a pitcher of water and matched them glass for glass. Except, while he drank water, their cups were filled with strong wine.

***

Near dusk, Mandonius slumped over the table and pointed an unsteady arm at Jace.

"Archer. Another trick," he demanded.

"My pleasure, War Chief."

From the tabletop in front of Mandonius, Jace took a pair of beeswax candles. Carrying them to the wall by his chair, he set them a hands width apart. The wicks wobbled in the early evening breeze, forcing Jace to cup them with his hands.

"A good trick," Mandonius slurred. "Do you plan to dance for us in the candlelight?"

"I do so wish I could," Jace replied. "But it's too soon."

Mistaking the term dance as entertainment rather than the Cretan term for maneuvering and fighting, the officers laughed at the hopelessness of the condemned man.

"Maybe later," a Captain teased.

"Maybe," Jace agreed as he pulled his hunting bow from the case. With his body blocking the view, he put the war bow and several arrows on the top of the wall. Then he bent and strung his hunting bow. During the turn to face the banquet, the tip of the hunting bow brushed the war bow. The heavy weapon and the arrows fell, unseen, off the wall. "Now if I can have your attention."

Hands pounded on the tables and more wine was splashed into glasses held askew. Missing lips, a good portion of the wine spilled onto the tabletops.

"This better be good," the big Lieutenant proposed.

"I'm not one to grade his own skills," Jace told the junior officer while notching two arrows on the bowstring. "But it does go quick. Pay attention."

"Pay attention," Mandonius insisted.

At the urging of the War Chief, the guests settled.

"What are you doing?" a Captain asked.

"Extinguishing two candles at one time," Jace said.

"That's easy," the officer scoffed, "all you have to do is blow."

"From across the patio?" Jace asked as he rotated the bow from a vertical hold to a horizontal position.

Zip-Thwack / Zip-Thwack

The pair of arrows flashed across the patio. They skimmed the tops of the candles, touching only the wicks. And as if the arrowheads had stolen the light, both flames died. The shafts continued for a short distance before tumbling to the level below the patio.

"And that, War Chief, concludes the evening's entertainment," Jace announced. He marched to the bow case, dropped the hunting bow in, and tied off the end of the case. "You don't mind if I keep these?"

"In fact, I do," Mandonius answered. "Guards, escort the Roman Tribune to his accommodations. And take the bows and arrows from him."

Jace grabbed a pitcher of wine from the table before walking away from the feast. Behind him, the War Chief chuckled at the theft.

Four spearmen escorted Jace to the steps. Down on the rampart, Jace glanced, ever so briefly, at the flat area beneath the patio. Then the guards pushed him to the next set of steps. They descended to the corridor where Jace doubled over.

"I had too much wine," he complained. "I'd gladly trade this pitcher of red for a waterskin. Any takers?"

"I have water," a spearman offered. He lifted the strap of a waterskin from his shoulder. "It's not a problem. I'll get it back in the morning."

Jace handed off the wine and dropped the strap over his shoulder.

"Thank you," he said before walking into the storage room.

While the spearmen placed boards over the entrance, Jace Kasia pulled out several slices of lamb he'd salvaged from dinner. Carefully, he wrapped them in a piece of leather before tying the ends to his belt.

"Water, a meal, arrows, and a bow," he whispered. "Everything I'll need."

Cretan Archer Kasia sat in a corner of the storage room to rest. Sometime in the middle of the night, when most of the occupants of the fort were asleep, he would leave – quietly, if possible.

***

In the Fort of Algerri, night noises were composed of men on watch whispering to each other, footsteps of a few more assigned to walking posts, and the snoring of sleeping men. Groans, like the ones coming from the storage room, were rare.

"Are you alright?" the young guard asked.

From the cracks between the boards, he received a reply.

"Water. If I don't get water, I'm afraid, ugh…"

"Afraid what?" the spearman inquired.

The voice, weak and pleading, responded, "I'll die, and your War Chief will be cheated out of…ugh."

"What? Cheated out of what?" the spearman questioned.

"Move one board, take the waterskin, and have someone refill it."

"I don't know about this," the spearman admitted.

"His retribution for having his wife spirited away. Oh, ugh, water."

A truth of all armies, the overnight guard for a single detainee was often chosen because he was the newest member of a unit, and most likely, the least experienced. Facing the possibility that his War Chief's prisoner would die before Mandonius could extract revenge for his wife, the guard slid the crossbeam away from one board.

Then he shifted the board, creating an opening just wide enough to pass an item through.

"Hand me the waterskin," he urged. "Quickly."

"I'm on my knees," the voice whined. "Reach in and take it."

The arm extended through the gap. With his fingers, the guard searched for the strap to the waterskin. For a heartbeat, the youthful spearmen thought, "this is a bad idea."

Then steel like fingers gripped the young spearmen's wrist.

Bang. Bang. Bang.

At the third jerk of his arm, and the third collision of the guard's head with the door boards, the spearman went limp. Jace released him, extended his arm through the opening, and shoved the crossbeam aside.

***

At the top of the steps, the Cretan Archer dropped to his belly. Crawling under the patio, he collected his war bow and the arrows. Then, he crept to the far wall. From the patio, the drop-off to the exterior of the fort appeared high and too dangerous for a leap.

Jace shoved the arrows in his belt, slung the war bow over his shoulder, and shimmied his legs off the wall.

Hanging by his fingertips cut the drop nearly in half. He let go and fell.

Once outside the fort, Jace headed for the dead birch tree, being sure he scuffed the dirt as he went. For good measure, he dropped the two broken arrows on the path as he scaled the slope.

***

Another truth of the military, a good NCO would wake early and check on his least experienced soldier. Following the standard, Sergeant Betin entered the corridor expecting to find his charge asleep. Silently, he approached the entrance to the storage room.

"Better me than the Lieutenant," the NCO uttered. "Wake up, soldier."

But the corridor was empty. And while the crossbeam still bolted the doorway, there was no guard.

A muffled plea from inside the storage room called, "Help. Help."

It came out welp, welp. But to an experienced NCO, like Betin, the meaning was clear. He pushed the beam off the brackets, drew his sword, kicked the boards aside, and found his missing spearman.

Naked, tied, gagged, and looking pitiful, the guard wiggled, trying to escape.

"The Roman is gone," Sergeant Betin bellowed. "Search the fort. Get up and get moving."

While the officers and commanders slept off the after-effects of too much wine, the spearmen and soldiers came awake and searched the fort. In moments, a report from the rampart alerted them to the tracks and broken arrows.

Betin and twenty spearmen left the fort, jogged around the back, and down the hill to where they picked up the trail.

"He went up the slope," a tracker advised. "He's not that far ahead."

"Be leery, the Roman has a short sword," Betin instructed. "Stay close."

Two abreast, with spears leveled, the tightly packed search party raced up the hill. Betin and the scout were at the front, both scanning the crest of the slope as they approached the old birch tree.

They didn't see the slim strips of linen and leather. Or how the rag rope held an arched branch that suppressed a twelve-foot-tall sapling. When Betin tripped over the rope, the branch released the young tree.

"I'm alright," the Sergeant assured his men. "Let's get after the…"

Ten feet above their heads the branches of the sapling slapped against the arrow shaft. As if pried with a lever, the shaft ripped away birch bark, exposing more of the hornet's nest. Angry at the intrusion, the entire nest of hornets swarmed down and attacked the twenty spearmen and their Sergeant.

Chapter 9 – Dangerous Curves

Daybreak found Jace east of the fort and deep in the mountains. He sat in the fork between two branches watching Ilergetes riders gallop up a ravine. Even after they passed, he remained hidden among the leaves and the limbs. Having pushed hard throughout the night, he decided to rest in the concealment. But it wasn't exhaustion keeping Jace in the tree. A Cretan Archer could run for days. Rather, he waited as part of his plan to evade the pursuers. From the ridge above, Jace knew the ravine ended at a pair of steep sided rocks. Too steep for climbing, meaning the riders would come back.

Sure enough, a short while later, they returned. But their rapid gait had been traded for surveillance methods. Of the five riders, two watched the dirt trail for signs of human footprints while the other three scanned the bushes and the slopes. A very effective tactic for catching a frightened rabbit. Not so good for tracking a Cretan Archer who was as sure of his fieldcraft as a lynx was while on the hunt.

Jace had eighty miles of rough terrain to cross before reaching the coast and the Legion at Tarasco. He doubted the Ilergetes Tribesmen would catch him, or even see his trail.

**

Unknown to Jace Kasia, he was one hundred and ninety miles northwest from Albarracín, a village at a pass through the Iberian mountain range. Albarracín happened to be the same distance from Cornelius Scipio. Except the General resided in New Carthage and the coastal city sat one hundred and ninety miles southeast from the mountain village.

**

A breeze off Cartagena Bay sent fresh air through the streets of New Carthage. To the east of the city, a pavilion snugged against the hills, rocked in the gust. And while their commander prepared, nineteen Centuries of Legionaries and four Centuries of Velites waited on the road.

"Are you sure this is wise, General?" Sidia inquired.

He took a light riding cloak from a chest, shook out the white garment, and held it out at shoulder level.

"I've prayed on it," Cornelius replied. He allowed his bodyguard to rest the material on his shoulders and then pin the ends together at his throat. "And I received no negative signs."

"How often do the Gods warn you if there's a problem?" Sidia asked.

"Optio Decimia, almost never," Cornelius admitted.

He marched from the tent, glanced at the clear blue sky, and scanned the four wagons on the causeway. Then he mounted his horse.

Waiting for General Scipio was Titus Quaeso, the Battle Commander for the Steed of Aeneas, and Centurion Ceionia, the Legions' standard bearer.

"We're ready to march, sir," Colonel Quaeso reported.

"Unfurl the guidon," Cornelius directed.

Cornelius urged his horse into motion. Colonel Quaeso, Centurion Ceionia with the standard waving in the breeze, and Optio Decimia followed. Each held their mounts back to allow General Scipio to review the nineteen Centuries as he rode by. While the command staff cantered to the head of the infantry, cavalry officers dispatched two hundred horsemen. Some raced ahead to scout the line of march, others rode to the rear to secure the baggage train, and the rest trotted to the flanks to guard against an attack from the sides.

When the command staff reached the lead Century of heavy infantrymen, Cornelius reined in at the head of the columns.

"Steed of Aeneas, standby," Senior Centurion Thiphilia shouted after a gaggle of Junior Tribunes settled around the General.

His voice carried to the light infantry Centuries charged with vanguard duty.

In response, Tribune Justus Furia ordered his standard bearer, "Centurion Usico, free the Wings of Nortus."

When both the Steed and the Wings waved in the morning breeze, Thiphilia thundered, "Centuries, forward."

The junior staff officers galloped back and ahead to officially pass on the order to begin the march.

***

As the columns of fifteen hundred heavy infantrymen and their officers stepped off, the four wagons on the causeway rolled towards the formation.

In the lead wagon, Sucra mentioned to Aurunica, "He's very brave to make this trip."

"His generosity and motives are untested," the beautiful bride cautioned. "Although he is trusting enough to bring a small detachment. However, let's wait and see what develops before we dismiss our duty to our sisters and the Goddess Trebaruna."

The handmaiden bowed to Aurunica's wisdom. They rode in silence as their wagons joined the center of the march. Soon, the walled city fell far behind as the half Legion hiked away from the ocean and journeyed into the wilds of Iberia.

***

Twenty miles from New Carthage, the detachment entered a narrow pass. On their left, high above the rough wagon trail, a crown of rock jutted from the tree line.

"What's that," Cornelius questioned a Junior Tribune.

The young noblemen shifted his eyes to the land feature and back to the General.

"Sir, I don't know," he said.

"Senior Tribune Zeno," Cornelius asked the Legion's top staff officer, "what is that?"

Without looking at the rock formation, Zeno answered, "That sir is the Castillo De La Asomada. Our engineers estimate it's a thousand feet higher than the trail. But the steep sides of the rocks prevent it from being used as a fortification."

"An excellent rendition of facts," Cornelius allowed. "Now I ask you, Senior Tribune, why don't your junior officers know it? Have they never seen a map?"

In another setting, in Rome perhaps or another Republic capital, Zeno would push back against the brash young man. But this wasn't the Republic and Scipio wasn't just any youth.

"Sir, when we set up camp tonight, I'll hold a lecture on our route," Zeno promised.

"In almost ten years of fighting, Hannibal has butchered our top commanders and one out of every five able-bodied Latin men," Cornelius reminded him. "These youths are the future leaders of Legions. Our duty is to train them. Teach them to be aware of their surroundings and how to use the land to defeat an enemy."

"Yes, sir, I understand," Zeno acknowledged.

Cornelius twisted in his saddle to face another junior staff officer.

"What is the order of march for entering a narrow gap?" he inquired.

"Sir, two Centuries of skirmishers through to check for ambushes," the Junior Tribune replied. "Followed by two squadrons of cavalry to return and report any trouble. Velites on the high ground to the sides, and two Centuries of heavy infantry at the rear to guard against an attack on our supplies."

"An excellent answer," Cornelius announced.

As he spoke, skirmishers raced ahead of the columns, light infantrymen climbed the hills to the sides of the trail, and two Centuries of heavy infantrymen fell out of the line of march. The Legionaries would wait and close in behind the supply wagons at the rear.

What no Centurion or Tribune witnessed was an NCO of light infantry who kept pace with the bridal party. From high on the hill, he waved down at the women in the wagons and made rude gestures towards them. In his defense, Optio Obellie had been drinking since the day before.

"Women like me," he boasted to one of his Veles.

"I'm sure they do, Optio," the light infantrymen agreed.

But as everyone did when Obellie began drinking, he shifted as far away as possible from the obnoxious drunk.

***

Once through the gap, a unit of Tribunes, Centurions, and skirmishers separated two wagons from the supply transports. They rushed ahead of the march and crossed the Segura River.

Five miles on the far side of the gap, Castillo De La Asomada was still visible behind the detachment. From a distance, the natural formation on the heights resembled a fort, but it wasn't. Ahead of them, the low walls of Murcia did not appear to be the ramparts, but they were.

"Why build a marching camp? Why not camp in that town?" a Junior Tribune inquired. The youth pointed at Murcia. "With those knee walls, they wouldn't turn us away. No, I stand corrected, they dare not refuse us."

"They don't need high walls," Senior Centurion Thiphilia told him. "Notice the tall grasses between the clumps of trees. They signal swamplands. If we attacked down the road, they could hold us off for days. And if we went off the road, we'd be up to our knees in sticky mud for a week."

"Then we should avoid the city and find dry ground for the marching camp."

"And that's what we'll do," the Legion's senior combat officer stated.

Shortly after the talk, they walked their horses down the embankment and swam the animals across the Segura River.

***

A half mile beyond the river, the advance party set stakes for the corners of the marching camp. Inside those boundaries, they designated bivouac areas for the tents of infantrymen, the headquarters pavilion, spaces for more tents for Centuries, a wagon park, and an animal pen.

Back in the marching columns, the wagons of the bridal party reached the river.

"The light infantry will push them across," Obellie directed, waving off the nearby heavy infantrymen. Then he assured Aurunica, Sucra, Ylli, and the last member of the bride's party. "Ladies, you are in good hands. We'll get you across safe and dry."

As the Velites ran to the wheels, the sides, and the backs of the wagons, a Centurion from third Maniple noted the assistance. Typically, his Tribune would supervise the crossing. But his staff officer, a more senior Tribune, remained back in New Carthage with the other half of Steed Legion. With the wagons being helped, and even though the Optio in charge kept taking streams from a wineskin, the veteran combat officer figured everything was running well. He crossed with his Legionaries and ignored the bridal party.

From the wagons, Ylli observed, "That Optio might be trouble."

"Sucra," Aurunica remarked.

"I noticed," she responded. "If he gets out of line, something will have to be done."

Propelled by the horses and the muscles of the light infantrymen, the four wagons plowed through the water of the Segura River, climbed the far bank, and rolled towards the marching camp.

The NCO who oversaw the crossing jogged up beside the lead wagon.

"I'm Optio Obellie. It has been a great honor to help. Perhaps…"

Drunk and overly excited, the NCO's wet combat sandals crossed, and his ankles locked together. He dropped face down into the grass as the wagons rolled by.

"Come on, Optio," one of his Veles said as he yanked the NCO to his feet. "The Centurion has us scouting to the east."

"I was just trying to be polite," Obellie whined while struggling to stand. "Some people don't understand gratitude or appreciate the work of others."

"If we don't get moving, the Centurion will come over to see why we're still here," the light infantrymen urged. "You don't want him to see you like this."

"Women are trouble. Dangerous curves, I tell you," Obellie slurred. Then the words of his man sank into his wine-soaked brain. "Hades. Do I look that bad?"

"Red eyes, wine breath, you sound like a bent file being pulled along the edge of a sheet of copper, and you can barely stand."

"Pretty bad?"

"Nothing a good hike won't cure," the infantrymen assured him.

With the intoxicated NCO in tow, the Veles marched him to their squads. After everyone had a good laugh at the mishaps of their Optio, they jogged off to the east. A pair ran on either side of Obellie to keep him upright and moving.

***

In the almost completed marching camp, the bridal party was directed to the area where wagons were parked. Animal handlers unharnessed the horses, and a staff officer greeted the women.

"Ma'am," the Tribune invited Aurunica, "General Scipio has requested the pleasure of your company this evening."

"What if I don't want to join the General?" she inquired.

"In that case, ma'am, I'm ordered to select a seasoned Century and assign them to protect you for the night," the officer replied. "You'll be safe with eighty Legionaries sleeping around you."

Ylli, the youngest of the bridal party, made a sour expression and offered, "Men snore. And eighty will sound like a tempest."

Sucra bristled at the impetuous description. Before she could voice a reprimand, Aurunica placed a hand on Sucra's arm.

"We will be joining the General, once we've collected a few things," Aurunica told the Tribune.

"Very good ma'am, he'll be expecting you."

On one side of the wagon park, cavalry horses, mules, and draft animals were enclosed. Beyond the rope pens, cavalry squadrons pitched their tents. On another side of the animal pens, a minor argument broke out.

"My Century has been digging trenches," a Centurion complained. "Your people are out hiking in the countryside. You take the spot next to the animals."

Weak as a combat officer, a poor leader and defender of his men, the other Centurion folded.

"Fine. I'll let Obellie know when the Century gets back from their patrol."

***

The addition of four women to the command mess kept the Tribunes and senior Centurions on their best behavior. Of all the attendees, Cornelius seemed to enjoy the female companionship the most.

"The worst part of campaigning is being away from family," he proposed.

"Then why do it?" Aurunica questioned. "Your enemy is Hannibal Barca and he's in your Republic. Not in my Iberia."

"Your Iberia sends silver, copper, and gold to finance the Carthaginian," Cornelius answered. "Grain to feed his forces, and men to swell his ranks. And that is why I am here, far from my wife and children."

"As much as I dislike the outcome," Aurunica commented, "your argument is valid."

Behind Cornelius, Sidia stood silently, his eyes catching any quick movement. About halfway through the meal, a Tribune jumped to his feet to make an impassioned plea for his side of an argument. At the swift rise, Sidia looked for a drawn weapon or a threatening gesture. Then, he noticed Sucra's eyes. They were scanning the loud staff officer as well. After the man regained his seat and his composure, Sidia paid additional attention to the handmaiden. More than once, their gazes met as they both examined the guests for threats.

"The way she's acting, I wonder who she's guarding," Sidia Decimia thought to himself.

When the feast broke up, servants guided the women to a separate tent, and Sidia followed Cornelius Scipio to his quarters.

"That was a delightful evening," Cornelius declared. "I am sorry you didn't have a chance to speak with that lovely young woman, Sucra."

"As odd as it may sound, sir," Sidia told him. "We shared a few moments during the evening."

"That's good," Cornelius offered.

***

In a separate tent of the pavilion area, Aurunica gathered her three handmaidens to her.

"What did we learn?" she asked.

"General Scipio is well protected," Sucra explained. "Not once was his cup unguarded. And there was never an opening for a blade to reach his neck or his chest."

"I agree," Aurunica granted. "What else came to light this evening?"

"General Scipio is a family man," the other stated. "He speaks fondly of hearth and home. That combined with the way he's treated us, reveals a man of honor."

"But he allowed savagery and brutality when his Legionaries captured New Carthage," Ylli cautioned. "He is dangerous."

"Excellent points. Now ladies, we should pray to the Goddess of Hearths and Mysteries," Aurunica announced. "Ylli, please present the image of Trebaruna for our prayer circle."

The youngest of the wedding party stepped back while clamping her hands over her mouth. Wide-eyed at first, she blinked as tears welled up.

"I left our lady in the wagon," she sobbed. "I'm so sorry."

"We are a small group," Aurunica informed her. "Far from home and away from our sisters. To be without the light of our lady, is disheartening."

Ylli ran to a stand and snatched her hooded robe from the wooden peg. After throwing the robe over her shoulders and the hood over her head, the young woman slipped out of the tent.

Sucra smirked and indicated the exit with a nod of her head.

"No. She is young," Aurunica said. "She must learn her duties."

"In a camp with two thousand warriors," the fourth woman emphasized. "Full of men who savaged New Carthage."

"Ylli is the least mature of us," Aurunica proclaimed. "She has to learn responsibilities. We'll let her amend this sin of forgetfulness."

"Late at night, in a Legion camp," Sucra advised.

***

At the wagon park, Ylli wandered between transports. When they rode in, the sun was up. Now, in the middle of the night, the wagons were dark shapes on wheels.

"They all look the same," she sobbed. Terror at not being able to find and retrieve the statuette of the Goddess sent shivers through her body. Not thinking, Ylli ranted. "Where are you? You, stupid wagon."

"Can I help you?" a voice from behind her slurred. Ylli shook in fright, when he added. "Not so high and mighty down in the dirt with us animals."

Ylli spun to face the speaker. In the dark she couldn't make out his features. But that was unnecessary, by then she knew it was the rude Optio from the hills and the river.

"I have to go," the young woman announced.

Obellie reached out and clamped his hand over her throat. Squeezing, so she couldn't scream, he walked her backwards to the end of the wagon park. At the animal pen, he dipped them under the corral rope.

"You treated me like an animal," Obellie growled in her ear. "Now, I'll show you how an animal treats you."

As much as she struggled, the fingers pressing into her throat controlled her body. And when he spoke, the sour wine stink took her breath away. The only thing the young woman had control of was her faith.

"Goddess Trebaruna, preserve me," Ylli prayed before everything went black.

Act 4

Chapter 10 - Imagine a Fourth Threat

Dawn in the Legion camp found Legionaries packing their tents and gear. As the four women and their servants strolled from the command pavilion, the men along their route stopped work to stare. And who could blame them? Each member of the bridal party was prettier than the other.

During their passage, a shout of alarm came from the animal pens.

"We have a body," a handler screamed. "Looks like an infantryman."

Centurions raced around, shouting for a roll call of their Centuries, to be sure everyone was accounted for. A light infantryman from a squad near the pens ducked under the rope and approached the dead man.

"It's Obellie. I think," the Veles called to his squad.

"What do you mean think?" his squad leader insisted. "Is it the Optio or not?"

Stomping over, his Lance Corporal reached the infantryman and shoved him aside. From a forceful entrance onto the scene, the squad leader recoiled and backed away.

A once human form had been splayed open from his crotch to his throat. The lower entrails had been cut free, stretched out, and wound around his head, covering his face. Angry slashes were visible on both of his hands.

"How do you know it's Obellie?" the squad leaders asked.

"His feet. I recognize the combat sandals."

Tribune Furia and several Junior Tribunes lifted the rope and entered the animal pen.

"What happened here?" he questioned.

"Optio Obellie was hunted," the squad leaders replied.

"Hunted?"

"Yes, sir. As sure as a deer is field dressed or a boar, Obellie was stalked, knifed, and gutted."

"Do we know who did this?" Justus Furia inquired.

He didn't expect an answer. But when Senior Tribune Kasia returned from his mission, he'd expect a full report.

General Scipio and Sidia pushed aside two horses and strutted to the body.

"Sir, we've had a man killed," Furia reported.

"I can see that," Cornelius sighed. "Did anyone hear anything?"

Furia glanced around to see if he could find someone in charge of the Century. Noticing the Corporal, he beckoned him over.

"Your Century is next to the pens. Was anything reported last night? Strange noises? The sound of a struggle?"

"No, sir," the Tesserarius assured him. "No one on watch reported anything."

While the questioning was going on, Sidia squatted beside the body. With two fingers, he lifted a flap of stomach skin and studied it.

"Optio Decimia," Cornelius inquired.

"Just a moment, General."

Then Sidia rolled the body over and examined the corpse. Locating a hole on the lower back, he put a finger in the gash, and probed it.

"The wound is wide," Cornelius offered, "most likely from a Legion dagger."

"No sir," Sidia corrected. He held two fingers side by side. Then, as if outlining a wiggling snake, the bodyguard allowed the fingers to trace a twisting path downward. "There wouldn't have been any sound. Other than the dead man gasping a final breath. He was stabbed in the kidney by a serpent dagger. The pain would have frozen him. A strong back and forth action as the blade was removed left the wide wound."

"Who would carry that type of weapon?" Cornelius inquired. In the distance, he noted the four women and their staff heading towards the wagon park. "Get the bridal wagons harnessed and moved out before they see this monstrosity."

Grooms raced to sort out the proper draft horses. After the rush, Cornelius looked at his bodyguard.

"Well?"

"You won't see this on the hip of a Legionary or an Iberian infantryman," Sidia explained. "A serpent dagger is not good for chopping food or making kindling. It's designed for assassins and always hidden from sight."

***

While burning was preferred, it would take most of the day. No one complained when Optio Obellie was dumped in a hole and dirt shoved in over his mutilated body. After a prayer, his Century ran to catch up to the rear of the Legion detail.

Near the front, Cornelius looked at the sky, letting his horse select the path for both of them. After a long time reflecting, Scipio lowered his head.

"Optio Decimia, we have an assassin in our midst," he stated.

"Yes, sir, it appears that way," the bodyguard agreed.

"Is there anyway to flush him out?"

"None that I can think of, sir," Sidia admitted. "We'll have to wait for him to act again."

***

At midday, on the fourth day of traveling, the vanguard called a halt. Moments later, Tribune Furia rode to the command group.

"Sir, we've made contact with a war band from the Oretani," Furia reported.

"Were they expecting us?" Cornelius inquired.

"Yes, sir. But they're blocking our path," Justus Furia said with a sly smile, "until they meet King Scipio."

Cornelius gnashed his teeth together for a heartbeat. Then he gathered his wits and told the Tribune, "They want to meet King Scipio? Then they shall meet King Scipio."

Cornelius and Sidia nudged their horses into motion. Ten riders from First Century went with them. But Justus Furia held back for a moment, savoring the details of the exchange. The exact words would go into his next report to the Senate of Rome.

***

After two days marching in Oretani Territory, the Legion detachment followed the local guides off the plains and into the Iberian Range. The grades grew steeper, and the sides of the valleys rose in tree covered greens and browns. For a section, where they travelled along the bank of a mountain river, the gravel was mostly smooth. But when they left the riverbank, the trail proved hazardous. Weather erosion exposed rocks and loose stones while creating gullies. For all the speed of crossing from New Carthage, their progress slowed in the mountains.

"I don't like it, sir," Senior Tribune Zeno disclosed. He studied the rising slopes on both sides of the trail. "We've no room to set up a proper marching camp. And the Oretani scouts said we have another day of this."

The midday break allowed the Centuries to catch their breath and rest. And it gave the command staff a chance to meet.

"Suggestions, Senior Centurion?" Cornelius requested of the Legion's senior combat officer.

Thiphilia drew a circle in the dirt with the toe of his hobnailed boot, then another, and then a third.

"Let each Century create a perimeter and where two are near a wagon, have them link their defensive circles," he described. "We can't build walls, but we can protect each group with shields."

"It's the best plan until we reach another valley," Colonel Quaeso concurred. "What about security for the Bastetani bridal party? They only have drivers."

"Select the most reliable Century we have and put it at the wagons," Cornelius directed. "I don't anticipate trouble, but better safe than sorry."

"I'd trust the Twenty-fifth Century with the assignment," Thiphilia suggested. "Their Centurion is an excellent leader who maintains discipline in the squads."

"Pull them from the line of march and position them at the bridal wagons," Cornelius directed. "If there's nothing else, gentlemen, get some rest before we move out."

Too rough and steep for horses, the Junior Tribunes hiked up and down the trail delivering instructions about the night's formation. One of the young staff officers walked downhill to the last third of the detachment.

"Centurion Arathia, compliments of Senior Centurion Thiphilia," the young nobleman advised.

From across the trail, a voice offered, "This can't be good."

"Save it, Optio," Arathia told his Century's Sergeant. Then to the staff officer, he urged. "Go ahead, sir."

"The Twenty-fifth Century is to move up and secure the Bastetani bridal wagons."

Without hesitation, the combat officer pushed to his feet, lifted his bundle to a shoulder, and stood still for a moment. The simple act of standing drew the attention of his Legionaries.

"Twenty-fifth Century, your vacation is over," Arathia shouted. "Optio. Tesserarius. We have a protection mission. And I expect every Legionary to act like he's in his mother's kitchen."

"Suppose we don't have a mother, sir?" an infantryman asked.

"Then act like you're still in the nest, bird brain," Arathia snapped back. "Twenty-fifth, move out."

Before all eighty infantrymen could shoulder their spears and gear, their Centurion was hiking away.

"Move it, move it," the NCOs shouted. "If the Centurion gets there first, he'll begin counting. And you do not want to be the last man to arrive."

Some officers badgered assuming if they kept their men unbalanced and mentally beat down it would deliver results. Others used the fear of sessions on the punishment post. They figured frightened men would react as directed. But a few, like Centurion Arathia, understood neither intimidation nor fear created true strength and pride in a Century.

The challenge of matching him in climbing the trail caused the eighty infantrymen and their NCOs to scramble after Arathia. None complained, that would be a waste of breath. And they needed every breath as they rushed to catch up with their leader.

***

Aurunica watched as a combat officer marched rapidly up the slope. Behind him, and strung out along the trail, came a string of heavy infantrymen. Between the armor, helmets, weapons, and personal gear, it was amazing how fast they moved.

"In a hurry, aren't they," the bride said to her bridesmaids.

"I wonder what's going on?" Ylli questioned. "Have we been attacked?"

Sucra noted the relaxed Legionaries on the trail below their wagons, and ahead of them.

"There doesn't appear to be an all-out alert," she offered.

The four women watched in silence as the combat officer marched up to them, came to a halt, and saluted.

"Centurion Arathia of the Twenty-fifth Century," he reported. "We are here to keep you safe. I only have one rule."

"You have a rule," Aurunica cooed. "Just one? How delightful."

"What rule?" Sucra questioned.

"When I tell you to get behind a shield, you do it without question," Arathia told them. "Do that and my Legionaries will do the rest."

"Sounds simple enough," Aurunica noted.

"There's nothing simple about it, ma'am," the Centurion remarked. While looking down the trail, he explained. "We've trained hard for two years in order for me to have confidence in my men. And, to know the rule will keep you safe."

"Then we will follow your directions," Aurunica agreed.

Arathia spun towards the arriving men and pointed downhills.

"Optio, I'll have words with Legionary Turtle, when he finally arrives."

"Better him than me," a Legionary said to a companion.

The last Legionary arrived, bypassed the Optio, and marched up to Arathia.

"Centurion. I should probably hike back and help the squad servants with the Century's gear."

"That would be most generous of you, Legionary Turtle," Arathia confirmed.

"Turtle? That's a unique name," Ylli mentioned. "And he seemed so willing to be helpful."

"His name is Geno, ma'am," the Optio informed her. "Legionary Turtle is a slur for the last man to complete a challenge. And the Turtle gets to name his own punishment."

"Is that another one of Centurion Arathia's rules?" the third bridesmaid asked.

"Yes, ma'am," the Sergeant told her.

A moment later, orders were shouted up and down the line of march to move out. When the bridal wagons rolled forward, they were surrounded by the proud Legionaries of the Twenty-fifth Century.

High above the trail, five Celtiberi tribesmen watched the movement.

"That's her," one said. "You can't miss the black hair and the air of superiority."

"She's surrounded by infantrymen," another warned.

"We only have to get one blade by the guards to save Prince Allucius and the Celtiberi people."

"Tonight," a third suggested.

"Tonight," the first confirmed, "when the infantry falls asleep."

Below them, the Legion detachment crawled up the steepest part of the trail.

***

Dark came early in the mountains. But due to the plan, the half Legion continued the march until the shadows grew long.

"Halt and form your defensive circles," Thiphilia shouted.

The Senior Centurion's words were repeated forward to the scouts at the vanguard and back until it reached the last pair of infantrymen in the columns.

While most of the Centuries gathered in loose circles, the Twenty-fifth split. Forty men moved to one side while overlapping the back of the main wagon. And the other forty shifted to the other side of the wagon and the front.

"Every other man eats," Arathia ordered. "Everyone else, stand by your shield."

"Sir, we're in the mountains and far from anything," his Tesserarius pointed out. "Why keep forty men standing after a hard day of marching?"

"Good question," Arathia granted. "The answer can be summed up in four words, bears, wolves, and lynxes."

"Sir, that's only three," the Corporal ventured.

"Can't you guess at the fourth?"

"No, sir. I can't imagine a fourth threat."

"Neither can I," Arathia admitted, "and that's why we'll maintain the vigil all night. Because, why?"

"Because the unseen spear is the one that puts you down," the Tesserarius repeated from lesson by his Centruion, "the unseen blade is the one that cuts deepest. And the unexpected threat is the one that murders you in your sleep."

"Maintain the watch," Arathia ordered before he walked off to check the positions of his Legionaries.

***

On a ridge above the sleeping Legion, five pairs of eyes watched the cookfires blaze to life. From their vantage point, the fires appeared to be torches lining the mountain trail.

"Easy enough to find in the dark," the leader noted.

"Is this the only way, Aluth?" one inquired.

"Our borders are strong because we stand firm against invasion," Aluth answered. "What else is a joining between a Bastetani Priestess and our beloved Prince, but a soft invasion of Celtiberi lands?"

"The marriage must be stopped," another commented.

"Yes, it must," Aluth confirmed. "Now, make your way to that wagon and slay the she-demon."

Four of them slipped downhill and vanished in the dark bushes. Aluth, having set the deed in motion, strolled over the hill to his horse. A heartbeat later, he walked the mount away from the ridge, leaving his assassins to their work.

Chapter 11 - Red Limestone

Images of teeth, fangs, and claws coming out of the night kept the Legionaries alert. But as the night wore on, the exhaustion overcame the danger. Every guard in every Century, in the middle of the night, fought to remain awake. One advantage the Twenty-fifth had, beyond the threat of bears, wolves, and lynxes, their Centurion prowled the night.

"Are you ready?" the combat officer asked.

From inclining against his shield and resting his head against the spear, an infantryman straightened at the question.

"Sir, I am prepared to die in combat for my Century and the Republic."

"Wrong answer, Legionary," Arathia corrected. "Your job is to make the other guy die in combat. You, stay awake and live."

"Yes, sir."

As he navigated around a sleeping infantrymen, Arathia staggered. It had been a long, long day. And cracks were forming in his veneer of the tireless commander. But he needed his NCOs fresh in the morning to manage the march. Figuring he could rest while he hiked, Arathia shrugged off the fatigue. Before he took the next step, a voice whispered from the back of the bridal wagon.

"Centurion, don't you every sleep?" Ylli inquired.

Arathia walked to the back of the wagon. One of the young women from the bridal party sat on the tailgate with her skirt covered legs dangling outside the wagon.

"Ma'am, I might ask you the same thing."

"I was asleep," she remarked. "But there is tension in the night. Don't you feel it?"

"A Centurion holds the lives of eighty-two warriors in his hands," Arathia told her. "For me, every day is filled with tension. Tonight, shouldn't be any different."

Ylli extended an arm and rested three fingers on Arathia's cheek.

"You sense more than you'll admit, Centurion," she stated.

Withdrawing her hand and then her legs, Ylli retreated into the wagon.

The brief encounter, deep in the night, refreshed him. With renewed clarity, Arathia returned to checking on his infantrymen. A moment later, a figure dressed head-to-toe in black dropped from the back of the wagon.

Once on the ground, the person crouched next to the rear wagon wheel. At first the squatter focused on the noise of men shifting and trying to stay awake, or those sleeping and snoring. After isolating and discarding the nearby noises, the dark figure cast a wider net.

Insects dodging bats, and small creatures scurrying from cover to cover while avoiding owls, combined to create a uniformed hum. But like a ripple in the corner of a pond when a fish broke the surface to eat a water bug, a disturbance in the night created a hole. Animals trembled in place and insects swarmed away from several intruders.

***

Two of the men tasked with murdering the demon bride, assumed the guard was listless and sleepy. They came from the dark in a headlong rush. One slammed into the armored chest and stabbed with his knife. The second man stepped to the side, using the fight to hide his approach to the bridal wagon.

But an edge of the big Legion shield slammed into his hip before he got by the scuffle.

"Rah," the Legionary roared. He swung his shield at one and hammered the forehead of the other attacker with his right fist. "Tonight, you die."

The circling assailant rolled into a sleeping infantryman.

Even though he was wrapped in the arms of Morpheus, the words Rah and Die reached his subconscious. Yanked away from the God of Dreams, the Legionary came around with his helmet and crushed the skull of the second assailant.

The first attacker dropped from the guard's punch. In the light of a campfire, he saw the face of his companion. But it was oval rather than round. Then, before the spear took his life, he understood. The other assailant's head was cracked open like a crushed melon.

In a heartbeat, the Twenty-fifth Century linked shields and lowered spears, creating a ring of hardwood and sharp steel around the bridal wagon.

"Your shoulder is bleeding," the Optio said to the sentry who had been attacked.

The Legionary lowered the tip of his spear and indicated the dead assailant.

"That's just a scratch, Optio," he exclaimed. "I let the other guy die for his cause."

"Rah," shouted the infantrymen on either side of him.

While the barrier prevented another attack from outside the perimeter, it didn't stop the two assassins already inside the ring of shields.

***

Although it provided barely any cover, one killer lay under the wagon pole with his head by the yoke. Relying on the wood and the harnesses for the draft horses to break up his form in the dark, the executioner remained still. Around him, the awake NCOs and the combat officer shifted to encourage individual Legionaries. Once the excitement faded, he would crawl, literally backwards, to the front of the wagon. Once there, he'd enter and murder the demon and her handmaidens.

A pair of hobnailed boots stopped next to the yoke, and the wearer shouted, "Twenty-fifth, count off."

"One"

"Two"

The boots didn't move. The counting grew fainter at the rear of the wagon but increased in volume as the men nearer the pole and yoke responded.

"Seventy-eight"

"Seventy-nine"

"Eighty"

One boot slid away, and the assassin smiled. He'd avoided detection. But when the sound of a steel blade being drawn reached him, he thought about moving. The thought only lasted an instant before he arched his back against the pain of a sword penetrating his spine.

"It's not a bear," the Tesserarius proclaimed while drawing his gladius from the man's back. "It's another one of Turtle's playmates."

"Is he dead, Corporal?" a Legionary inquired.

"I am proud to announce," the Tesserarius replied, "he unwillingly died for his cause."

"Rah," the forward section of the defensive line shouted.

Neither the Centuries securing the livestock and the other wagons, nor their officers were willing to leave their defensive line. They had no way of knowing who the Twenty-fifth was fighting. However, the victory cheers told them the Legionaries were winning.

***

At the rear of the bridal wagon, the fourth assassin waited. He's located a maze in the Century's pile of tents and extra gear and crawled in between a gap. From the cries of Rah, he realized his three companions in the venture were gone.

Not afraid to die, but leery of falling short, he recalled Aluth's words for encouragement.

"What else is a joining between a Bastetani Priestess and our beloved Prince, but a soft invasion of Celtiberi lands?"

He listened for the Legion officer and NCOs to make another round. When the Centurion moved off, the murderer scrambled out of the labyrinth. In a crouch, he ran for the rear of the wagon. Leaping, he gripped the top of the tailgate while drawing his long knife.

"Assassin?" a soft voice called to him from under the wagon.

He would have ignored the voice and completed his mission. Except a length of cold steel in his gut held him in place.

"Slayer," he growled. A shove drove the blade up to the hilt, and the failed murderer moaned. Although he knew the answer, the assassin inquired. "What now?"

The voice answered, "you die for your cause."

The serpent dagger twisted as it rotated upward, piercing the man's heart. Releasing his grip, the assassin fell from the tailgate. Quickly, the black clad figure ran to his head, grabbed the arms, and pulled the body to the pile of gear. In a final act of butchery, the wavy, double-edged dagger was jerked downward and across the dead man's stomach. Then, as silently as the figure emerged, Slayer slipped back into the bridal wagon.

***

Normally, after a violent engagement, Legionaries suffered a letdown. It was especially true when dawn chased away the shadowy night. But three bodies told the tale of their brush with danger, and it motivated them.

"Standdown," Arathia ordered. "If they want to try their merda in the daylight, we'll welcome them with bare steel. Rah?"

A surge of "Rah" came back to him.

"Centurion," the Optio called from the rear of the wagon. "We've another corpse, but no one is claiming the kill."

Fearing the deceased was an animal handler or a wagon driver who stumbled into the wrong camp, Arathia jogged towards his NCO. The death of a servant wouldn't end a career, but it would dilute the pride his Century was experiencing.

When he arrived, the Optio informed him, "He's a Celtiberi, sir. You can tell by his height and the light-colored hair."

Arathia held his NCO in high regard. And never more so than at that moment. While the Centurion squinted at a disemboweled gut and cords of intestines spilled on the ground, his Optio managed to notice other details.

"Who is he?" Arathia inquired. He pulled his eyes away from the gore and examined the ground for footprints.

"Not one of our drivers or mule handlers," the NCO informed him. "From the way he's dressed, and the long knife, I'd say he's one of the assassins."

"Then who killed him?"

"That sir, is an excellent question."

***

News of a nocturnal attack reached the command staff. Not long after receiving word, General Scipio, Optio Decimia, ten Legionaries from First Century, and Senior Centurion Thiphilia reached the area controlled by the Twenty-fifth. Immediately they were drawn to the rear of the wagon by the presence of the Centurion and his NCOs.

"What happened here?" Cornelius inquired.

He pointed at the mutilated corpse.

"Sir, he's one of four murderers we intercepted last night," Arathia stated. "Two were killed on the defensive line by my infantrymen. Another was discovered under the harnesses by my Tesserarius and sent to Hades before he could do any harm."

Sidia Decimia moved to the body and began probing the gash.

"And this one?" Cornelius asked.

Sidia twisted to face Cornelius and whispered, "the assassin was killed by our assassin."

Overhearing the declaration, the Senior Centurion bristled.

"How can you say that?" Thiphilia demanded. "The Legionaries of the Twenty-fifth did a magnificent job last night. Perhaps, in the fog of battle, one of them struck down the killer but can't remember doing the deed."

Sidia clamped his mouth shut and locked his eyes on his General. Ever aware of his status among the men, Cornelius Scipio lifted his arms into the air.

"After an intensive investigation, I've decided the Twenty-fifth Century shall be awarded a unit citation," Cornelius announced. "For gallantry while on special assignment, the men of the Century valiantly defended people under my care against an assault in the night. Killing four, they drove off the rest in as brutal a manner as one would expect from Republic infantrymen. In doing so, they showed bravery, skill, and discipline while upholding the honor of the Steed of Aeneas Legion. Let their praise be voiced far and wide by order of Cornelius Scipio, General of Iberian Legions, the Prorogatio of Iberia."

Following his speech, Cornelius handed Arathia a pouch of coins.

"For your Century's funeral fund, or a feast when we return to New Carthage," he explained with a salute. "For now, toss the bodies on the side of the trail so we can get the detachment moving."

"Yes, sir," Arathia acknowledged. After handing the pouch to his Tesserarius, the Centurion exclaimed. "They tried and they died. And the Twenty-fifth? We survived. Drop them on the side of the trail as a warning to others, then gear up. Our day is just starting. Rah?"

Joining the eighty Legionaries, and the two NCOs, Cornelius and his party added their voices to the resounding "Rah."

After the General and his company left, Centurion Arathia looked at the ground for footprints. But the multitude of hobnailed boots had marred the area, destroying any trace of the fourth assassin's real killer.

"Are we leaving soon?" Ylli asked from the rear of the wagon.

"Yes, ma'am," Arathia confirmed.

***

At midday, the vanguard of skirmishers from Wings Legion, Tribune Justus Furia, and the Oretani scouts reached the top of the mountain. As each stepped onto level ground for the first time in days, they beheld a wonder. Below, a river with wide banks ran through a lush green valley. The land offered almost flat trails, fresh water, and space for a marching camp and safety at night. Yet, the bottomland wasn't the most spectacular feature of the basin. At the end of the valley, the trail vanished between slopes glowing orange red in the sunlight.

"Celtiberi territory," one scout stated.

"Where?" Justus Furia asked.

"At the start of the red limestone walls," the Oretani told him. "We'll leave you there. The Celtiberi aren't fond of visitors."

"We're visitors," staff officer Furia remarked.

"Like I said, Tribune, they aren't fond of visitors."

As if a mosaic in a fine Roman villa, the high bare rocks set atop the evergreen trees on the lower elevations seemed more art than nature. The vibrant colors and contrasts fascinated Furia. Distracted, he tripped on a rock and dropped to a knee.

To cover for the Tribune, First Centurion Turibas rushed to his side, and knelt on a knee, as if praying. Then he pulled Furia to his feet.

"Did you hear about the citation, sir?" Turibas asked, as if they were discussing the vista.

"I heard a Century had contact," Furia proposed, "but nothing about an award. What happened?"

"The Century killed four and the rest ran away," Turibas answered. "No one knows why the Celtiberi would attack us."

Remembering the scout's words, Furia instructed, "Send a messenger back to General Scipio. Have him forward the engineers to lay out a marching camp."

"Yes, sir," the First Centurion stated. After the courier left, he added. "The citation is for bravery by order of Cornelius Scipio, General of Iberian Legions, the Prorogatio of Iberia. Pretty impressive."

"Too bad it's not a royal decree," Justus Furia whispered.

***

By early afternoon, the rear of the detachment dropped through the pass and marched into the valley. The movement was so quick, the stockade walls and defensive ditches were only partially constructed.

"Give me a half maniple across the valley," Cornelius directed.

Senior Tribune Zeno of Steed Legion pointed at the head of the valley and also at the rear.

"Might I suggest another half maniple behind us," he offered.

"Seal the valley," Cornelius agreed. "But leave the Twenty-fifth with the

Bridal wagon. At least until the walls are up."

***

The six Centuries of the first maniple jogged by the Legionaries constructing the camp. Two hundred feet down the valley, the columns split with two hundred and forty infantrymen going to the left and an equal number going right.

They formed two rows with six combat officers spaced behind the defensive lines. The single Tribune for the right side of first maniple galloped from his Eight Century on the left to his Thirteenth Century on the far right.

After the quick inspection, he reined around, and trotted back the way he came. Each of his six Centurions received a salute as their staff officer rode by.

In a mirror image of the first maniple, the third maniple stretched across the valley to the rear of the camp.

"The valley is sealed, sir," Colonel Quaeso reported.

Cornelius twisted and looked back at the wall of shields and Legionaries. Then he shifted, peered beyond the camp, and declared, "Your spears are appreciated, Colonel."

The comment puzzled Titus Quaeso before he noticed the high pass at the end of the valley.

Streaming down through the red limestone gap were columns of Celtiberi heavy cavalry. Their lances held high, allowing the sunlight to reflect off of a thousand steel tips. And each of their tough mountain horses pranced in anticipation of battle.

Chapter 12 – Swallowed My Pride

Justus Furia also noticed the aggressive greeting party.

"Centurion Usico, pull two Centuries off the construction work and take them to first maniple," the Tribune instructed. "I'll check with the General for more specifics."

"Yes, sir," the standard bearer for Wings Legion acknowledged.

In the few moments it took Furia to reach Cornelius, Usico had mounted, waved the standard, and gathered one hundred and sixty light infantrymen.

"General Scipio, I've sent two Centuries to the battle line," Furia informed Cornelius.

The two Centuries ran to the rear of first maniple, and clustered on the riverbank in the center of the valley.

"Keep them behind the heavies for now," Cornelius advised. "I don't want to initiate a battle if all the Celtiberi want is to intimidate us."

Furia sent a Junior Tribune with instructions for the Velites to hold behind the Legionaries.

"If that's all they want, sir," Steed's Senior Centurion suggested, "it wouldn't hurt to open a gap in our lines."

"What are you thinking?" Cornelius asked.

"Give them an advantage," Thiphilia explained. Despite the scoffs and snickers from the command staff, Thiphilia continued. "Open an easy route through our lines."

"You mean offer their horsemen the riverbed," Cornelius said, his eyes opening wide with understanding. "And let our Velites use javelins to keep them in the water. That's a dangerous test, Senior Centurion."

"It's better than trampled light infantryman, and our front line of shields dodging hooves while battling lances," Thiphilia stated.

"Take your standard bearer and make a show of keeping Legionaries out of the water," Cornelius ordered the senior combat officer. "The infantrymen will appreciate it. Let's see if the Celtiberi do."

Ceionia unstrapped the Steed of Aeneas standard and allowed it to dangle in the windless air of the afternoon. Only when the standard bearer and the Senior Centurion galloped towards first maniple did the cloth lift, and the banner flutter against the pole.

"That should get their attention," Cornelius mentioned.

"Sir, not to be argumentative," Battle Commander Quaeso remarked, "but half a maniple of heavies, two Centuries of light, and our two hundred mounted, isn't attention getting. At least not against a thousand heavy cavalrymen. Let me send second maniple forward."

While the Legionaries were stacked two deep in order to span the valley, the heavy cavalry mounts facing the infantrymen were in files six deep. By sheer mass, the Celtiberi had already won the battle of intimidation. But they hadn't won the war, as the war hadn't started.

"Not yet," Cornelius responded. "We need the second to finish the stockade walls. Plus, I'm curious about what the Celtiberi have in mind."

"If they get it in their minds, sir," Zeno warned, "they could ride over the first and be on you quick."

"Senior Tribune, if that's all they wanted, we'd be elbows deep in blades and bodies by now," Cornelius told him. "I think they're waiting for something."

"Maybe an excuse to attack, like a flight of javelins from our skirmishers," First Centurion Rosato guessed. "Or an advantage, like that one."

A gap opened between the Tenth Century and the Eleventh. Legionnaires moved out of the stream and up onto the dry land of the embankments. Left behind was a gaping hole in the center of the Legion line.

"There it is," Cornelius pointed out. The opening may have been a wet, river rock strown pathway, but it would allow riders to get behind the Legion's shield wall. "Will they take it?"

From the ranks of Celtiberi riders, a few trotted out and approached the stream. More joined them but none charged down the watercourse.

"What's missing, Battle Commander?" Cornelius questioned.

Hyped up and focused on which Centuries to move to the attack line first, Titus Quaeso missed the meaning of the inquiry.

"Excuse me, General?"

"Look at the cavalry," Cornelius urged. "What's missing?"

"They haven't taken advantage of the breach," Quaeso guessed.

"That's obvious. I'm asking, where is their command staff?"

A reply came when a trumpet blared from the gap. Riders in bright armor with banners flying overhead came galloping through the opening in the red limestone.

"I'm going forward to talk with them. You stay here," Cornelius instructed. "If I'm attacked and go down, Colonel, you're in command. Make the Celtiberi pay. Then get my men safely out of this valley."

The officers in the command staff were impressed by Scipio's lack of concern for his own safety. And while the Centurions and Tribunes appreciated the bravado by a General of the Republic, the Legionaries in the group came to a different conclusion. They would repeat Cornelius' order to get his men safely out of the valley. His words would be repeated often along with an oath of fidelity to General Scipio.

"We'll be there with you, sir," Rosato proclaimed.

"No, First Centurion. Keep First Century around the Colonel. Just give me three veterans," Cornelius said. "I've already got Steed's and Wings' banners and Optio Decimia."

"That's not a very impressive entourage, General," Senior Tribune Zeno remarked. "You're very courageous to put yourself in harm's way. But shouldn't you take a bigger party to display your status?"

"Aristotle taught that courage is a virtue," Cornelius responded. "It's a virtue that moderates our instincts. On one hand it directs us towards recklessness, and on the other, cowardice. In the end, the Greek philosopher believed the courageous person feared only things that were worth fearing. Do you really think a handful of junior staff officers, several Tribunes, a cluster of Centurions, and a hundred veteran infantrymen will elevate me in the eyes of a thousand Celtiberi riders and their commanders?"

Cornelius nudged his horse and the mount cantered away from the staff. Sidia galloped ahead of the three veterans and caught up with Cornelius.

"I've been with you long enough to know you aren't reckless, General," Sidia speculated. "Therefore, I assume you see something in this situation others missed."

"They came through the gap as if expecting a fight," Cornelius replied. "When we didn't offer one, they formed ranks and sat around as if waiting for an inspection."

"You don't think the Celtiberi came to fight?"

"They've invaded Oretani territory and that seems wrong. Plus, the cavalry arrived without a command staff. And for no good reason, they acted like a bully trying to start trouble," Cornelius explained. "Someone was looking for an opportunity."

"An opportunity to do what, sir?" Sidia asked.

"If I knew that, I'd be a wealthy seer and not a General," Cornelius proposed. "Signal the standard bearers to join me."

Scipio slowed his mount to a walk. As he approached the first maniple, the two standard bearers fell in off the haunches of his horse, and the guards flanked the banners.

"Make a hole," Cornelius commanded. Then, as he rode by the two rows of inexperienced infantrymen, he leaned over and spoke to the Legionaries. "If I have to retreat, I'm depending on you to hold the line. Rah?"

His voice didn't carry far. But as Cornelius Scipio moved through the assault lines, a rolling cry of Rah came from the Centuries. It sounded as if the infantrymen were spontaneously cheering their General.

***

Prince Allucius rode with a vengeance and curses on his lips. On either side of him, his cavalry Captains kept pace with the Celtiberi noblemen. And behind the commanders, their standard bearers fought to keep the poles upright during the race through the red gap. And farther back, trumpeters blared notes signaling the cavalry to hold their location.

"Thank you, Reue," the Prince prayed to the God of Justice and Death.

The invocation came from seeing his one thousand heavy cavalrymen waiting in ranks. Across from them, the Romans dangled a pitiful double line of four hundred and eighty heavy infantrymen with a breach in the center of the defensive lines.

"The scoundrels tempt us with weakness," Captain Amaina shouted.

"Was it you who sent the cavalry out early?" Allucius roared back.

"No, my Prince," the officer assured him.

"Somebody did," Allucius growled.

Yet, he felt the same way. Obviously, the weak defensive formation of the Legion begged to be trampled and lanced. It cried out for his brave cavalrymen to ride through the first lines, and destroy the light infantry clustered together in the rear. But then the trap became apparent.

With a new stockade fort anchoring the battlefield, the Romans had placed another five hundred heavy infantrymen there, along with almost two hundred light. And deeper in the valley, a third group of heavies waited to close the door on his cavalry should they fall for the trap.

"The area between the fort and the rear infantrymen is the killing ground," his other cavalry officer confirmed, as if reading the Prince's mind.

"Kunbiur, did you order the cavalry forward?" Allucius bellowed.

"I did not, my Prince," Captain Kunbiur promised.

As the seven riders reached the valley floor, a lone figure in a helmet with a white plume and white cape, broke away from a collection of mounted men near the stockade. Before the man in white reached the lines of Legion infantrymen, the standards from two companies joined him.

"They have wisely sent out a negotiator," Amaina advised. "Perhaps, my Prince, you should accept their surrender and save them the embarrassment of begging."

"But first, you should inform him that his General's tricks wouldn't work on Celtiberi tribesman," Kunbiur suggested.

Allucius slowed his horse, giving him time to weigh his options. To go forward and deal with the negotiator himself, or to send his Captains? It made a difference for one of his status.

***

Sidia fought the urge to break formation. Although he didn't, he did shout to Cornelius, "General Scipio, I should be by your side."

"Remember when you said, you didn't think of me as reckless?" Cornelius replied. "You didn't know me when I was younger. You should ask around the next time we're in Rome."

"God Averruncus, protect him," Sidia prayed to the god who averts calamity.

His plea came in response as two Celtiberi officers, their two standard bearers, and eight lancers cantered forward to meet Cornelius.

***

"Why are you here on our frontier, Latian?" Captain Kunbiur demanded.

Before Cornelius could reply, the other inquired.

"Why do you tempt my cavalrymen with weak formations?" Captain Amaina questioned. "Do you think we're stupid."

Cornelius Scipio reined in and sat, silently, staring straight through the Captains.

"I'm talking to you, envoy," Kunbiur snapped.

His sharp tone caused the mounts of Cornelius' escorts to prance. It took a few moments for the Legion riders to settle their horses. During the disturbance, Cornelius remained quiet and stationary.

"Perhaps the Roman's cut out the tongues of their negotiators," Amaina proposed. "It does cut down on the small talk."

The Celtiberi group laughed at the thought of a mute messenger.

"He doesn't talk," Kunbiur emphasized. "Do you think he bleeds?"

Sidia Decimia placed a hand on the hilt of his gladius and lifted his heels in preparation to rush in and protect his General. But a wave of Scipio's hand stopped the bodyguard.

The nineteen mounted men sat staring at each other until Amaina threatened, "If you don't want to talk, we will ride you down, and butcher every Latian in the valley."

Cornelius raised an arm and swept his hand in a circular motion. In response, he and his escorts began to turn their horses. Halfway around, Cornelius stopped his mount.

"Tell Prince Allucius that in the morning, I'm taking my Legionaries and his bride back to New Carthage," he advised. "We've already been attacked once on the trail by Celtiberi assassins. Tell your Prince, if I'm attacked again, we will bring forth Hades on every Celtiberi we meet until the end of time."

Cornelius kicked his mount, and the beast trotted back towards the Legion lines.

"Wait," Kunbiur called, "who are you?"

Cornelius didn't reply to the cavalry Captain. But he did order Sidia, "Optio Decimia guard my back. I don't trust those cowardly, disloyal Celtiberi."

"Yes, General Scipio," Sidia shouted as he galloped across the entourage to put his body between the stunned and confused Captains and the General of all Roman forces in Iberia.

Kunbiur glanced at Amaina with a pained expression on his face.

"What do we tell Prince Allucius?" Amaina questioned.

"That we lost his bride," Kunbiur proposed. "But what did the Latin General mean by him being attacked by Celtiberi assassins?"

"Come on, let's go confess," Amaina proposed. "I was a good Lieutenant before the promotion."

"If we're lucky just to be demoted," Kunbiur said. "He may have us shoveling horse manure before sundown."

***

Cornelius held up three fingers as he passed through first maniple. The two rows collapsed until the inexperienced Legionaries were in their rightful triple ranks. On the other side of the defensive line, he held up two fingers and indicated the compressed defensive formation. Near the stockade, Colonel Quaeso issued orders. An instant later second maniple jogged by Scipio as they moved forward.

Before the General reached the marching camp, the valley was sealed by a wall of spears and infantry shields. No cavalry would dare attack the triple layer of a Legion assault line.

"I had swallowed my pride to come here," Cornelius admitted. "The Celtiberi took Carthaginian coins and deserted my uncle. For their deceit, I've a mind to advance across the valley and bleed the pigs."

"Sir, we can, and we will," Titus Quaeso assured him. "But it'll be a costly fight."

With his hands shaking from anger, Cornelius lifted his face to the sky. At first his chest rose and fell rapidly. But the longer he regarded the heavens, the more shallow his breathing became. When his rage finally subsided, he lowered his face and smiled at the Colonel.

"But I'll settle for keeping her father's ransom, and selling Prince Allucius' bride into slavery," Cornelius stated before riding into the completed stockade camp.

Act 5

Chapter 13 – League of Old Men

Titus Quaeso passed through the main pavilion, exited the tent, crossed a causeway, and entered the bridal tent. His arrival brought Aurunica and her handmaidens to the sitting area. Accompanying the women was a pleasant aroma of flowers and spices.

"I want to apologize for the absence of General Scipio," Quaeso explained. "His temper is still hot. Not having an emotional attachment to the situation, he chose me to deliver an unfortunate message."

"Colonel Quaeso, you are always welcome," Ylli assured him. "Whatever you have to say, we're ready for it. And honored that General Scipio picked such a distinguished herald."

Caught between the message, the platitude, the expressive eyes of the handmaiden, and the heady fragrance, Quaeso hesitated. A moment later, he composed himself and squared his shoulders.

"In the morning, the Legion detachment will break camp and march for New Carthage," the Battle Commander announced. "Once in the city, Aurunica from Bastetani will be sold to slavers."

The three bridesmaids shouted at once, interrupting the Colonel. Only after Aurunica hushed her attendants did she speak up.

"What of the ransom my father paid for my freedom?" she inquired.

"About the silver bars? General Scipio said it wasn't sufficient to replace, Gnaeus Scipio, the uncle of the General of Iberia."

Titus Quaeso stepped back, preparing to leave when Sucra held up an open palm.

"What of us?" she asked.

"The bridesmaids will be free to return to their villages," Quaeso answered before ducking out of the tent.

***

Once alone, Sucra nodded at the tent flap.

"You questioned Scipio's generosity and reminded us that his motives are untested," she said to Aurunica. "After this news, are you ready to honor our sisters and the Goddess Trebaruna."

"First we must pray to the Goddess of hearths and mystery for guidance," Aurunica proposed.

"We can't wait for too long," Ylli warned. "Tomorrow, Scipio will have us heading in the wrong direction."

"But can Quaeso be trusted to do the right thing?" Sucra inquired.

"Contemplation sisters," Aurunica advised. "Let us pray."

The third bridesmaid silently dipped her head in solidarity with Aurunica.

***

During the nightly staff dinner, a rainstorm blew through the valley. The sides of the pavilion flexed tight in gusts and collapsed when the wind subsided.

"It's a good night to be inside," Justus Furia mentioned.

Cornelius set down his glass and cocked his head in the direction of the Wings' Tribune.

"You aren't wrong," he said. "But your concept is in error."

"How so, General?" Furia asked.

"As pleasant as it is inside this tent," Cornelius answered as he stood, "on the defensive line, our Legionaries are wet, cold, and sleeping in mud."

Cornelius walked to a servant and took an oiled goatskin tarp from the man. He tossed the wrap over his head, grabbed two wineskins, and made for the exit.

"Where are you going, sir?" Colonel Quaeso inquired.

"To share a tonic against the weather with our infantrymen."

"I should go with you," Quaeso volunteered.

"You stay and entertain the staff. I'll be back later."

While the Colonel remained at the feast, Sidia Decimia sprinted from the General's private quarters. Racing from the tent, he ran to catch up with Cornelius.

***

No one feels the blessing of the Goddess Miseria like an infantryman on a combat line. And never was her presence felt more acutely than when sleeping in the mud between sessions of standing watch.

The guard from second maniple, Steed of Aeneas Legion, shifted. The move dumped a fold of cold water down his back.

"That'll wake you up," a voice said from behind the line.

When the rain started, it doused the open air cookfires. A few creative infantrymen had placed covers over their flames. But rain driven by wind reached under the awnings and drowned those fires. The absence of heat and light left each man wet and cold, and feeling isolated.

"Who are you?" the Legionary demanded.

He fumbled his spear before leveling the shaft at the dark shape standing in the rain.

"Just a staff officer checking the guard positions," Cornelius answered, by far understating his position. "Can my Optio and I come forward?"

"Yes, sir," the Legionary allowed.

Cornelius and Sidia stepped close to the infantryman.

"You look miserable," Cornelius said while handing the guard a wineskin. "A little of this will help cut the cold."

"Thank you, sir." At half a stream, the Legionary lowered the skin and attempted to hand it back. "Sir, that's really good, I mean excellent, red. You must have taken the wrong container of vino."

"No, Legionary, I took exactly the one needed for a night like this. Drink a little to take the chill off. But not so much that you end up on the punishment post."

"Look around, sir," the infantryman urged after he swallowed a second gulp. "Isn't this punishment enough?"

"I can't argue with you on that," Cornelius agreed.

After retrieving the wineskin, Cornelius and Sidia moved down the line to the next guard. Along the route, they carefully stepped around sleeping infantrymen.

Once the visitors were away, the guard's Centurion slipped up next to him.

"Do you know who that was?" the combat officer asked.

"A staff officer," the infantrymen informed his Centurion.

"No Legionary. Not just a staff officer," the Centurion corrected. "That was General Scipio and Optio Decimia, his bodyguard."

"What was a General doing out here in this weather?"

"Obviously, he was delivering vino to his infantrymen."

Still damp, and still cold, yet the idea of his General caring enough to share vino with an infantryman warmed the Legionary's heart.

***

Deep in the night, a soaking wet General and his equally damp bodyguard returned to the pavilion. A couple of low burning braziers provided weak light and a little warmth for their hands.

"Get some sleep," Cornelius directed as he rubbed the feeling back into his fingers.

"Yes, sir," Sidia replied, "once you're secured in your quarters."

"I'm surrounded by Legionaries," Cornelius remarked, "how much safer can I be?"

"Asfáleia, sir," Sidia mentioned.

"Asfáleia?" Cornelius asked.

"It's a Greek word Jace, rather, Tribune Kasia uses," Sidia replied. "He likes it because it has a lot of meanings but all of them revolve around protection. For instance, safety, security, insurance, assurance, safely locked, and safeness, as in the act of being safe. Understand?"

"I get the message," Cornelius admitted. "If you're going to tuck me in, hurry up. I'm beat."

They crossed the meeting room. Before entering the narrow passageway to the General's private chamber, Sidia reached out and gripped Cornelius' arm. A gentle pull backward stopped Scipio in midstride.

Moving forward alone, Sidia entered the smaller tent. He found two more braziers burning low and casting pools of light on the simple furnishings. Before he ran to catch up with Cornelius and join the tour of the assault line, Sidia had practiced his version of asfáleia.

A brass candle holder on the corner of the camp desk had an unbroken trail of beeswax connecting the metal rim to the desktop. A leg of the desk chair remained on a specific edge of a bronze coin. On the bed, the edges of a folded silk scarf retained the twisted peaks instilled by Sidia. But the two chests that carried the General's belongings were out of alignment. Four pieces of straw on the floor marked the original corners, but not anymore.

Sidia drew his gladius as he rushed across the room. On his last step before reaching the chests, he swung the flat of the blade as if it was a club. Sweeping behind the containers, the steel connected with an object.

"Ugh," a high-pitched voice emitted.

Along with the vocalization of pain, a black clad figure popped up and attempted to jump the chest. But the swing had been hard, and while a larger person might have absorbed the blow, the smaller body simply collapsed over the chests.

Not sure what he was dealing with, Sidia rapped the assassin on the back of the head. Leaving the black clad figure disoriented and draped over a chest, the bodyguard searched the corners of the chamber for another assailant.

Once sure the assassin was working alone, Sidia called softly, "General Scipio, you have a visitor."

***

Cornelius Scipio balanced the serpent dagger on his palm and admired the wavy curves of the blade.

"It's a fine weapon," he declared. "And your description is apt Optio Decimia. It's not good for slicing meat or chopping kindling."

Sidia finished using the silk scarf to tie the black clad figure to the chair. Standing, he reached out and gripped the hood.

"Sir, with your permission?" he requested.

"Please. I'm curious about our assassin," Cornelius informed him. "And who wanted me dead."

Sidia lifted the hood and revealed Sucra, the bridesmaid and Sidia's former dinner partner.

"Young lady, would you like to explain this?" Cornelius inquired.

He tapped the blade on his palm.

"I am a slayer. A bringer of death to enemies of the Goddess Trebaruna," Sucra hissed.

"Sir, perhaps it was the bump on the head," Sidia offered. "It seems she doesn't realize the situation."

"I know my fate full well," Sucra boasted. "I am ready to die for my Goddess."

"Optio Decimia, before I awaken the First Century, please clarify for the young lady the reality of what is about to happen," Cornelius urged.

Sidia squatted so he was at eye level with the assassin.

"You can continue to spout fanatic phrases right up until we put you on the cross."

"I am ready to die for my Goddess."

"Yes, we heard you," Sidia assured her. "But you won't be alone on the wood. Aurunica, Ylli, and the silent one will be joining you. At your feet, we'll cut the throats of your chaperones, your drivers, and your other servants."

"But they had nothing to do with this," Sucra protested.

"You attempted to murder the Prorogatio of Iberia," Sidia accused. "And you claim it was just you and the Goddess Trebaruna who planned it? That's not likely. Without further understanding, we'll let First Century handle it going forward. But know this, everyone in or connected with the bridal party will be taken into custody. General, I think we have room in the donkey pen to hold them until morning."

"Optio, it's wet, and muddy, if that's the word for what's mixed in with the soil, plus the wind's up and it's cold tonight," Cornelius pointed out.

"Yes sir, and none too good for a band of ungrateful thieves and murderers."

"We aren't thieves or murderers," Sucra snapped.

"Perhaps, we can come to some other arrangement," Cornelius proposed. "If I had more to base my judgement on. Let's start with your party not being thieves and murderers. Present company excluded."

"The Goddess of the Hearth and Mysteries calls to a select group of women in each village," Sucra divulged. "When our men go off to war or raiding, we protect the citizens against marauders."

"That explains the serpent dagger and you as the slayer," Cornelius guessed. "What about the others?"

"Aurunica is the priestess of our cult," Sucra informed the General. "Ylli the face should we need a distraction. The unnamed one is our recorder. She listens and remembers, but rarely speaks. And I am the Slayer. You know my duties."

"So far, you've spared the lives of your servants," Cornelius allowed.

"Wait," Sidia commented. "At dinner, you said you were all from different villages."

"And we are," Sucra confirmed, "and from different cults of Trebaruna. But we were selected to travel with Aurunica on an important mission."

"To kill Prince Allucius," Cornelius concluded. "I might save you the trouble and kill him myself."

"No. General Scipio please, no," Sucra begged.

***

It was the first instance where she had shown any real emotion.

"If you aren't here to kill the Prince," Sidia asked. "Why are you here?"

"To protect Aurunica and the Prince and stop anyone from interfering in the wedding."

"Like me?" Cornelius inquired.

"Yes, General Scipio," Sucra confirmed. "Much to my dismay, someone exactly like you.

"Why is this marriage so important?" Cornelius questioned.

"The Celtiberi tribe is landlocked," Sucra explained. "They need a harbor for trade and fishing. If they move directly west, they'll get into a protracted fight with the Edetani and the Contestani. That'll leave them open to an attack by the Ilergetes from the north."

"Another of my favorite tribes," Cornelius said, his voice dripping with sarcasm. "Go ahead."

"But if the Celtiberi attack to the southeast, they'll trip an agreement between the Oretani, and my people, the Bastetani," Sucra described. "The only way to prevent all-out war, is for a Bastetani to marry into the Celtiberi Tribe. Aurunica can open trade routes that will benefit everyone and prevent a massive loss of life."

"And keep your men at home," Sidia stated.

"Yes," Sucra confirmed.

"Untie her and send her back to her people," Cornelius ordered.

"I don't understand," Sucra admitted.

"The General doesn't want to throw people into the mud and then post some poor Legionaries to guard you," Sidia told her. "But remember these two things. If you come within an arms distance of the General ever again, I will cut you down. And then, I'll personally direct a Legion assault line through your hometown. We will kill every man, woman, and child as well as the livestock."

"I'm keeping the serpent dagger," Cornelius told her. "Now go before I change my mind."

Walking stiffly, maybe from nerves, or from the blows by the gladius, Sucra marched from the chamber. With the failure of her mission, the future looked bleaker than before the attempt.

***

Sleep evaded Cornelius. Indecision twisted his gut, as his mind remained undecided. A war between eastern tribes would bring havoc to the region. And the weakened state of the local tribes would create opportunities for a Carthaginian army of western

Iberians. Contrasted with a deep primal need to avenge his uncle and father and his wounded pride, the twenty-five-year-old felt almost crushed under the weight of the obligation.

"He was twenty years old," Sidia whispered from the passageway.

"How long have you been there?" Cornelius inquired.

"Since I changed into dry clothes, General Scipio," Sidia told him.

Cornelius paced the chamber twice more before stopping and asking, "Who was twenty years old?"

"King Alexander of Macedon was twenty when his father was assassinated. Tribune Kasia told me about him. After the death of his father, the new King murdered his rivals, then campaigned across Macedonia and Greece before arriving at the gates of Corinth. In the Greek city, Alexander convinced the old men from the League of Corinth to let him lead the Greek army against Darius III. And, as recorded by historians, he was very successful against the King of Kings."

"What does that have to do with me?" Cornelius questioned.

"What else is the Senate of Rome but a league of old men," Sidia proposed. "And what is Iberia but a collection of unlawful kingdoms?"

"I can't wage war against all of them."

"Sir, there's only one battlefield you need to conquer," Sidia offered. "Find victory on that one, and the rest are simple problems of logistics."

Cornelius stretched out on his bed and stared at the dark ceiling of his chamber.

"How long until daybreak?" he asked.

"Not long, General," Sidia replied. "Do we march backward to New Carthage and prepare for a long siege? Or do we march forward to Albarracín and witness a marriage?"

"That skirmish, Optio Decimia, is still being contested."

"I understand, sir."

***

A short while later, a Junior Tribune dashed into the passageway from the pavilion.

"General Scipio. A Celtiberi in ceremonial armor and two runners are outside the stockade walls," the youth shouted. "The duty Optio wants to know if he should open the gates for them, sir."

"Sidia, I asked Jupiter for guidance," Cornelius mentioned as he swung his legs off the bed. "Do you suppose this is the sign?"

"You won't know sir, if you don't order the gates opened."

"Yes, of course. Tribune, open the gates for the Celtiberi and have him escorted to my pavilion."

"Yes, General Scipio."

"Optio Decimia. Help buckle me into my ceremonial armor," Cornelius instructed. "For whatever Jupiter has sent me, I want to look like a General. Not a sleep deprived politician.

"An excellent choice, sir," Sidia acknowledged.

Chapter 14 – Of a Priest and an Assassin

The ceremonial armor glowed in the rays of the rising sun. Although the storm had passed, the ground was muddy. To remain unsoiled, Cornelius waited on the platform in front of his pavilion. And while he remained clean, it wasn't an apt description of a rider and a pair of runners approaching from the main gate.

Wet dirt, tossed up by the horse's hoofs, clung to the animal's legs and underbelly. Additionally, the mud coated two men holding onto straps on either side of the saddle. Pulled along, they easily kept pace with the horse even as their legs churned faster than was comfortable.

"It's a light infantrymen's trick, sir. They're using the horse to pull them at a faster rate and for a longer distance than they could without the aid," Sidia whispered to Cornelius. Then aside, he warned the Legionnaires of the First Century. "Watch those two. If they draw weapons, ignore the blades, and guard the General."

"We know what to do, Optio," a veteran infantryman assured him.

"A naked blade to a Legionary is a challenge," Sidia related. "I'm reminding you, so you don't attack the man and ignore your duty. Rah?"

"Rah, Optio Decimia," several First Century veterans responded.

"Do you really think the Celtiberi would only send three men to kill me?" Cornelius inquired.

"Three or a thousand, General," Sidia answered. "It only takes one to remove the head of an eagle."

"So noted," Cornelius agreed. "Those two hanging onto the saddle, they look familiar."

"They should, sir," Sidia advised. "They're the arrogant Captains from yesterday's meeting."

***

Cornelius saluted as the rider reined in at the pavilion.

"Welcome. I am Cornelius Scipio, General of the Iberian Legions and Prorogatio of Iberia."

The rider returned the salute. As he acknowledged Cornelius, the runners stepped away from the flanks of the horse. They saluted as well.

"I am Allucius, Commander of the King's cavalry," the rider exclaimed, "Prince of the Celtiberi, and fiancé of Aurunica from Bastetani."

Cornelius dipped his head in understanding before inquiring, "Have you come to say goodbye to me or to your bride?"

The question rattled the young Prince. His arm shook, jiggling the reins in his hand, and as if he had a fever, he licked his lips to replace the moisture.

Cornelius assumed the same blank stare, and far off expression he'd used during the first meeting.

After a long, strained pause, Allucius announced, "They have something to say."

The two Captains braced, and after collecting as much dignity as possible considering their unarmored and filthy state, the pair saluted again.

"I am Kunbiur, Captain of the King's Cavalry," one officer introduced himself. "I offer my apologies for my bad manners and my insults."

Cornelius looked at the man's mud encased feet and legs, and the splatters on his tunic. After inspecting that officer, he turned his attention to the other cavalryman.

"And I am Amaina, General Scipio," the other stated. "A Captain of the King's Cavalry and I want to beg your forgiveness for my actions during our meeting. And it goes without saying, my rude behavior."

"Well, that's that," Cornelius declared. He extended his arm and pointed back down the road. "There's the gate. Thanks for coming."

Cornelius was half turned when Allucius pleaded, "General Scipio. We need to talk. Or rather, I need to speak with you."

Squaring his shoulders to the Prince, Cornelius informed him, "Yesterday, I rode out to talk and wasn't given the opportunity. Today, you ride into my camp and apologize. And now, I'm supposed to forgive and welcome you with open arms?"

"I might point out that I've put aside your remark about the Celtiberi being cowardly and disloyal," Allucius interjected. "Can we not come to some sort of truce?"

There were three possible ways to end the adversarial exchange. Should Cornelius Scipio walk away, in all likelihood, the action would trigger an armed conflict. At his core, Cornelius welcomed the fight and an opportunity to avenge his uncle. Another possibility was to hear the Prince's side and glean some insight into the Celtiberi as an enemy or an ally.

Or, most satisfying, Cornelius thought while looking in the direction of the red limestone pass, he could order the deaths of the Prince and his Captains then march on the cavalry. From yesterday's example, he doubted the Celtiberi cavalry were prepared for an attack. In his soul, family pride screamed for revenge.

But just as he started to order Allucius' death, Sidia's words came to him, *"There's only one battlefield you need to conquer. Find victory on that one, and the rest are simple problems of logistics."*

Gritting his teeth against the urge to murder the Celtiberi, Cornelius addressed the First Centurion, "Centurion Rosato take Captains Kunbiur and Amaina and allow them to wash. Then supply them with clean tunics. When they're presentable, have the Captains join Prince Allucius and me in my pavilion."

"Yes, sir," the veteran combat officer acknowledged. "Captains, this way please."

"We're talking?" Allucius inquired.

"Not out here," Cornelius replied, looking up at the mounted Prince. "It's never a good idea for men to look up at, or to look down on, other men during negotiations."

As the Centurion and the Captains walked away, the Prince dismounted and followed Cornelius into the pavilion.

***

Pitchers of wine and ale, along with glasses, were placed on the table. After serving, the aides faded back against the far side of the pavilion and out of hearing range.

"What we say should be private," Cornelius submitted. After Allucius agreed, he continued. "Yesterday, your cavalry charged into another tribe's territory. They gathered in ranks, then sat leaderless, aimless, and idle until you arrived. Why?"

Of all the possible topics, Allucius hadn't planned on discussing the failings of his command structure. He almost changed the subject until he noted the intensity in the eyes of the Latian General.

"At dawn, a priest of Bandua held a sacrifice and invited the Lieutenants of the cavalry," Allucius explained. "Somehow, during the prayers to the God who protects cities and towns, the junior officers got it into their heads that you came as an invader."

"But they didn't attack," Cornelius remarked.

"Their maneuver created a defensive formation to block the pass," Allucius described. "Unless attacked, they would have remained in ranks while waiting for me and their Captains."

"That explains the cavalrymen. Why were your senior officers so insolent?"

"I'm sure you noticed my hesitation to discuss this," Allucius said. "The night before last, Kunbiur and Amaina attended a dinner with a priest. I didn't know they were primed to mistrust, and yes, to mistreat you. To my horror, I sent them to speak with a man I thought was your emissary, and not you in person."

"You know there's a common thread running through this situation," Cornelius proposed.

"It took half the night to identify the, as you call him, the thread," Allucius stated. "His name is Aluth. And the priest of Bandua was the speaker at the dinner and the one who officiated at the morning sacrifice."

"Is he against your marriage to Aurunica for personal reasons?" Cornelius asked. "Or, just opposed to prosperity for your people?"

"Aluth is a leader in the Celtiberi first alliance. He and his types believe the Celtiberi culture is superior and should remain pure and unpolluted by other tribes."

Cornelius refilled the Prince's cup. As he poured, he locked eyes with Sidia, before shifting his focus, indicating the rear of the tent. The bodyguard stepped away, about faced, and marched for the back exit of the pavilion.

"I understand the personality," Cornelius informed the Prince. "There's a politician in Rome who believes the Latin culture is the only civilized one. We've debated on other subjects, but every time at its core, Cato and I tangle over the philosophy of change."

"But you're a Republic General. Everyone knows you are, and forgive me, arrogant and unbending in your Latian ways."

Cornelius took sips of wine to delay revealing his beliefs. Finally, he placed the cup on the tabletop.

"You know that my homeland is under attack by Hannibal Barca," he divulged. "Every Latin commander who has gone against the Carthaginian has suffered defeat. It appears the old, strict ways no longer work. I'm learning to embrace other cultures. Once I have the skills of Hannibal, I'll command an army as diverse as his, and I will defeat him."

"Then you understand?" Allucius questioned.

"I understand I can't build Legions if the eastern tribes are warring with each other. I understand the Carthaginians will be emboldened by my failure. And I understand the wedding must take place to calm the situation. Is there something I missed?"

"One thing," Allucius replied. "You understand why I can't punish Aluth."

"It would create a breach between the ruling family and the priesthood," Cornelius guessed.

Before he could say more, Captains Kunbiur and Amaina, along with Centurion Rosato marched through the front entrance. At the same instance Aurunica, the silent one, Ylli, and Sucra strolled into the main pavilion from a back entrance.

***

Allucius and Cornelius stood, faced the bridal party, and hoisted their glasses. Aurunica and her bridesmaids stopped to listen.

"To the marriage of Aurunica of Bastetani and Allucius, Prince of the Celtiberi. May their joining bring prosperity to both tribes," Cornelius announced. Then he offered. "To express my best wishes, as a wedding gift, I am presenting the silver Aurunica's father paid for her release. Silver increases perception and helps regulate emotions. Things a married couple often need. And silver can be polished to a mirror shine allowing one to see themself from outside the body. May you both be temperate with each other and look upon the other with kindness all the days of your life."

As Cornelius and Allucius drank a toast, Aurunica and her bridesmaids curtsied at the generous gift. When they started forward, Sidia hooked Sucra's arm and pulled her aside.

He handed her an object wrapped in a roll of fine leather.

"I believe, Slayer," the bodyguard told her, "shortly, you'll learn where the serpent dagger will do the most good."

Sucra batted her eyes at Sidia, then winked, and rushed to catch up with the bridal party.

Chapter 15 – Good to be Home

The last day of Priest Aluth's life, he sacrificed and schemed, while publicly soliciting the Gods to bless the marriage of Prince Allucius and the Priestess Aurunica. As Cornelius Scipio watched the bridesmaids escort the beautiful bride in her black wedding dress, the final day of the Priest's life dwindled to a conclusion. For not long after sunset, the Slayer would remove him and his threat to the marital bliss of the newlywed couple and the commercial result of their union.

As Cornelius Scipio was witnessing the marriage ceremony in the town of Albarracín, a warship backstroked to the north beach at New Carthage. When the keel touched the shallows, half the oarsmen jumped into the surf and pushed the quinquereme onto dry land. Once the ship settled, Jace Kasia leaped from the stern of the warship. A moment later, his bundles landed beside him.

"Good to be home," he mentioned to the empty shoreline.

Then Jace realized he only used the phrase because his Legion was stationed at the island city. He'd have said the same thing if Wings of Nortus was positioned at Tarraco, or Rome, or on the Island of Crete. Until that moment, he hadn't realized the emotional connection he had to the mixed-use Legion.

Jace waved to the sailor who threw the luggage. Then he picked up the bags and marched towards a hill on the far side of the road. Four men slept under a tarp. Farther up the slope, a cocked onager baked in the hot sun.

"Firewood?" Jace inquired.

"Are you blind?" one of the dozing men answered. "Can't you see those stones and the weapon? We're a shore defense installation."

None of the four bothered to open their eyes to see who was speaking. Jace dropped his bags and climbed to the weapon.

"A good torsion cable," he announced. After tapping the taut horsehair and sinew cable, he observed. "In another day, this will all be firewood."

"What are you talking about?" one of the men challenged.

Coming to his feet, he took a step towards Jace. Then he stopped short.

"Senior Tribune Kasia, I didn't recognize you," the artilleryman said.

"Save your weak excuse and tell me why this weapon is sitting under tension?"

"We were told that we'd have a drill, today," the Legionary explained. "So, we prepared the catapult."

"And left the beams to warp, the pins to loosen, and the cable to stretch beyond its usefulness?"

"It's taken longer than expected to start the drill, sir," the Legionary offered.

"How often do you hold drills?" Jace inquired.

"Never, sir. Although we prepare every other day."

The answer troubled Jace. But he'd rectify that later. At the moment, he needed to save the catapult.

"I want this onager dismantled, the beams rubbed down with olive oil, and allowed to rest," Jace ordered. As he spoke, the other three crewmen joined him on top of the hill. "And while it's in pieces, you four will carve new pins to assure the fit is tight."

"But we have a drill coming up, sir," one insisted.

"Do you enjoy digging latrines?" Jace warned.

"No, sir," all four replied.

"Then follow directions," Jace said.

He walked down the hill, picked up his bags, and marched towards the gates of New Carthage.

***

Senior Centurion Ceradin put down the pen and stared at the parchment.

"How am I supposed to write a report when there's nothing to report?" he complained.

From the reception area, Jace answered, "You start with getting out of the office and inspecting your men."

Ceradin jumped up in surprise. The last time he checked, the staff had gone for their midday meal. The headquarters of Wings Legion should be deserted.

"Senior Tribune Kasia am I glad to see you," the senior combat officer said when Jace came into the office. "Without support of a senior staff officer, I'm at a loss."

"Where is First Centurion Turibas, Centurion Usico, and Tribune Furia?"

"General Scipio took them, our cavalry, and half a maniple of Velites on an expedition," Ceradin explained. "He left a few days ago."

"Just a half maniple from Wings and most of our command staff," Jace summed up. "That's an odd detachment for a General, even for Cornelius."

Ceradin flinched at the easy reference to the General's style.

"He also took half of Steed of Aeneas' heavy infantry and their command staff," the Senior Centurion added as if to provide cover for Scipio.

"Let me guess. He took the Lady Aurunica to her wedding and didn't want to take a large force. But for pomp and ceremony, he wanted two standard bearers."

"I believe that was his thinking, Senior Tribune."

"Now that I have an overview of the situation," Jace allowed. "Tell me why you're here, in the office, and not walking the positions of our onagers and bolt throwers. Or checking the guard posts of our Velites."

Ceradin's shoulders slumped, and his chin fell. Jace recognized the posture of a defeated man.

"I understand, Senior Centurion, that you're an Iberian officer," Jace sympathized with the senior combat officer. "And I realize that a lot of Republic officers and Legionaries resist your orders."

"That's not the issue, sir."

Between the undisciplined onager crew, the dejected Senior Centurion, and having rumors control his artillery emplacements, left Jace in a quandary.

"Then what is the issue?" he inquired.

"Sir, I don't want to get you in trouble," Ceradin proposed. "Or cause more issues for Wings Legion."

Before he questioned the Iberian further, Jace walked to the outer office and retrieved his bags. Then, he pulled out his best armor and a new Battle Commander's helmet. The red horsehair comb still stiff and bright from the drying rack.

"Sir, is that a…"

Interrupting and avoiding the combat officer's question, Jace instructed, "Help me strap on my armor."

Moments later, Colonel Kasia finished transferring his skinning knife to a custom sheath on the armored skirt. Then he held the helmet, identifying him as a Battle

Commander, under one arm and asked the hard question, "Why aren't you in command of Wings of Nortus Legion?"

"General Scipio left Colonel Nabars from Trumpet of Aeneas in charge of New Carthage," Ceradin informed Jace. "Nabars, like me, is Iberian and I assumed we would get along. But Metie, his Senior Tribune is an Etruscan. He felt that Wings Legion wasn't a true Legion and that we needed the guidance of a Republic officer. They marched their Centurions over and took command of our light infantrymen, the artillerymen, and confined me and the junior staff officers to our headquarters."

"Senior Centurion Ceradin. You will go and interrupt the midday meal of my Junior Tribunes," Jace growled, barely keeping control of his temper. "Send them around New Carthage. I want every combatant, animal handler, servant, and driver in Wings Legion assembled outside the main gate before I arrive. And Ceradin, I don't plan to dither. So, they better hurry."

"Yes, Colonel Kasia," Ceradin responded while saluting.

He ran from the office with fire in his eyes and a smile on his face. Seemingly contradictory expressions unless one understood the emotions of a combat officer. Being relieved of duty and parked in an office had been hard on the man. But with the return of his Senior Tribune. No, that was wrong. With the return of his Battle Commander, Ceradin's authority had been given back and he was exuberant.

***

Junior Tribunes from Wings Legion ran or rode to every part of New Carthage and delivered the order to assemble, immediately. From the defensive walls and installations around the island city, onagers and bolt thrower crews raced from their weapons. Velites threw down shovels or other tools and left whatever undesirable job they had been assigned. Wagon drivers, animal handlers, and servants shuffled to the main gates and got in line behind the officers, the Velites, and twenty heavy infantrymen from First Century. They had been left behind to heal injuries and to guard the headquarters of the Legion. Everyone waited impatiently for their senior officer. But it wasn't Jace Kasia who came through the portal.

"What's the meaning of this," Senior Tribune Metie demanded. He reined in hard. Hard enough that the front hoofs of his horse came off the ground. And moments later, five heavy infantrymen from Trumpet jogged through the gates. With shields and spears to enforce his authority, Metie threatened. "Ceradin. I'll have you on the punishment post for this act of mutiny. The rest of you get back to your jobs."

"I am the Senior Centurion of Wings Legion, and you will address me as such," Ceradin reminded him.

"And I'm a Senior Tribune," Metie began. But a tug on his boot stopped the rebuke and made him look down.

Jace Kasia allowed his hand to linger on the boot as if preparing to pull Matie off the mount.

"But I am Colonel Kasia, Battle Commander of Wings of Nortus Legion. Why are you addressing my formation?" Jace inquired. Without taking his eyes off Metie, Jace asked. "Senior Centurion Ceradin. Did you invite the senior staff officer from Trumpet of Aeneas to give a speech to my Legion?"

"Colonel Kasia, I did not," Ceradin assured him.

"Well, I know I didn't," Jace declared. "Metie. Be a good lad and run along. Oh, and tell Colonel Nabars I'll call on him once I've finished an inspection of my Legion."

Matie started to argue. But the heavy infantrymen from First Century Wings Legion jogged to Jace and placed their shields between the two officers.

"Sir, it's good to have you back," a Legionary said with a quick turn of his head.

"It's good to be home," Jace replied.

Then, ignoring the Senior Tribune from Trumpet, Jace marched to the front of his formation and bellowed, "Wings Legion."

As if released from bondage, the specialty Legion roared back, "Wings Legions."

***

In a Legion that had been browbeaten, overworked, insulted, and generally abused, the healing wouldn't come from cuddling.

"That onager is filthy," Jace informed the crew and the section Centurion. "I want it disassembled. And the parts and pins oiled. Only after Senior Centurion Ceradin inspects it for dry spots, will you reassemble it. Rah."

"Rah, sir," the artillerymen acknowledged.

Halfway down the hill, Ceradin inquired, "You aren't going easy on them. If anything, you're more demanding than Metie."

"To weak officers, fear means respect," Jace answered. "I can be tough on the men because we are Wings Legions. And they know I only want the best from them."

"I can't argue that, sir," Ceradin stated.

"After we inspect the onagers on the south wall," Jace directed, "I'm going to visit Colonel Nabars. You get back to each position and inspect the work."

At the bottom of the hill, five veteran Legionaries followed Jace and five trailed Ceradin. With bodyguards present, the command staff of Wings Legion wouldn't be removed if Metie decided to try.

***

At the villa serving as the headquarters for Trumpet of Aeneas, Jace was stopped by infantrymen from Trumpet's First Century.

"Sir, you can go in, but your Legionaries must remain here," a Optio instructed.

"Colonel don't go in that house," a Wings Legionary warned. "We can't protect you from here."

Jace hung back so his voice only reached his five guards.

"I'll tell you a secret," he divulged to the veterans. "A couple of weeks ago, I was locked in a hillside fortress by the War Chief of the Ilergetes Tribe. He couldn't hold me. Do you think Trumpet can?"

"No, sir," another infantryman answered.

"Wait here," Jace ordered. "I'll be back, one way or another."

***

Battle Commander Nabars, Trumpet's Standard Bearer Caldur, and Senior Tribune Metie stood next to a table. Displayed in miniature was the city of New Carthage, the docks, the bays, and the causeway.

"Gentlemen, pardon the intrusion," Jace greeted the trio. He stepped into the main room and took off his helmet. "Colonel Nabars, I apologize for the delay in letting you know I was back."

"You should arrest him for mutiny, sir," Metie asserted.

"That would not be advisable," Jace insisted.

"And why is that Senior Tribune Kasia?" Nabars asked, being sure to emphasize the rank.

"For two reasons," Jace told him. "The rank is Colonel Kasia by order of General Scipio. If you don't believe me, ask the General."

"Unfortunately, he is away," Nabars reported. "What's the second reason?"

"Your artillery is not available to defend the city," Jace informed him. "Until I allow the crews to resemble the onagers and bolt throwers, the weapons are nothing except carefully shaped beams."

"This never happened under my command," Metie boasted. "I maintained our long-range defenses. Not one was out of action, ever."

"That's true," Jace agreed. "And to keep the artillerymen alert, Senior Tribune Metie floated rumors of pending drills. Of course, he never ran the training, that would take leadership. But it did serve to lessen the readiness of the crews. And as he boasted, he never allowed the crews to break down their weapons and do maintenance. It's a good thing I got back when I did. Another two weeks of stupid, and your ranged weapons would fail during an attack."

Metie stepped towards Jace with his hands curled into fists.

"Before you take another step," Jace commented. "Have you ever been in a fighting circle?"

"You can't talk to me like that," the Senior Tribune proclaimed.

None of the commanders of Trumpet Legion had seen Jace move his arms. Yet, when he finished talking, a thin skinning knife appeared in his hand, and he began cleaning his fingernails.

"The Spartans before they go into battle clean their nails, and comb and braid their hair," Jace described. "I've always thought it showed their lack of fear and displayed supreme contempt for their enemy. Don't you agree?"

When faced with the truth that he was no match for Jace Kasia, Metie stepped back to the map table.

"By early tonight, all the catapults and bolt throwers will be oiled, repaired, and assembled," Jace promised. "Now if you'll excuse me, I've inspections to make. Good afternoon, gentlemen."

Jace left in such a hurry, Trumpet's Battle Commander, Standard Bearer, and Senior Tribune stared at the doorway as if expecting Kasia to come back.

He didn't, but from the courtyard outside, Jace shouted, "Wings Legion."

Beyond the walls surrounding the house, five voices replied, "Wings Legion."

***

With his five guards in tow, Jace turned down a street, heading for the north wall. After being hard on the artilleryman, he wanted to go by each position and praise their work.

Part way along the block, and in the yard of a big house, an old man spoke to a youth. To the Legionaries, it was gibberish. But Jace had served in the land of the Numidia and understood the language.

"You must remain patient," the old man advised.

"I'm sick of this place," the youth insisted. "I demand to go home to my father's house."

"Soon, my Chief. We'll make arrangements soon."

Jace stopped, pivoted, and pointed at the pair.

"Seize the boy and the man," he ordered. "But don't hurt them."

The Legionaries jumped the short garden wall. The old man and the boy were herded as if sheep, and quickly corralled by the big Legion shields.

"King Masinissa or King Syphax?" Jace asked.

"Master, I don't know what you're talking about," the old man lied in Iberian.

Switching to Numidia, Jace warned, "Tell me the truth. Or I'll take the boy's right hand. He'll never throw a spear from a horse and will never lead a war band."

The old one shivered with indecision. Seeing the confusion, the boy puffed up his chest, and addressed Jace.

"I am the nephew of King Masinissa," the boy announced. "Friend of Carthage, enemy of Rome until the day I die. I am Shuphet."

"No, my Chief," the old man screamed. He threw his frail body between Jace and Shuphet.

"Very commendable, Grandfather," Jace granted. "But I have no interest in a dead hostage. That is how you got here, isn't it?"

"Chief Shuphet was in New Carthage visiting. He was a guest of General Mago Barca when you Latians came over the walls."

"We're pretty good at ruining people's vacations," Jace jested. "Legionaries. Three of you take them to headquarters."

"Sir, Trumpet is just two streets from here," a Legionary suggested.

"King Masinissa is the ruler of the Massylii and a great friend of Carthage," Jace told him. "I fully intend to have our Legion, Wings of Nortus, hand this prize over to General Scipio. Certainly not Trumpet."

"We'll escort them," three infantrymen volunteered. "They'll be safe until you're ready to present them to General Scipio."

"I'm headed for the north wall," Jace told the two remaining guards. "And we've got a lot of ground to cover before dark."

"Wings Legion, sir,"

"Wings Legions," Jace confirmed.

Act 6

Chapter 16 – Storm of Ink

The first sign of General Scipio's return were the Velites. Ranging far ahead of the main body, the light infantrymen strolled in front of Tribune Furia. Just behind the Tribune, Wings Standard Bearer Usico and First Centurion Turibas rode in front of the Legionaries of First Century. Much farther back, General Scipio rode with the heavy infantry of Steed Legion.

Seeing the walls of New Carthage, every man in the detachment increased his pace. Waiting for them were hot meals, beds under roofs, and evenings on the town.

As much as the infantrymen and their officers were thrilled to see the city between the bays, none were more excited than Justus Furia. The trip had provided him with another set of crimes by Scipio and he was in a hurry to send the condemning letter. Perhaps, the latest report to his contact would get him recalled. The thought of leaving the barbarians of Iberia behind and returning to Rome carried Furia to the causeway.

Jace Kasia waited beside the roadway. Interestingly, Senior Tribune Kasia wore a Colonel's medal. And on his helmet, the red comb ran from front to back. For a heartbeat, Furia considered starting a chain of letters listing Kasia's crimes. Although intriguing, Tribune Furia feared starting that scroll, as the act would delay his departure from Iberia.

***

"Tribune Furia, First Centurion Turibas, and Centurion Usico, guide our men to the Wings area," Jace Kasia instructed. "Give Senior Centurion Ceradin a list of wounded or dead, then go clean up. He'll handle the return inspections."

"Where will you be, sir?" Furia inquired.

"With General Scipio, I assume," Jace told him. "If not, I'll be in the headquarters office waiting for his summons."

When the infantry of Steed Legion came abreast of Jace, he saluted General Scipio. If he had any doubt as to Cornelius' state of mind concerning the hostages and the brothers from the Ilergetes tribe, the General answered the question.

"Ride with me, Colonel Kasia," Cornelius invited. Then before leaving the march, he addressed Steed's commanders. "Gentleman, thank you for your help. We'll meet for dinner tomorrow to discuss the future. For now, express my gratitude to the Legionaries of Steed Legion for a job well done."

Cornelius nudged his horse out of the ranks followed by Sidia. Jace joined them and the three circled around and were soon cantering along the south bay road. None of Steed's First Century followed. The guard duty had passed to the five Legionaries from Wing's First Century.

"A thing I miss from my days as a Tribune," Cornelius mentioned, "is the ability to go for a ride alone with my thoughts."

"The thoughts you had while praying for Legions to command, sir?" Jace inquired.

Cornelius looked at the sky and inhaled.

"The exact ideas I am trying to put into action as a General," he admitted. After a humorless laugh, he described. "There once was an old man. Poor and barefooted, he went to the woods every day and collected sticks to sell as firewood. One day, bent and exhausted, he dropped the bundle and sat on it. Dejected, feeling at wits end, and having nothing to live for, he exclaimed, Master Death come and end my misery. To his horror, in a flash a terrible apparition appeared. You called for Death, the ghoul said. What can I do for you, old man? Terrified by the result of his hasty statement, the old man changed his mind. He said, the bundle is heavy. Can you help me pick up the branches, and load them on my back? The moral to this story, Jace, is to be careful what you wish for. You just might get it."

"That's very profound of you, sir," Jace offered.

"That's Aesop, not me. He was a Greek slave, a storyteller, and a wise man," Cornelius clarified. "And now that I have my Legions, I must be careful what I wish for. Because I might get a battle with Hannibal before I'm ready. But you, Colonel Kasia, can I assume you're about to report on a successful mission?"

"King Indibilis needs his daughters to secure support for his throne. And his brother, War Chief Mandonius, requires the companionship and counsel of his wife to sleep at night," Jace reported on the value of the hostages. "However, General, before you turn over Budarica and Betina to the King and return Ama to the tribe's War Chief, I have a suggestion."

"I'll go with any advice you have," Cornelius relented. "Afterall, you were in their camp."

"That's one way to put it, sir," Jace granted. "Before you give up the hostages in a storm of ink while trying to forge a treaty, understand this. The brothers, or rather the Ilergetes tribe, only respect strength."

"You're saying just returning valuable hostages isn't enough?"

"A treaty under those circumstances, General Scipio, will last until you turn your back on them," Jace warned. "Let history be your guide. Ten years ago, your father defeated a war party and captured Indibilis. After a year, the future King made promises and was released."

"And Indibilis returned the favor of freedom by attacking and murdering my father," Cornelius summed up the history lesson. "Your point is well taken."

"You could always bleed and burn the hostages," Jace suggested. "No one in Rome, and very few in Iberia, would blame you."

"I've just swallowed my pride to maintain peace in the east," Cornelius stated. "It makes no sense to create a vengeful enemy in the north to satisfy a burning in my gut. It's a fire, I'm afraid, that wouldn't be extinguished by cutting the throats of a woman and a pair of girls."

"Then we'll need to formulate a plan to get their attention," Jace said.

"And actions, General Scipio, to make them fear crossing you in the future," Sidia advised.

They reached a four-man artillery installation. Sporting a fresh coat of oil, the beams of the onager glowed as if the weapon was a piece of fine furniture. Plus, a new cable hung slack, ready to take the tension required to launch a large stone. Standing next to their catapult, the four artillerymen held a brace while saluting.

"That, Legionaries, is a beautiful machine," Cornelius praised the onager. He returned the salute, wheeled his horse around, and added. "With professionals like you on the defensive line, I have renewed faith in the survival of our Republic. Thank you."

As General Scipio, Colonel Kasia, and the others rode back towards New Carthage, the artillerymen buried their mouths on their forearms.

"Did you hear that?" one got out by suppressing an urge to yell. "Do you hear what the General said about us?"

"We are professionals," another repeated for the crew, "the General said so."

Far away, Cornelius glanced at Jace.

"Did I go overboard?" he inquired.

"No, sir. Your sentiment was what an isolated onager crew needed to hear."

"That's good. Sometimes I think my commitment to the strategy of being popular causes my comments to get flowery."

"There's nothing extravagant about giving credit to a crew that's done a good job," Jace told him.

***

Near dark, a Legion officer strolled through the southern gate. On the dock, he searched for a specific merchant ship. Once located, he hopped onboard and greeted the Captain.

"We're near the end of this charade," Justus Furia whispered while handing the skipper a scroll. "Another month and we'll be done. I can't wait to be away from here."

"Speak for yourself," the Captain countered. "This is the best assignment I've had in years."

"How can you say that?" Furia demanded. "Iberia is a place of savages."

"With the addition of the seventeen captured ships-of-war, General Scipio has forty-seven warships patrolling the coast," the merchant Captain answered. "In the Adriatic Sea, I have to contend with Illyrian pirates. Everywhere else, I'm a target for Carthaginian ships-of-war. But along the coast of Iberia and around to the Republic, my ship is as safe as if it's docked at Ostia."

Furia reached out and tapped the scroll with a finger.

"Don't forget your job is to deliver the message, as quickly as possible," he threatened. "Fail in that and you'll be lucky to land a job as a deckhand on a trader off the coast of Illyria."

"I know my job. But understand I can't go anywhere until they load my cargo tomorrow. I'll row out on the morning tide the next day," the Captain described. "Now go before people start asking questions."

Justus Furia leaped to the pier and strolled through the gate and back into the city.

***

The next evening, Cornelius indicated Jace.

"Colonel Kasia and his cavalry will accompany me," he explained, "but not the rest of Wings of Nortus. The Legion is needed for the defense of New Carthage. Colonel Nabars will come along with Trumpet of Aeneas Legion."

"What of Steed Legion, sir," Titus Quaeso inquired.

"You, Battle Commander Quaeso, are charged with the protection of New Carthage in my absence."

"Sir, who will be in charge of the onagers and bolt throwers," Tribune Furia asked.

"I understand we had some issues the last time we left a Senior Centurion in command," Cornelius answered. He glanced for a moment at Centurion Metie before saying. "I've decided the defensive weapons and light infantry rate a staff officer. So, I'm promoting you to senior staff officer, Senior Tribune Furia. Congratulations."

"But I need to go with you," Furia blurted out.

"Commendable. However, you'll best serve the mission from here. Now gentlemen, let's eat. Tonight, we feast because we march the day after tomorrow."

Furia leaned over and asked Jace, "Colonel Kaisa, is their anyway to get me on the staff for the campaign?"

"I understand you want to be involved in the glorious parts," Jace said. "Trust me, Iberia is far from settled. They'll be more battles for you in the near future."

"That's what I'm afraid of," Furia mumbled into his stew.

Mistaking the remark for a complaint about being left behind, Jace told him, "The plan is to march to Ilergetes territory and exchange Ama and the girls for a peace treaty. So, you'll avoid marching and sleeping in the mud just to stand in the rain outside a treaty tent. Count yourself blessed of the God Caerus. And be grateful for receiving his luck and his gift of favorable moments while sleeping in a bed at night."

Discussions continued late into the night. In his anger about not being included in the mission, Senior Tribune Furia fumed silently throughout the meal. As with anyone holding an emotionally charged internal dialogue,

Furia missed the nuances of the conversations. They included an overemphasis on how peaceful the handoff of the hostages would be while lacking details on just what General Scipio expected from a treaty with the Ilergetes tribe.

***

When the feast ended, Justus Furia rushed to his quarters and lit a beeswax candle. By the light of the tiny flame, he wrote an addendum to his first message.

"Obviously timid, Cornelius Scipio, as well as being undemanding of his allies, habitually frees those who fought against him and the Republic. And due to his soft nature, Scipio handed over hostages that would give the Iberian Legions an advantage in men, food, and access across tribal lands. Disorganized and overly friendly, his latest misadventure has him blindly handing over a wife and two daughters to the Ilergetes tribe for nothing more than empty promises. I feel my job in Iberia is complete. I await orders to return home to Rome."

Once finished with the storm of ink, Furia marched to the southern gate.

"Open it," he demanded.

"Yes, sir, Tribune Furia," the Veles acknowledged.

"Keep it open," Furia ordered while waving a piece of parchment. Light from a torch reflected off the message. "I'll be right back."

The staff officer went through the gate. And as good as his word, he came back from the docks a short while later, but without the piece of parchment.

"Have a good evening, sir," the guard said to Furia's back.

The Senior Tribute was quickly lost in the dark streets of New Carthage. For a brief moment, the sentry had the information to stop the spying. But three drunk sailors approached, and the guard forgot about the parchment to deal with the men.

***

On the appointed morning, Wings Legion trotted out ahead of the march. Once away from New Carthage, Jace Kasia and his cavalrymen dispersed to a wide front.

Later that day, an officer from Wings Legion eased up besides Jace.

"Colonel, shouldn't you be riding with the General?" Sinebe inquired.

"General Scipio didn't leave me much to command on this campaign," Jace replied. "But he did allow me two hundred Legion cavalrymen. And for that I am grateful. Because you and the others give me a reason to stay away from the General and his staff."

"I can't argue with that, sir," the Centurion of Cavalry told him.

They rode together in silence, both scanning the riders on their flanks. A pleasant day with dry ground and lots of grass, the environment made for relaxed movements of man and horse.

"For the start of a long march, Colonel," the officer proposed, "it's too perfect to last."

"Centurion Sinebe, are you always this optimistic?" Jace teased.

"After years of riding for my tribe, a few for the Carthaginians, and now six years as a Legion cavalryman," the officer confessed, "I always expect the worst."

"Then you rode with one of the Scipio brothers," Jace offered.

"Yes, sir, General Gnaeus Scipio. He was a leader who knew how to command men," Sinebe reminisced. "Until those no good Celtiberi infantrymen deserted us."

"With you being Iberian, I wondered how you felt about fighting certain tribes. Now I know about the Celtiberi. What are your thoughts on the Ilergetes?"

Delaying, as if to collect his thoughts, it was a few heartbeats before Sinebe asked, "Colonel, what do you call people who stir up conflict, create drama, and then enjoy watching agitated people cut each other's throats?"

"I guess you could call them backstabbers," Jace remarked.

"No, sir, they would be Ilergetes. Does that answer your question about my feelings?"

"I believe it does," Jace stated.

A breath later, the calm was shattered.

"Trouble," Sinebe declared.

The cavalry officer kicked his mount into motion and guided it off to the left. Jace was an instant behind. They headed for a scout who was driving his horse in a headlong rush back to Wings' command.

Converging quickly, they reined in as the scout arrived.

"Cavalry," the breathless scout informed them.

"A war band," Jace asked. "What tribe, could you tell?"

"Not a small war party, there are a thousand of them if not more," the scout reported. "Lots of big men on mountain horses, followed by supply wagons. They look like they mean to stay."

"What tribe?" Sinebe questioned.

"As near as I can tell, sir," the scout stated, "they're Celtiberi heavy cavalry."

Sinebe spit as if to get a bad taste out of his mouth.

"Orders, sir?" he asked.

"Pull our riders back to Trumpet's light infantry," Jace instructed. "The scout and I'll go directly to the General."

"Celtiberi, sir," Sinebe advised. "Here's a chance for General Scipio to get some revenge for his uncle."

"I don't think he's looking for revenge."

"He should be, Colonel. I know I'd like to sink my blade into a few of them."

"Pull us back," Jace reminded the cavalry officer. "Don't lose men to your passion."

"There are two hundred of us and over a thousand of them," Sinebe commented. "We're pulling back."

Chapter 17 – The Low Price of Peace

Legionaries didn't run when they shifted into a defensive formation. They shuffled, jogged, sprinted for short distances, and generally hurried, but they didn't run. Mainly because from columns of march, the maniples unfolded like wings. Once extended, the infantrymen closed the distances between rows until they create three distinct assault lines.

Twelve Centurions prowled behind the First Maniple watching for guidance from their left and right Tribunes. The staff officers in turn watched for signals from the Senior Tribune of Trumpet Legion. And the senior staff officer coordinated with the Battle Commander, who was looking to the General for orders.

"Cavalry, even heavy cavalry, would be foolish to charge a prepared assault line," Nabars pointed out. "But their arrival has us stopped in the road. Any advice, General Scipio?"

"Let's allow the Celtiberi to dictate the terms of battle for today," Cornelius offered. "If they delay, when they camp for the night, we'll march in and change the terms."

"Senior Tribune Matie, have the maniples hold positions," Nabars instructed. "Get extra javelins to the third lines. If the cavalry comes at us, I want them to pay a steep price for their stupidity."

"Yes, sir," Metie acknowledged. He pointed at a ring of junior staff officers. "Four additional javelins for the rear ranks. Everyone holds where they are. Go."

The six Junior Tribunes galloped away to inform the maniple Tribunes of the decisions.

"What are you thinking, sir?" Jace inquired.

"It's not what I'm thinking but what I fear," Cornelius answered. "Could my agreement with Prince Allucius have fallen apart this quickly?"

"If it has," Nabars warned, "the Celtiberi will be missing a thousand cavalrymen by dawn."

As they talked, two long columns of riders appeared from the northwest. At the sight of the Legion battle formation, the columns halted. Six cavalrymen trotted away from the formation.

"They want to talk, sir," Battle Commander Nabars observed. "Metie and I'll take a squad and go forward."

"No, Colonel. It's my nonaggression pact that's been violated," Cornelius asserted. He held up a hand to hold Sidia in place and addressed Jace. "Battle Commander Kasia, care to take a ride?"

"You're the client, sir. I'll be wherever you need me," Jace responded.

"In that case, let's go talk to their delegation."

***

As they trotted through the lines of infantrymen, Jace remarked, "six against two, not good odds, sir."

"Last night, I thought of Hannibal," Cornelius mentioned. "He commands different tribes yet finds ways to connect with their officers. But his power stems from more than the respect of Captains and Lieutenants. Somehow, Hannibal manages to inspire spearmen and soldiers. It's the only explanation for how he gets men to follow his complicated battle plans."

"And you think by sacrificing yourself, you'll inspire your Legions?"

"Of course not," Cornelius assured him. "I'll sacrifice you while I ride away."

For an instant, Jace couldn't process the statement. Once he did, he replied, "That's a different pay scale."

"Was that comedy or tragedy?" Cornelius questioned.

"General, I'm not following you," Jace admitted.

"First, I don't think anyone is going to get sacrificed today," Cornelius pointed out. "The cavalrymen aren't carrying lances and haven't drawn their swords. And so, I ask you, how was it?"

"How was what, sir?" Jace inquired.

"The joke. I'm working on humor to enhance my accessibility to the men," Cornelius explained. "For Aristotle, comedy represented man at his worst. Deserting you in a fight would be me at my worst. That made my comment humorous. Which was yours?"

"If humor is worst, what's the opposite?" Jace inquired.

"Comedy shows men at their wickedest while tragedy displays real life and man at his best."

"I'm afraid, a Cretan Archer is trained in mercenary ways," Jace described. "There is a price for every life. Sometimes it's high, and other times the cost is low."

"Then I declare your phrase, that's a different pay scale, as tragedy," Cornelius announced.

"Sir, if I might make a suggestion."

"Go ahead, as you pointed out, we're two against six."

"You have a reputation as being able to communicate with the Gods," Jace offered. "When you grow silent and gaze at the sky, as if you're consulting with a deity, the men are enthralled. At that moment, you become an inspiring figure."

"But I'm not doing anything except carefully weighing choices," Cornelius protested.

"Not to your Republic or Iberian Legions," Jace assured him. "To them, you are a conduit to the Gods. Stay with that."

"And leave the comedy to others," Cornelius guessed.

***

Cornelius and Jace reined in as the six riders approached then halted.

"General Scipio. I am Bekeres and he is Darsosin, Captains of Cavalry," one of the Celtiberi riders greeted them. "We carry best wishes from Prince Allucius. And a gift."

Cornelius straightened his back and used a forward and a rear saddle horn to lift up. He peered at the columns of cavalrymen in the distance.

"A gift, you say?"

"Yes sir. Fifteen hundred cavalrymen from the heart of Celtiberi," Captain Darsosin answered. "The Prince trusts that you will have a use for us."

"Colonel Kasia, can you fit fifteen hundred heavy cavalrymen into Wings Legion?" Cornelius asked.

"Sir, it's better than the alternative," Jace replied.

For a moment, Cornelius started to lift his eyes to the sky and ponder the statement. But realizing he needed to get his Legions moving, he directed, "Captain Bekeres. Captain Darsosin. Good to have you with us. We're marching north to Tarraco. Take the forward position. I'm sure Colonel Kasia will be along to introduce himself later."

"Yes, sir," the two officers replied.

They pulled their horses around and trotted back to the columns of cavalrymen.

"It's better than the alternative," Cornelius repeated Jace's words from earlier. "I'm not sure if that's comedy or tragedy."

"Perhaps, sir," Jace uttered, "it's a little of both."

***

A week later, the Legions reached the fort at Marçà outside of Tarraco. During the eight days of traveling, Jace worked with Bekeres and Darsosin to ascertain the skills of the Celtiberi cavalrymen.

"Centurion of Horse," Jace called to Wings top cavalryman, "I've good news and bad."

"There always is," Sinebe acknowledged.

"The Celtiberi are masters of breaking other mounted formations," Jace described. "Riding shoulder to shoulder at a gallop, they'll smash the opposing cavalry with a wall of lances and armored horses."

"What's the good news, sir?" Sinebe inquired.

Jace studied the man to see if he was jesting. By the set of the cavalry officer's jaw, he could tell the Centurion was serious.

"I thought that was the good news," Jace told him.

"No, sir. Legion cavalry is utilitarian," Sinebe explained. "We're not swift like the light cavalry from Numidia. Or solid like the heavy cavalry from Celtiberi."

"We're not fighting the Celtiberi," Jace reminded him.

"No, sir. Not this year."

***

That night after the Legions were secured from the march and quartered, Jace reported to Cornelius.

"Sir, you'll be pleased to know, the Celtiberi can break most formations with a cavalry charge," Jace bragged.

"That's not how Hannibal did it at Cannae," Cornelius proposed. "He sent his heavy cavalry out wide. Close in, on our flanks, he used his light cavalry to screen the movement of his light infantry. By the time the dust settled, our maniples were infiltrated by infantrymen. To copy the movement, I need the Celtiberi to be swift around the infantry line, to be aggressive and run off the enemy's cavalry, then to attack him from the rear."

"How long do I have?" Jace asked.

"We're three days march from the Segre river and the town of Lleida. And I don't plan to stay here while the Ilergetes prepare for us. Figure you have about three days before we come into contact with a force of any size."

"Yes, sir. If you'll excuse me."

"Aren't you staying for the officers' mess?"

"No, General. The grains in the sandglass are running."

"I understand. Dismissed."

Jace saluted, turned about, and ran from the command pavilion.

***

Scipio's three Legions consisted of almost six thousand heavy infantrymen, twenty-two hundred light infantrymen, and two thousand cavalrymen. Between the combatants and the supply caravan, it could have been mistaken as an invasion force.

Seven miles southwest from Lleida and the Segre river, Indibilis and Mandonius planted their banners and dug in their heels. Based on the ranks of Ilergetes spearmen and cavalry gathered, the brothers decided it was an invasion.

As the front ranks positioned themselves a long bow shot from each other, tents and pavilions went up behind the combat lines. On the Legion side, Cornelius called his commanders together.

"If you beat them here, General," Gaius Laelius of Eagle Legion mentioned, "you can hammer out a treaty and be free of the hostages."

"A quick march in, sir," Colonel Nabars agreed, "and out with minimum casualties. I would call that a successful campaign."

Ignoring the Battle Commanders of Eagle and Trumpet, Cornelius looked over the collection of staff officers and Colonels.

"Kasia, where are you?"

"Back here, sir," Jace called from the rear of the crowd.

He stood by a basket of fruit. After cutting a plum in two, he pulled out the seed, and popped a half into his mouth.

"Everyone has advice for me," Cornelius said. "What about you?"

Plunk, Jace dropped the seed into a bowl, and paused for a moment while chewing.

"It's under ten miles from here to the Segre river," Jace said after swallowing. "My advice, sir? Turn the land between here and the river into a killing field. And burn everything to the riverbank."

Laelius and Nabars protested as did their Senior Tribunes.

"For what purpose?" some demanded. "You beat them here and be done with it. Why make an enemy of the Ilergetes?"

Jace shoved the other half of the plum into his mouth and chewed while they complained. When the noise faded, Jace replied, "You want peace, so choose. The price of peace is high, or it is low. If you want to return season after season and pay the high price, we should leave now. We'll be back to fight them later. However, if you want a low price for peace, drive the Ilergetes to the river and leave ash and bodies in our wake. Give their women nightmares and make their poets cry when they sing of the horrors."

The pavilion fell silent, and all eyes turned to Cornelius. The advice went against the General's habit of releasing foes, and his willingness to discuss a treaty, even when the details favored his adversary. Typically, in a situation like this, Scipio would set up a treaty tent and call for talks before the javelins flew and the shields clashed.

"Senior Centurions of Supply," Cornelius requested, "I want two wagons filled with barrels of vino."

"We can do that, sir," one of the supply officers assured him. "Where do you want them?"

"I want the Ilergetes spearmen to have the vino before dark."

"You're giving our vino to them?" Senior Tribune Metie scoffed. "What about our Legionaries? They deserve extra vino if anyone does."

"Matie will drive one rig," Cornelius announced. "Kasia, I want two riders with extra horses to pull him and the other driver out once they've delivered the vino and the message."

"Message, sir?"

***

The comedown from commanding six maniple Tribunes, and being second in charge of a Legion, irked Matie. Plus, his Legionaries and Centurions were witnesses to the spectacle. At the moment, he hated the Ilergetes, his infantrymen, and Cornelius Scipio.

"What's this," a spearman shouted.

Along the defensive line, the Ilergetes braced with spears in hand, ready for an attack. But all that approached their lines were two wagons.

"What's this?" another demanded.

"Wine for the mighty Ilergetes," Matie sneered, barely able to get out the complimentary words. "Your power on the field of battle is renowned. Please accept these gifts."

"The Legion and the boy General send us wine," a spearman declared. He patted the barrels. "They are afraid of us."

As directed, Matie said, "Your words carry weight."

"And look who the driver is," a war leader noted. "He's a Senior Tribune."

Before the tribesmen could surround Matie and the other driver, Jace and Sinebe arrived with the mounts.

"Sir, we should go," Jace stated.

The Senior Tribune and a Centurion, selected to protect Matie, jumped on the horses. Followed by a rain of insults and laughter, they galloped back to the Legion lines.

"It's not even enough to get all of them drunk," Matie complained.

"They're Ilergetes, Senior Tribune," Jace explained. "Most of the spearmen won't even get a taste. But their war chiefs and commanders will drink a bellyful."

Matie fumed all the way to Trumpet Legion. But as he approached, shouts went up.

"Rah to our Senior Tribune," the infantrymen yelled. "Matie rode right up to the enemy and spit in their eyes. Rah."

Senior Tribune Matie sat a little straighter as he approached the headquarters tent of Trumpet Legion.

***

"It's always like this in the Legion," an infantryman whined. He indicated the cookfires of the Ilergetes. "Somone else gets our vino and we're stuck with vinegar and water. It's always like that."

"But we got extra rations," another member of the squad said. "I'd rather have a full plate than a few sips off a wineskin."

"Eat and rest," their Optio warned. "I've never seen a Battle Commander give anything without expecting something in return. That means get some rest before the Colonel collects."

"It's always like that in the Legion," a Legionary stated.

The NCO walked to the cookfires of his squads and checked on each infantryman. He would make his rounds until everyone at every cookfire, except a guard, slept. Then he went to his tent, took off his armor, and stretched out.

Before daylight, the Optio rose and nudged his Tesserarius.

"Get the squads up and dressed," the Optio instructed. "Remember, no fires and keep the noise to a minimum."

"We're heavy infantry," the other NCO offered. "Quiet is not a normal state for Legionaries. And they'll want breakfast."

"Tell them to eat it cold. Remind them that last night they got extra rations. And this morning, the Colonel is collecting for his generosity."

***

While the heavy and light infantry dressed in the dark, Jace Kasia tugged on the reins of his mount. He and five hundred cavalrymen led their horses through the trees, skirting to the southwest of the battlefield.

"I see a villa," a cavalryman mentioned. "Is that our destination?"

Beyond the trees and far to the right, numerous campfires illuminated the walls of a compound and a bonfire inside outlined the roof of a big house.

"We're headed for the Segre river," Jace replied. "You'll know when we get there."

Chapter 18 – Make Their Poets Cry

The empty ground between Legionaries and Ilergetes filled, too quickly. As one side surged across at first light, the other side slept. They dozed, unaware of the attack, until twenty-four Centurions barked out, "First maniple forward."

Even if the two dozen voices went unheard, the following crescendo of the orders, being repeated by infantrymen, brought the spearmen to their feet. By then, unfortunately for the Ilergetes, the officers from the first maniples of two Legions ordered, "Advance, advance, advance."

A line of six hundred and forty hardwood shields smashed forward. Getting a face full of Legion shield rocked the few spearmen alert and on the line. Some went down. They joined those slow to awaken. And just as they struggled to their knees and prepared to stand, the shields withdrew. And the wood of six hundred and forty infantrymen got replaced by the cold, sharp steel of their gladii. Stepping forward into a field of bodies and wounded, the Legion lines completed the first advance.

By the start of the second advance, the Ilergetes in the rear stormed forward. But haphazard reinforcements proved no challenge for a well-disciplined wall of Legionaries. This repetition of the hammering shields had the aid of spear thrusts from the second row. And while six hundred and forty short blades delivered devastation, the overhand thrusts with an equal number of spearheads destroyed the resistance.

"Second line, rotate forward," the twenty-four Centurions bellowed. "First line, rotate back."

After months of practice and a thousand sessions of rehearsals, the Legions put fresh arms and legs on the assault line. And after only a slight delay, they began the third advance.

Ilergetes reeling from confusion or injury remained on the defensive line. They absorbed the hardwood and went down. And as they did for each advance, the gladii stabbed in unison, as if a single axe blade. The action chopped down the remaining spearmen. In turn, those tribesmen still alive were stomped to death by three lines of hobnailed boots.

***

"They've broken," a staff officer exclaimed. "Congratulations, General Scipio, you've won the day. Should we hold?"

Cornelius looked from the slaughter and the fleeing tribesmen to the heavens. But unlike the normal pause to consider choices, he prayed.

"God Aeneas, the Terrible, grant me the strength to see this through," he implored. A moment later, Cornelius Scipio lowered his eyes and with an icy calm, he ordered. "Send the Velites down the center for the stragglers. Followed by the Legionaries. And start the flank attacks by the Celtiberi cavalry."

After a gentle nudge, the General's horse began picking its way through the broken and bloody bodies.

"Surely, this will make their poets cry," he whispered.

But in the distance, the routed spearmen joined other tribesmen. Together, they formed defensive ranks on either side of a walled compound. And farther away, on the horizon, Cornelius noted wisps of smoke drifting into the sky.

***

From concealment, Jace Kasia and his cavalry detachment peered through the trees. A camp of better than eight hundred Ilergetes and their horses covered the field to their front. The tribal cavalrymen squatted around cookfires eating a dawn meal. Behind them, the eastern half of the city of Lleida served as a backdrop for the horse camp.

"If they get a hint that we're here before the attack begins," a Legion cavalry officer warned, "we'll be chopped meat."

Across the Segre river, the other half of Lleida slept. The presence of Ilergetes cavalrymen, however, brought out vendors from the town on this side of the river.

"Their communications protocol is poorly designed," Jace remarked.

"Excuse me, Colonel?" a Centurion inquired.

An inbound messenger slapped reins on the flanks of his mount. Driven by the panic of its rider, the horse raced into the Ilergetes camp. The courier guided the horse towards the command tents in the center.

"The rider with a report of the attack is late," Jace advised. He looked at the streaks of light in the sky. "If the Legion had been attacked, I'd hope my cavalry officers would be sober enough to send out couriers with the report before midmorning."

"It appears the vino had the desired effect," a cavalryman offered. Next, he observed. "When they go to help their spearmen, we'll have the privilege of sacking a fully stocked camp."

"Hold that thought until we see how many riders respond to the attack," his Optio suggested. "If they keep too many in reserve, we could still be outnumbered."

The courier rushed into a pavilion. A moment later, War Chief Mandonius emerged. He was fully dressed in armor and lively.

From the woods, Jace lifted his arm. Sighting along the top of his fist, he proposed, "It'd be a long flight, but I could do it."

"Do what, sir?" a cavalryman inquired.

"Nothing," Cretan Archer Kasia lied.

Mandonius ran from cookfire to cookfire kicking and shouting at his cavalrymen. Not long after the messenger arrived, the entire compliment of eight hundred riders galloped towards the fighting.

"That's considerate of them," Jace commented as he walked his horse out of the tree line.

"What's considerate, Colonel?"

"They left us burning branches," Jace declared. "Everyone, take fire. Toss any loose valuables into wagons then destroy the camp and burn the city."

In short order, whisps of smoke from burning tents and flaming buildings drifted into the sky.

***

Outside the walls of the compound, the spearmen reestablished their defensive positions. Meanwhile, inside the house, King Indibilis stormed around the great room.

"Yesterday, my Captains told me the boy General was sending us gifts," he shouted. "Obviously as a means to garner favor before we negotiate for my daughters."

Indibilis kicked a wicker basket. The container of woolen yarn flew up chest high. It tumbled causing balls of yarn to spill out and unspool. In the blink of an eye, streamers of yarn covered the floor as if spider webs. In a fit of rage, the King of the Ilergetes kicked at the thin lines of fiber.

The residents, staff, and neighbors, who sought shelter in the compound, huddled against the walls.

"And now," the King growled while trying to untangle his foot from the yarn, "I learn my army is being driven back to my headquarters. And no one has thought to contact my brother."

"Sir, we sent a courier for the War Chief," a Captain told him. "He should be here shortly with the cavalry."

Before the tribe's War Chief arrived, the sounds of steel on steel, shields on shields carried into the house. Moments after the fighting reached the compound, a member of the King's guard rushed into the room.

"Sir, you need to go," he announced.

"I've got walls and thousands of spearmen outside," Indibilis challenged. "Why would I move?"

"Sir, the Captain said to inform you that using the compound as a defensive point has failed," the guard told him. "The Legionaries are peeling us away from the bricks and doing damage. The War Chiefs feel we need a solid line to stop the attack. And before the Republic infantry comes over the walls, you need to be away from here."

"Where's my brother and the cavalry?" Indibilis complained as he took his helmet and ran to where his guards waited. "We'll ride to the rear and create a fallback position."

Indibilis mounted. A moment later, he led his fifty bodyguards out through the gates. As he made the turn towards the east, he noted smoke rising into the sky. Behind him, Legionaries scaled the walls of the compound and dropped into the courtyard. With the enemy close and a battle on his mind, the King couldn't be bothered with the source of the smoke.

***

Cornelius saw his infantrymen climb the brick walls. Not an easy task while lugging a big infantry shield, but enough did to chase the last defenders from the compound. And although overjoyed to see the walls taken, he was more excited by the second retreat of the Ilergetes assault line.

"Sir, we've taken the compound," a Junior Tribune reported. "Colonel Nabars wants to know if we should hold the advance here. The house will be good for your negotiations."

"I know a poet," Cornelius said to the junior staff officer. "Quintus Ennius gets emotional about a few things, mostly injustice and misinterpretations of history. That's because the spirit of Homer speaks to him."

"Yes, sir," the youth said although he was confused by the statement. "General Scipio, sir. What about the compound?"

"In all the years I've known Ennius, I've never seen him shed tears," Cornelius continued as if the junior staff officer hadn't asked the question again. "I don't suppose for a man, who trades in emotional speeches, it's easy to cry."

"Sir? Are you well?"

"Tell Colonel Nabars to bar the doors to the main house, the stables, and every shed in the compound," Cornelius ordered. "Then burn them all."

"Sir, there are household staff and families in the compound."

"I said to burn them all," Cornelius exploded on the youth. Faced with the ferocious response by the General, the youth galloped away. Alone for a moment, Cornelius proposed. "Maybe that will make their poets cry."

***

Assuming he had a few miles to go to reach the fighting, War Chief Mandonius jerked on the reins when he came upon the King's entourage.

"Have you drawn them into a trap?" Mandonius asked. "What's the plan?"

"Scipio is not like his father or his uncle," Indibilis described. "He has none of their diplomatic skills. Last night, he sent a Senior Tribune forward with two wagons of wine."

"A peace offering," Mandonius suggested. "A way for the boy General to grease us up before we take back our women."

"No, brother. A way to get our Captains drunk and slow their response to a predawn attack," Indibilis stated. "He's chased us to here and burned every farm and field along the way."

"What is he an animal?" Mandonius scoffed, "or a madman?"

Just as the War Chief of the Ilergetes finished, flames crawled up to the roof of the main house. Other fires inside the compound told the tale of incineration with a purpose.

Spearmen from the area attempted to rush back to the compound. They were held down by friends as their families burned. Crushed by the slaughter of their loved ones, they dropped to the ground and cried.

As he witnessed the massacre of innocents and the heartaches of his warriors, a memory of whips of smoke came to Indibilis. He twisted in the saddle to face eastward. Above Lleida, a layer of black smoke hung, as if clouds heavy with rain. But the dark sky didn't hint at rain from crops and relief from the heat. Rather the smoke told of the destruction of half his capital city.

"General Scipio is neither an animal nor a madman," Indibilis informed his brother. "He has the stone heart of an Ilergetes. And the iron will of a War Chief of the people. I believe, it's time we begged General Scipio to join us in a treaty tent."

"I have eight hundred cavalrymen and you command thousands of spearmen," his brother protested. "And in two days, we'll have twice as many warriors."

Although far off, Legion riders came from the east, and heavy cavalry closed in from the sides. While the mounted forces moved in, lines of Legionaries approached, further defining, and sealing the kill box.

"In less than a day, we'll join our ancestors in the ground," Indibilis countered. "No, brother. We will ask for a treaty."

"And then?" Mandonius questioned.

"Would you break your word to a man committed enough to burning his enemies and scorching the very earth under their feet?"

"Truthfully, no," Mandonius admitted. "I would not break my word to a man like that."

***

Veterans from third maniple formed a passageway. Down the center, a wagon rolled slowly, carrying Budarica and Betina, Indibilis' daughters, and Ama, Mandonius' wife. Still surrounded by infantrymen, the wagon stopped behind the treaty tent.

"I am out of patience," Cornelius snapped, "and have no more days to waste on the killers of my father."

He marched into the tent with Sidia behind his left shoulder. No other bodyguards accompanied the Legion General.

"You're very brave to come into the tent unescorted," Mandonius noted.

Indibilis and Mandonius were seated at a table. Behind them, six spearmen stood as guardians over their King and War Chief.

"Sidia. What happens if I fall in this tent?" Cornelius questioned.

"Your veterans, General, will execute the girls and the woman," the bodyguard replied. "Then Colonel Kasia will take command."

"I believe you know Jace Kasia," Cornelius offered.

"We've met the archer," Mandonius grunted.

"He's my strategist," Cornelius informed them. "I don't listen to all of his advice. It's often too brutal. For instance, we're here and not meeting on the ruins of Fort Algerri. Do you understand?"

"We understand, General Scipio," Indibilis stated. "What do you require for peace between us and for the return of the hostages."

"I want silver. Plus, a thousand spearmen for my Legions," Cornelius listed. "And your oaths, sworn on the lives of all you hold dear, to never raise a weapon against me."

"In that case," Indibilis agreed, "all that's left is the counting."

"What guarantees do we get?" Mandonius asked.

"My word that I will not come in the night," Cornelius promised, "to kill your children, burn your cities, and erase you from history. Is that enough?"

"It's enough, General Scipio," Indibilis agreed.

They both lifted their eyes to the wagon and the waiting hostages.

"It's enough, General Scipio," Mandonius vowed.

***

To the east of the treaty tent, the Legion cavalry sat on their mounts, maintaining the blockade. And there was the issue. Waiting drained the energy from both man and beast. Jace grew bored and eased his horse away from the Centurions of Cavalry.

"Let me know if anything develops," he requested.

"Where are you going, Colonel?"

"I want to look over the things we took from the big pavilion."

"There are some nice gold and silver items," a combat officer suggested.

"Those aren't the riches I'm seeking."

Jace trotted to a column of transports. Filled with treasures from the Ilergetes horse camp, the wagons, although hurriedly loaded, were stacked high. As Jace approached the teamsters, all but one watched him closely and trembled. They had been drafted at the point of a lance to drive the wagons. He couldn't blame them for being afraid. But an unresponsive driver caught his attention.

"What's his problem?" Jace asked.

He swung out a leg, slid off the horse, and stepped onto the bed of a wagon.

"He's a poet, sir," a teamster answered. "And the thoughtless destruction has overwhelmed him."

"Look at me," Jace ordered.

The poet slowly raised his face to reveal tear-stained cheeks.

Raising an arm, Jace waved at an Optio of Cavalry.

"I need two riders and a third horse," Jace instructed. "Take the poet to General Scipio. Tell him, this poet wept."

After the cavalry escort left, Jace pulled back animal skin covers and sorted through the items from Mandonius' tent. At first, he couldn't find it. But then the quiver appeared. And a moment later, he located the bow case holding his hunting bow.

He started to turn from the pile of goods when a voice from his past came to him.

"A Cretan Archer always earns a profit," Zarek Mikolas had recited often.

Jace went back to the pile of loot and selected a gold cup. He dropped it into a hip bag. Before jumping off the wagon, he announced, "profit earned, Master."

***

The Legions jogged back to their marching camps, carrying their wounded. Although General Scipio had an agreement, no one trusted the thousands of Ilergetes warriors milling around. Before sundown, guards were posted, and the gates closed and barred shut.

In the morning, General Scipio would march his victorious Legions out of Ilergetes territory. In a few days, they would reach the Legion fort outside of Tarraco.

"I need to coordinate with Junius Silanus about our next campaign," Cornelius told his staff. "I'm out of useful hostages. And with the Carthaginian Generals away from Iberia, I'm not sure of the next tribe we should target for pacification."

But due to circumstances beyond his control, Scipio, the Prorogatio of Iberia, would not meet with Silanus, the Magistrate of Iberia. Fate and the Senate of Rome had other plans for Cornelius.

Act 7

Chapter 19 – The Judgement Trap

A mile from the fort and drill fields at Marçà, Cornelius Scipio, Sidia, and ten veteran Legionaries galloped away from the columns. Angling off the trail, they rode cross-country until they reached the base of the hill with the four shrines. At the top, Cornelius turned his horse and gazed down on his Legions.

Jace Kasia's mounted detachment of Republic cavalry rode the vanguard. Next in the march came the fifteen hundred Celtiberi cavalrymen. Cornelius felt bad about placing all those horses in front of the infantry of a Republic Legion. He could imagine the cursing by the Legionaries as they stepped in horse manure. But he wanted Colonel Laelius' Eagles adjacent to the thousand Ilergetes spearmen. And with Colonel Nabars' Trumpets, an Iberian Legion, positioned behind, the two Legions boxed in the newly recruited Ilergetes.

"It's an impressive display of military might, sir," Sidia offered.

"Two full Legions, plus auxiliary troops and riders," Cornelius remarked. "It's not enough to even threaten Hannibal."

"But General, you have five more Legions under your command," Sidia reminded him.

"And five more of those," Cornelius declared. Those referred to the long line of transports with loaded donkeys and spare mounts interspersed between the wagons. While Cornelius could see all his martial forces in one sweeping glance, the file of supply wagons and pack animals stretched back into the hills and out of sight. "This operation was a test of my command abilities. I learned a lot and have identified several problems. Chief among them is my slow and lumbering supply caravan."

Cornelius spun his horse from the marching men and faced the four shrines. Running along the crest of the hill, the altars were visible from the surrounding area and the Legion fort on the far side.

"Will you be praying, sir?" Sidia inquired.

"In all four shrines," Cornelius answered. "After this campaign, I believe it's warranted."

As befitting the father of gods, Jupiter's shrine crowned the hill. Planted at the entrance were duplicates of the Legions' banners. An Eagle on one side and a Lightning Bolt banner on the other adorned the altar. A little downhill, the shrine of Aeneas, The Terrible, displayed a Steed, and a Trumpet, banner. Next to that, the shrine of Deimos sat solid and not the least bit scary. But anyone going in knew full well, Deimos visited a terrible fear on warriors before a battle. Its banners were a Chariot and a Golden Cat. Last in Cornelius' compilation, Nortus, the God who blows wind from the north. Fittingly, the banners of Wings and Wind hung at the doorway.

Cornelius lifted up his left leg, preparing to pull it over the saddle horns and dismount.

"Sir, I'd wait," Sidia suggested. "You've got company coming."

Riding hard from the Legion fort, Lucius Marcius and five bodyguards galloped up the slope. Cornelius allowed his leg to lower. Then he sighed while waiting for the Battle Commander of Bolt Legion to reach him.

***

"General Scipio, I trust that you are well and full of vigor," Marcius proposed when he reined in.

"That, Battle Commander, is the opening for a formal letter," Cornelius noted. "Is there a reason for the ceremonial greeting?"

"Sir, the news is grim, and I wasn't sure how to go from a robust welcome back to a gritty, stuff it in your face, delivery."

"You succeeded in raising my curiosity and lowering my expectations," Cornelius assured him. "I'm braced for the bad news."

"Last week, a delegation of Senators arrived from Rome," Marcius told him. "They were heading for New Carthage to arrest Colonel Titus Quaeso based on a letter they received from Senior Tribune Furia."

"They what?"

"Exactly, sir. They arrested Colonel Quaeso and took him and Furia back to Rome," Marcius explained. "Fearing a break in command, Magistrate Silanus sailed to New Carthage with a detachment."

Cornelius sat very still on his mount. For long moments, the only movements were muscle twitches in the shoulders of his horse. Then a muscle flexed in Scipio's jaw.

"The last time I checked I was the Prorogatio of Iberia. And that title comes with specific authority over my command," Cornelius said. "How could they row in, ignore my position, and arrest one of my Colonels without asking my permission?"

Marcius extended a scroll to Cornelius.

"You've been recalled to Rome and stripped of authority, pending a ruling by the Senate, sir."

Cornelius took the missive but didn't read it.

"Did the delegation name a charge?"

"Yes, sir. You are being accused of creating an unlawful kingdom," Marcius answered. "And of declaring yourself, the King of Iberia."

For a heartbeat, Cornelius almost said sarcastically, "If I had set out to rule Iberia. By now, I would march on Rome and spank the old fools." But he held his tongue and his temper.

"Tonight, at the officers' mess, I'll designate the distribution of the Legions and the auxiliary units. And in the morning, I'll sail for Rome," Cornelius announced. Then he hesitated and commented. "Only if my plans, Colonel Marcius, meet with your approval."

"No one in Tarraco has seen that scroll or talked with the delegation, General Scipio," Lucius Marcius vowed. "It'll be a pleasure attending a feast in your honor, before you start your vacation in Rome."

***

Two weeks after rowing from the port of Tarraco, Cornelius Scipio and Sidia arrived at the Scipio Villa in Rome. A guard on the gate saluted, a stableman took their horses, and a house servant opened the door.

"It's good to have you home, sir. But your arrival has taken us by surprise," the villa's manager advised. "The lady of the house is at a ceremony for the Goddess Juno. We don't expect her until evening. Should I send a messenger for Lady Tertia?"

"Don't bother. I need a bath, a pitcher of vino, and a chair on the patio," Cornelius told him. "Find a room for Optio Decimia. He'll be staying with us."

"Yes, sir."

Near sundown, Cornelius Scipio reclined in the chair, stretched out his legs, sipped good red from a glass, and looked out over the city. For the first time in almost two years, he didn't have a Legion to train, a mission planned, or an enemy to fight.

"Sir, how long are we staying in Rome," Sidia inquired.

The bodyguard stood off to the right, pivoting his head, switching between the elevated view of Rome from Palatine Hill and the relaxed posture of General Scipio.

"Sidia, we may never leave, or we may go to a Legion that's chasing Hannibal," Cornelius told him. "Or, we might run for political office. How would you feel about being a bodyguard for a Senator?"

"We already know the streets of the city are dangerous," Sidia said. "Let me put it like Jace. You are the client, and I'll always guard your back. But doesn't a citizen need to be thirty-two to become a Senator?"

"And it's forty-two years to be a Consul and a General of Legions," Cornelius replied. "I did that at twenty-four."

Before they could talk more, a cry of pleasure reached them from inside the villa. A moment later, Aemilia Tertia raced across the patio and threw herself at her husband. Cornelius and the Lady of the Villa tumbled to the pavers, then rolled onto the grass. Sidia hurried back into the house, allowing the couple privacy for their reunion.

***

Twenty-four days later, Cornelius and Aemilia rested on sofas. Between them, the remnants of a midday meal lay scattered on a table.

"No doubt Cornelius, you have earned a rest," Aemilia mentioned before taking a sip of watered wine. "And the Gods know I love having you home. But there's a shadow hanging over your homecoming."

"I can't imagine what you're referring to, dear," Cornelius replied.

Aemilia rested her glass on the edge of the table. Then she leveled a stern gaze at her husband.

"For three weeks, you've been in the villa as if we're under siege," she pointed out. "Except for walks through the gardens, you sit on the patio looking at Rome as if it was in the distance and not just down the hill."

"The Senate recalled me from Iberia," Cornelius confessed, "and they want to hold a hearing about my actions. If I go to them, I could be stripped of my social position and exiled from the Republic. As ironic as that may be, considering the charge of building a royal region in Iberia, I don't want to be banished from Rome."

"I married a warrior. A man who survived the massacre at Cannae where my father died," Aemilia challenged. "Since when does Cornelius Scipio back down from a fight?"

Despite the demanding speech, she extended a hand, offering comfort. Cornelius interlaced his fingers with her fingers.

"If I stay in the compound, until it's time, I'm safe," Cornelius stated. "They don't have the courage to send

Legionaries with orders to drag a General of Legions from his villa."

"Until it's time?" Aemilia questioned. "Then you have a plan?"

"I have a belief," Cornelius answered.

Aemilia rocked their arms hard as if testing the strength of their bond. No matter how sharply she jerked, Cornelius' and Aemilia's fingers remained interlocked.

***

Two weeks later, Sidia received a package from Jace. He didn't open it. Rather, the bodyguard carried the bundle to the patio.

"General, as close as my cousin and I were when we were outlaws," Sidia announced, "he's not in the habit of sending me presents."

Cornelius gave a long side eye to the wrappings. Then he pulled the bundle onto his lap, unpeeled the leather cover, and glanced inside.

"Optio Sidia Decimia. Tomorrow you will dress in your best armor and display all of your medals," Cornelius instructed. "Then you will accompany me to the Senate of Rome."

"Is it proper, sir, that a citizen have an armed Legion NCO as a bodyguard?"

"In the morning, I will submit myself to my judgmental critics," Cornelius answered. "But they'll have to rule against a General of Legions and the Prorogatio of Iberia. And not a poor helpless citizen."

"Yes, sir," Sidia stated.

"Burn this before anyone can decipher the meaning," Cornelius ordered. He handed back the package and added. "I'm going to talk with Lady Tertia and get her sage advice. Then I'm going to pray for guidance from the Gods. But I have a feeling by then, I'll already have the best counsel possible."

After the General left, Sidia went to a firepit and lit the stacked wood. From the package, he pulled a wineskin. A sample told him it was sweet raisin wine from Carthage. After dumping the valuable wine, he tossed the skin into the fire. Next, being careful to hide the items, he pulled out three tiny spears carved from wood. Two had peacock feathers tied around the shaft while the third had a raven's feather twisted around the spear. He fed them into the flames. Once the items were ash, Sidia broke up their shapes with a stick to hide the message. Then he went to polish his armor.

***

The Senate of Rome began each session at daybreak. During the prayers and small sacrifices, most of the chamber was in shadows. But rather than hampering the opening rituals, the sacrificial flames glowed brightly in the dark. Once the Senators finished paying homage to the Gods, sunlight streamed in, illuminating the entire chamber.

In the bright sunlight of the next day, a General entered the chamber and marched to the top of an aisle. The helmet hid his face and the pale, front to back horsehair comb distinguished him from a Senior Tribune or a Battle Commander. Although a white cloak covered his armor, no one doubted it would be silver trimmed in gold. A decorated Legion NCO stood braced by his side.

"He's too young to wear that uniform. I prefer my commanders with wrinkles and white in their hair from years of experience," an old Senator commented. "But his Optio has seen some action."

"Consul Claudius Marcellus," Alerio Sisera called to the dais.

"The chamber recognizes Senator Sisera."

"Consul, I ask that the Senate recognize General Cornelius Scipio, the Prorogatio of Iberia, and the hero of the battle for New Carthage."

"Not anymore," a voice shouted from a back row.

"Do I have a second?" Marcellus asked, ignoring the outburst.

After a brief consultation between Quintus Fabius, Marcus Cato, Fulvius Flaccus, and others, a Senator from that side of the chamber offered, "I second the motion."

"The Senate of Rome welcomes General Scipio," the Consul declared. "Come stand before the body, Cornelius Scipio, and be recognized."

With an uncustomary flourish, Cornelius snatched the cloak from his shoulders. Giving it a jerk, he snapped it in the air before laying the garment over Sidia's arm. A gasp rose from the assembly. The ceremonial armor was not silver trimmed in gold, but gold plate trimmed in silver.

Following the showy uncloaking, in a slow and precise manner, Cornelius removed the helmet and handed it to Sidia.

"Ostentatious, just like his wife," a Senator complained. "Someone should bring those Scipio's down a rung."

"Just you wait for Cato to get done with him," another whispered. "By the end of the presentation, Cornelius will be in Sicilia managing a pig farm."

***

Cornelius marched down the aisle without acknowledging either friend, foe, or those uncommitted. At the front, he saluted Claudius Marcellus, then half turned, he faced the Senate.

"Why does he wear the garb of a General of Rome?" a Senator inquired. "Wasn't he stripped of his Legions?"

Sisera stood, pointed to the speaker, and stated, "the committee withdrew the Prorogatio title pending a hearing. And they took his authority as a Republic General in Iberia."

"That's right," Flaccus concerned. "So, wearing a General's armor is disrespectful as well as unlawful."

Cries of undress him or yank the armor off the youth came from different quarters. While the detractors shouted for extreme measures, Alerio Sisera remained standing by his seat. Finally, the rioters and their strong language settled.

"I see you're still on your feet, Senator Sisera," Claudius Marcellus noted. "Do you have more to say?"

"I do, Consul," Alerio replied. "While the Governor's title has been temporarily withdrawn and we've ordered him away from his Legions, we have not found a sound reason why one of Rome's best military minds should be slighted by the removal of his armor. More importantly, if anyone believes Cornelius Scipio is incapable of commanding Legions, they should speak up, before we violate and denigrate General Scipio further."

Valerius Flaccus jumped to his feet, raised a fist in the air, and shouted, "we have much to say on the matter. And none is complimentary to the underaged citizen named Cornelius Scipio."

Alerio Sisera shifted his focus to the front of the Senate. He expected to find Cornelius seething with rage. But the youthful General simply stood as he had since he marched down the aisle. Even Consul Marcellus noticed the lack of pushback by the general officer.

"Unless General Scipio has opening remarks," Marcellus hinted. He paused to allow Cornelius to voice an objection to the proceedings or at least to say something in his defense. Having been the target of dishonest charges himself, Claudius Marcellus wanted to give the accused every chance. But Scipio remained mute. After forcing out a breath in frustration, the Consul invited in the executioners. "The chamber recognizes Senator Flaccus."

Valerius Flaccus glanced around as if searching the nearby faces for something. Finally, he briefly stopped on one, before addressing the Senate.

"All this is unnecessary," Flaccus announced. "Everything the boy Scipio has done occurred before his twenty-fifth birthday. Not only was he underage to sign contracts or treaties. He had yet to reach the age for a Senator's position, let alone for a General of Legions. As such, I request a vote to have this hearing sent to a city magistrate for trial."

Low and deep, the growl from Alerio Sisera sent shivers through Senators who had served as infantrymen in the Legions. In training, the guttural sound marked the intent of a physical challenge followed by pain. In the Senate, it was taken as no less a sign of danger.

"I protest the circus juggling act being attempted by Senator Flaccus," Senator Sisera countered. "We've seen too much silver, copper, and gold flow from Iberia to the coffers of Rome to discount General Scipio's worth. To be clear gentlemen, understand that I will not permit a General of Legions to be tried in the Forum by a civil judge. I will not allow the judgment trap of an ambitious magistrate to abduct what rightly is the Senates to decide. We will not wash our hands of Cornelius Scipio. We will not forsake our responsibility to the Republic. If there is to be a trial, let it be here. Let it be now."

The chamber erupted with shouts of agreement. Enough in fact, there was no reason for Consul Marcellus to call for a vote to hand off the trial to a magistrate.

"We will hear the evidence and vote on the virtues or the vices," the Consul declared. "And, seeing as General Scipio is participating in spirit only, I call on Senator Flaccus to deliver the accusations."

Chapter 20 – Without My Warrant

Fulvius Flaccus bowed, then instead of speaking, indicated Quintus Fabius. The old Senator, famous for his strategy of following Hannibal but not engaging, nodded at the silent handoff.

"Because none of the Senators see value in this procedure," Fabius said in his dignified manner, "I will call on a contemporary of Scipio's to levy the charges."

"Don't include me in that group, Delayer," a Senator protested, using the insulting term. After the Legions suffered several catastrophic defeats, Consul/General Quintus Fabius instituted a tactic of following Hannibal and interrupting his supply lines, but not doing battle with the Carthaginian. Some citizens understood and cheered Fabius for his patience. Others thought of the delaying strategy as cowardly. The protesting Senator pointed out. "Cornelius has opened trade routes between Rome and New Carthage and protected them with Republic warships. If anyone deserves a hearing in the Senate, it's him."

"Present company excluded," Fabius allowed. The venerable statesman waved an arm as if sweeping away the insult and the argument. "I call on a contemporary of the disgraced Legion officer, Cornelius Scipio, to present the case. I ask that Marcus Cato be recognized."

"Marcus Cato, you have the floor," Consul Marcellus instructed.

From a campstool beside Fabius' chair, Cato rose and extended his arms.

"There are many clues to the crime," he stated. "And I will list them. But let me rush to the end to help you see the path we will travel together. For at the conclusion, surely, you will convict Cornelius Scipio of declaring himself the King of Iberia."

At the utterance of the hated title of King, the Senate dissolved into pools of anger and outrage. Since dethroning Tarquin, the last King of Rome, the Senate of the Republic had fought against the very idea of a Monarch. Three hundred years of resistance resounded throughout the chamber.

Inside, Cato's heart pounded with joy. He had triggered the Senators and swayed them even before presenting a drop of evidence. Externally, he maintained a grave expression on his face to show the gravity of the situation.

***

When the uproar settled, Cato nodded wisely.

"I ask you, Senators of Rome, how would a King act? Would he break with tradition? Bestow awards just to gather support?" Cato inquired. "Cornelius Scipio, after the fall of New Carthage, presented two Corona Murali medals. How could two standard bearers plant their Legion's banners on an enemy's wall at the same time? Obviously, King Scipio wanted support from his household Legions, the Eagle of Jupiter, and the Lightning Bolt of Jupiter. So, he trounced on tradition and bestowed one on each Legion."

In most cases, even men who haven't been to war would offer opinions after a battle. Especially true were the results of a siege. The proof came as clusters of Senators held two hands in front of their faces. With each, they reenacted climbing ladders then topping a wall. In every case, they agreed that it was unlikely for two standard bearers to scale two ladders during a fight and reach the top of a defensive wall at the same time.

"Test the theory yourself," Cato encouraged, although most had already. "In another grab at power, King Scipio assembled eight Legions. A Consul or a Proconsul commands just four Legions each. Yet, in Iberia, Scipio controls eight Legions."

"He could invade Rome," a Senator squealed in fright. "With eight Legions, Cornelius Scipio could finish what Hannibal started."

It might have been a damning exclamation. Except, the Senator sat near Flaccus and Fabius. Most of the Senators understood he was part of the prosecution and playing a role in the drama. Even so, a few Senators felt the panic in the back of their necks.

Cato cupped his forehead with one hand and waved the other, as if cautioning the Senators of a danger.

"Not only does King Scipio have an enormous royal army he possesses a massive navy," Cato warned. "With a commercial fleet of sixty-three captured transports plus a total of sixty warships, King Scipio can transport his army anywhere. To Rome to Alexandria, or to Carthage."

"If he's so strong," an old Senator demanded. "Why hasn't he invaded Carthage?"

"An excellent question," Cato conceded. "Additionally, he furthers his ties with Iberia against Rome, by treating his defeated enemies as if they were snakes, and he a Priest of Asclepius. Almost as if he worships our enemies, he frees them as soon as the battle ends."

Tongues clicked at the timid character displayed by releasing an enemy before asking for ransom.

"Did I say snakes?" Cato questioned. "King Scipio ordered his headquarters to be placed in the Temple of Asclepius. Typically, the temple is a place of healing and snakes. But in New Carthage, it's a shrine to the God Scipio, King of Iberia."

Accusations of blasphemy were leveled at Cornelius by several Senators. For a moment, Cato pondered adding the charge of dishonoring the Gods to Cornelius' crimes. But he had touched an emotional sore spot with the King line and decided to stay with it.

***

Alerio Sisera and Consul Marcellus turned to Cornelius. As he had done all morning, Scipio watched the critical speech and the reactions dispassionately.

Waving to his assistant, Alerio called Hektor Nicanor to his side.

"Find out what Cato is building to," he instructed. "I know he's pushing the King scenario. But he'll need something better than words to bring down a General. And while you're researching that, see if you can discover why Cornelius is so calm."

"Yes, sir," the assistant acknowledged before dashing up the aisle.

Two aisles over, he stopped behind Optio Decimia.

"What is Cornelius waiting for?" Hektor whispered.

"Sir, I have no idea," Sidia lied. "The General is a contemplative man. Perhaps he's praying."

"Too busy praying to save his career?" Hektor inquired. "I'll be back. Think on this. If Cato and his crowd succeed, your General will be a chicken farmer on the Island of Sardinia by Saturnalia."

The assistant moved away quickly, and a shiver went through Sidia. If Hektor had waited for another heartbeat, the bodyguard would have told him. But Hektor had left, leaving a bad taste in Sidia's mouth.

"I hate farming," Sidia whined.

***

Hektor Nicanor couldn't very well walk up to the opposition and ask what they had planned. While that approach was doomed, he did have a deep knowledge of the assistants for the Senators across the aisle from Senator Sisera. And at the moment, they were absent.

"During this presentation, you've heard me use King Scipio, a lot," Cato informed the Senate. "Those aren't my words. The local tribesmen and women call Cornelius,

King Scipio. And by all reports, he never corrects them. And why would he?"

Hektor ducked through the door and scanned the patio. At the base of the stairs, a Colonel and a Senior Tribune talked with the assistants for Fabius and Flaccus.

"Witnesses," Hektor thought.

At a fast walk, he retreated to the place behind the bodyguard.

"In a moment, two Legion officers will enter the chamber," Hektor alerted Sidia. "In short sentences, tell me who they are. And why they would want to hurt Cornelius."

"How would I know two officers from Rome?" Sidia protested. Then he stiffened and half turned his head. "Colonel Quaeso, the Battel Commander of Steed of Aeneas. He gets along good with the General. The other officer is Justus Furia. Senior Tribune of Jace Kasia's Legion, Wings of Nortus. Colonel Kasia trusted and promoted him."

"Ill placed trust," Hektor grunted before rushing away.

***

"On several occasions, Scipio mishandled funds," Cato was saying when Hektor reached Senator Sisera.

"He has two witnesses," Hektor told the Senator. "One of Cornelius' Battle Commanders and a newly promoted Senior Tribune."

While Alerio thought, Cato continued his talk.

"One of the instances of coins gone missing, has to do with three hostages. They were a women and two young girls, belonging to the Ilergetes Tribe. The tribe that murdered Proconsul Publius Scipio, Cornelius' father,"

Cato offered. "But maybe we shouldn't have been looking for coins. After all, who would sell the memory of their father? Perhaps, the real coin exchange for hostages will come when King Scipio declares himself. And to vouch for the validity…"

Alerio Sisera pushed out of his seat and shouted, "A moment, young Cato. If you're going to pile on more charges, I need to reflect on the seeds you've already planted. Consul Marcellus, I believe a pause is in order."

"Due to the heat near midday," Marcellus directed, "the Senate will take a recess until this afternoon."

***

Hektor collected Cornelius and Sidia. Together with Senator Sisera, they walked to a restaurant. In a private room, they were served lunch and left alone.

"Why aren't you defending yourself?" Alerio asked.

"Would it do any good?" Cornelius countered. "King is a colloquialism in Iberia. Every town has a King. Every tribe has a King. Every region has a King. Is it unreasonable for tribesmen to call a Legion General, King?"

"I can see the value in staying out of a battle with no substance. But you could at least make a statement."

"Senator Sisera, I've been listening," Cornelius informed him. "Someone has reported on my activities. But I don't know who. I was hoping that somewhere in Cato's speech, he would say something to give me a hint."

"Titus Quaeso or Justus Furia," Hektor mentioned. "Those are the two witnesses Cato has waiting when we reconvene."

"I find it hard to believe a harsh commander like Quaeso would also be a spy. When I sent Steed Legion into New Carthage, they were supposed to take Citadel Hill and the high ground with the Temple of Asclepius," Cornelius said. "Colonel Quaeso took both hills. But his infantry massacred townspeople between the objectives. Maybe being a Republic Legion, they didn't see the value of Iberian citizens. In any case, they butchered hundreds."

"That's settled," Alerio announced.

"Excuse me Senator Sisera, what's settled?"

"Justus Furia is the spy and Titus Quaeso will lie to protect himself from being prosecuted for murder," Alerio replied. "All we need now is a way to counter their false testimony."

"One way is to get Cornelius reinstated as the Prorogatio of Iberia," Hektor suggested. "As the Prorogatio, he could pardon Colonel Quaeso and free the man of the threat."

"An elegant solution for a dirty allegation," Alerio added. "Let's put aside the law for the time being and focus on the food."

They ate in silence. But just as they finished, a runner appeared at the doorway.

"Senator Sisera, Consul Marcellus has called for a full session of the Senate," the messenger announced. "You are to return immediately."

"The Delayer wants this over fast," Cornelius offered. "He must have another life to destroy before the end of the day."

***

At the Senate chamber, they pushed through crowds of Senators and assistants. To Cornelius and Alerio's amazement, the discussions had little to do with the Scipio trial. Instead, everyone questioned the early session.

"There's something in the air," Senator Sisera said. "And look at the Consul. You'd think he was standing on hot coals."

Claudius Marcellus shifted from one foot to the other. Either the soles of his sandals were uncomfortable, or he was preparing to go for a run. Neither action fit the current situation.

"I can interrupt the witnesses, and ruin their rhythm," Alerio told Cornelius. "But I can't stop them from testifying."

"I'm just learning how to handle murderous tribal leaders and women with daggers," Cornelius admitted. "I have no idea how to deal with the politicians in my own Senate."

"You're halfway there."

"How so, Senator Sisera?"

"You've got the descriptions right."

***

Cornelius marched to the dais, saluted, and asked, "Do I stand where I did before, Consul?"

"Scipio, call down your NCO and take back your helmet," Marcellus instructed. "I've received news. And after I deliver it, I'm calling for a vote."

"What news, sir?"

"You'll know soon enough," the Consul replied.

A wave brought Sidia down to the floor of the Senate. Cornelius took the helmet and tucked it under his left arm. Before Sidia could make his way up the aisle,

Claudius Marcellus grabbed his shoulder and spun the NCO to face the Senate.

"How long have you served General Scipio?" he demanded.

Sidia stammered trying to figure out the years and how to get away from the Consul of Rome. Finally, he guessed, "Sir, about four years, sir."

"Is General Scipio a good commander?"

"He brought the Ilergetes Tribe to their knees, made their poets cry, and burned half their capital," Sidia answered. "But mostly, sir. General Scipio left, Indibilis and Mandonius, the men who killed his father, afraid he'd return one night and finish the job."

Claudius Marcellus, the General who conquered Syracuse, scanned the Senators.

"Optio, take you place behind your General," he ordered. Then Marcellus produced a scroll and unrolled it. "I'll skip the opening and get right to the important matter. Colonel Kasia returned from a long-range patrol and reported the following. Recently arrived on Iberian soil are Hasdrubal Barca, Mago Barca, and Hasdrubal Gisco. Immediately after landing, the Carthaginian Generals began calling in favors and distributing coins. Their purpose is to raise three armies and throw the Legions into the sea. It's signed Junius Silanus, Magistrate of Iberia and Senior Tribune of Iberian Legions."

Marcellus lowered the parchment and raised his eyebrows in a questioning manner. When no one commented about the letter, he squared his shoulders.

"Gentlemen, what this means is the Republic treaties in Iberia are about to go up in flames," he described. "And the only military commander with experience in the region is standing here accused of running an unlawful kingdom. General Scipio, are you loyal to the Republic?"

"Yes, Consul."

"Why do you have eight Legions?"

"The Senate didn't authorize me a Roman Legion, sir," Cornelius answered. "Three of my Legions are from the Republic and four are Iberian. The eighth is a specialty Legion for my artillery and cavalry."

"Do you want to be King of Iberia."

"Consul Marcellus, Iberia has too many Kings as it is," Cornelius replied. "I am a citizen of the Republic and always will be."

His answer brought applause from the Senators accompanied by Rahs from Senators who had served as Legionaries.

"Will you return to Iberia and battle the Carthaginian threat in the name of the Roman Republic?" Marcellus asked.

Cornelius paused. In response, the Senators leaned forward, until he answered, "No, Consul, I will not."

From shouting for his armor, his neck, his exile, and even his soul, the Senate of Rome questioned why Cornelius Scipio would say no.

"Did I hear you correctly, Scipio?" Marcellus inquired. "You don't want the command?"

"Facing three Carthaginian armies, commanded by experienced Generals, is not a job for a committee," Cornelius responded. He slipped the General's helmet over his head and braced. From behind, Sidia placed the white cloak on his shoulders. "I was relieved by a committee of Senators. And for what? Sending gold, copper, and silver to Rome. Preventing pirates and foreign navies from attacking our merchants. And creating peace along the east coast of Iberia? No thank you, Consul. Give the job to another commander."

Claudius Marcellus sneered at the Senate as if they were schoolboys.

"Here's the opportunity. Take command in Iberia and earn your glory," he challenged. But no one stepped forward to assume the responsibility. Then Marcellus faced Cornelius and asked. "What would it take to get you to return to Iberia, General Scipio?"

"I won't go without my warrant," Cornelius told him. "Only as Prorogatio of Iberia, and General of all Iberian Legions, will I accept the responsibilities."

"Senate of Rome," Marcellus announced from the podium, "now, we vote."

Chapter 21 – Jupiter and His Eagle

The upper deck of the quinquereme was damp and glistening. Although a light rain, the deck boards collected moisture as if the warship was a long pan. And while the upper tier of oarsmen enjoyed the refreshing sprinkles, below them, the next level caught drippings from the boards and the oarsmen above. Even so, they brushed off the mist as they rowed. But like any pan, there was a bottom. At the lowest level, the rowers stroked between streams of flowing rainwater from overhead and ankle-deep water underfoot. As they worked, they cursed the weather.

On the steering platform, the ship's Centurion and First Principale watched the warship, the waves, the sky, and the murky horizon. Behind them, both navigators manipulated the rear oars. Despite the rain and low clouds, everyone in the crew was honored to be transporting the Prorogatio of Iberia.

"General Scipio," the ship's Centurion addressed Cornelius. "I heard about your stoic response to the vicious attacks in the Senate. I don't know if I could have held back. But you, sir, emerged victorious."

"Plato the Greek said the first and greatest victory is to conquer yourself. To be conquered by yourself is of all things most shameful and vile," Cornelius quoted to the ship's officer. "In my heart, I wanted a dog fight. To rip and tear at my accusers. To drag their carcasses across the chamber floor and gnaw on their bones. But that would not have been a victory. It would have been, as Plato stated, shameful and vile. Instead, I depended on the Gods to right the wrong."

"It is for sure the Goddess Fortuna blessed you on that day," The Centurion offered. "Speaking of luck, sir, this weather could get worse. I'd like your permission to beach the ship for the night."

"I'm good at planning campaigns with thousands of warriors," Cornelius admitted. "Not in commanding a warship in foul weather with four hundred citizens depending on me. Do what you feel is right."

"Thank you, General," the Centurion said. "First Principale, find us a sandy bed for the night."

"Third Principale, find us a beach," the ship's first officer notified the bow officer.

While the crew prepared to locate a berthing place for the warship, Sidia eased closer to Cornelius.

"I won't disregard the hand of the Goddess Fortuna in the vote," the bodyguard whispered to Cornelius. "But, sir, you knew from Jace's message the Carthaginians had returned. With the two peacock feathers representing Hasdrubal Barca and Mago Barca, and the raven feather Hasdrubal Gisco, you know about the Generals. It might have been beneficial for you to take a little credit for your own cunning."

"Optio Decimia, never argue with a man who places you in the company of the Gods," Cornelius instructed. "He's already given you authority far above anything you could claim for yourself."

"In that case, General Scipio," Sidia proposed, "I'll arrange a sacrifice for the Goddess Fortuna when we land."

"We should honor her involvement," Cornelius affirmed.

***

A week later, when Tarraco came into view, Cornelius had mixed feelings. Between the celebration feasts with supporters, and the victory galas put on by his wife, Cornelius had wallowed in the joys of Rome. Among them, making speeches in the afternoons to eager audiences, drinking vino, and talking until early morning, sleeping late, and hugging Aemilia whenever she came within reach. And his wife had made herself available for hugs, and consultations, plus introductions to the newest power brokers in the Republic. But the revelry ended, Iberia loomed ahead, and that made him a little sad.

Conversely, on his first assignment to Iberia, he was shorthanded, unsure of himself, and set up by the Senate to fail. But he persevered, built coalitions, and created eight Legions. Soon, under his watch, coins flowed to Rome and sea trade increased. Pride and a sense of destiny overwhelmed the sadness as the warship backed onto the beach at Tarraco.

"What's our first stop, sir?" Sidia asked.

"The shrines at Marçà," Cornelius answered.

"To pray for guidance, sir?"

"Not guidance, Optio Decimia. I'm asking the Gods for help in shattering the three spears of Carthage against the shields of my Legions."

Unfortunately for Cornelius, his appointment with the Gods was cut short. In his absence, rumors circulated that General Scipio had fallen ill and was on his death bed. The long visits to the shrines were replaced by in-depth and personal inspections of his Legions and auxiliary forces.

***

Starting with the garrison at Tarraco and extending to the garrison stationed south of New Carthage, Cornelius Scipio spent the next month assuring the men under his command and the leaders of allied tribes of his robust health. Pausing at New Carthage before returning to Marçà, Cornelius and Junius Silanus talked over dinner.

"King Indibilis and War Chief Mandonius have stationed spearmen on their border and are using them to raid their neighbors," Junius told Cornelius. The Senior Tribune of Iberia appeared gaunt and pale from stress. "I thought about sending a Legion to warn them. But then considered it might cause an unnecessary war. I weighed the benefits against the cost but couldn't find the balance point. I fear I've come up short as a General."

"Without your support Junius, we'd still be in a defensive posture around Tarraco," Cornelius assured him. "The Ilergetes brothers were always going to be a problem. Let's send them a couple wagons of saltwater fish to remind them of our agreement."

"We'll need a lot of salt in this weather," Junius pointed out, "or the fish will rot."

Early fall along the coast held onto the heat of the Iberian summer. In a matter of weeks, the night temperatures would fall, but for the present, the sun maintained its strength. An unsalted wagon of fish would last two days at most before the stench would warn off potential diners.

"No salt. Just a scroll telling the brothers to eat the rotten fish and die," Cornelius described. "Or to send me a message informing me when I should march to their homes and cancel their bloodline."

"Do you think two transports of smelly fish will get the desired result?" Junius Silanus asked.

"The fish are just the message," Cornelius uttered. "I'm depending on Colonel Kasia, six hundred heavy cavalrymen, and five hundred of his light infantry, and Bolt Legion to make my point."

"The heavy cavalrymen and light infantry are here in New Carthage and Bolt Legion is in Marçà," Junius mentioned. "Plus, we already have cavalry up there."

"You're correct, of course. But moving cavalry and light infantryman from New Carthage will appear to weaken our defensives."

Junius Silanus thought for a moment. Then he lifted his glass in salute.

"If we're weak, we can't attack the Carthaginians, and they'll let down their guard," he summarized. "It's good to have you back, General Scipio."

"It's good to be back, Senior Tribune Silanus."

***

The long days of travel gave Cornelius the opportunity to plan a course of action. After much consideration and praying while riding, Cornelius envisioned a campaign against the Carthaginians using the brothers from the Ilergetes tribe. To inform his Colonels of the strategy, Cornelius sent out messengers with invitations. Some only needed to cross the fort to attend. Others would ride from New Carthage for the appointed day in a large and impressive force.

After his whirlwind tour, Cornelius returned to the Legion fort at Marçà. He relaxed with a glass of wine while waiting for his seven Battle Commanders and Senior Tribune Zeno from Steed of Aeneas to arrive. Shaken by the vicious politics, Colonel Titus Quaeso declined to return to Iberia. And Junius Silanus, having commandeered a warship from New Carthage, arrived a day early. But instead of the two commanders meeting, Cornelius sent him to Tarraco to dine with the mayor.

***

"Master Silanus, you seem despondent," the mayor's wife noted. "I hope it's not the company or the food."

Ten people dined at the long table. Caikonbe, the Mayor of Tarraco, sat at one end, and the Roman officer occupied the opposite end of the table.

"Lady Sicounin, the companions are pleasant and the feast delicious," Junius assured her. "I'm afraid my malaise is a professional malady."

"What a curious use of words," Sicounin commented. "Please tell us about it. It's said that unburdening your mind helps bring solutions to the forefront."

"As is identifying the cause of your issues," Caikonbe proposed. "I've always found the answer to every problem lies in the details."

Junius took a healthy drink from his wine glass and held it out. A servant immediately refilled it. The Senior Tribune took a sip before setting it on the tabletop.

"Most of the summer, I have been acting Governor of Iberia," Junius slurred. "And I think I've done a good job."

"Most assuredly," Caikonbe remarked. "Trade is up and shipments of metals to Rome were uninterrupted."

"And you've provided security along the coast," Sicounin conceded. "Our fishing fleet is safe thanks to you."

Of the seven other attendees at the feast, five were leading citizens of Tarraco. But two were merchants with deep connections to tribes on the interior of Iberia. And while the residents were slightly curious about the conversation, the merchants focused on remembering every word uttered by the Roman.

"I really shouldn't, it would be disrespectful," Junius said.

"Come, Senior Tribune, you're among friends," one of the traders urged. "Allow us to be a sympathetic audience for you."

Junius Silanus drummed the fingers of one hand on the table while downing his glass of wine. A waiting servant quickly refilled the glass.

"I held the Legions together when he left for Rome," Junius complained. "And as he frolicked with the elites, I did the work here. And suddenly, he's back and I'm told to wait for tomorrow's meeting like one of his Battle

Commanders. And he spends all of his time in the shrine of Jupiter, thanking the God for my work."

"How awful," Sicounin gushed.

Murmurs of agreement from the guests supported the sentiment. Junius bobbed his head, stopped to take another slurp of wine, and opened his mouth to speak. He hesitated briefly before telling them the tale.

"It's those Ilergetes tribesmen," Junius revealed. "He blames me for not punishing them. Now, he's pooling resources to march on the tribe and butcher them into extinction. And he's punishing me because it delays his plans to deal with Hasdrubal Barca, and the other Carthaginian Generals. He's so incensed with Indibilis and Mandonius that he's weakened New Carthage to punish the brothers. And crippled my Legions and my ability to strike at Hasdrubal from New Carthage."

"He should be grateful to have an administrator like you to lean on," Sicounin told him. "Without you, we'd all be slaves of Carthage. Even if he doesn't, we appreciate to you, Junius Silanus."

Junius lifted his glass to his mouth and smiled before taking a tiny sip. For him, the evening couldn't end soon enough. But until the feast broke up, he'd have to maintain the appearance of a disgruntled Legion officer.

***

Sidia Decimia and five Legionaries from First Century idled away the night. A couple of times a patrol had questioned them, but once made aware that he was the Generals' bodyguard, the city guards continued their rounds.

The six infantrymen sat on the patio of a closed café. They had a good view of Tarraco's night gate a half block away.

"I sure hope the proprietor is an early riser," a Legionary commented. "I could eat."

"You can always eat," another pointed out.

"That's because I'm always hungry."

"Can you stop thinking about food for the moment and ponder the rider and the wagon?" Sidia asked.

From the dark city, a wagon rolled into view. Beside the transport, a mounted man kept pace with the driver.

"The rider might be a caravan guard," an infantryman suggested.

"What guard carries extra waterskins but no armor or long weapon," the hungry Legionary questioned. "He looks more like a courier."

"Come daylight," Sidia promised, "I'm buying you breakfast."

"That'd be great," the Legionary replied.

The rider and wagon rolled to the city gate, and after speaking with the gate guards, they vanished through the portal.

"I think that's it," Sidia announced.

But from down the street, another rider trotted towards the gate. Light in the saddle with feed bags and waterskins hanging off the horns, the man wasn't equipped for anything except fast traveling.

"Now that Optio, is a messenger," a Legionary reasoned. "It's a very busy night in Tarraco."

"Now I hope the owner is an early riser," Sidia said.

"Why do you say that?" two infantrymen inquired.

"Because we're going to be here all night."

"Watching for more couriers?"

"Right you are, Legionary," Sidia stated.

***

Late the next morning, Cornelius rode to the shrines overlooking the fort. Without the protection of Sidia, he brought two veterans to watch his back.

"I'm accustomed to peace while I pray," he told them. "Unless it's important, I'm not to be disturbed."

"Yes, sir," they replied.

The bodyguards took positions on either side of the entrance. With an Eagle banner waving over one infantryman and a Lightning Bolt standard flapping over the other, Cornelius strolled between the banners and entered the shrine.

***

Copied from the small shrines of Rome, the structure had relatively high walls, a stone floor, benches for worshipers, and a stone altar for small sacrifices and gifts. What the shrine lacked was a roof. Open to the heavens, the style allowed for uplifting sunlight, fresh air, and access for the God to look in on his flock.

What no one planned on, including his Ilergetes uncle, was a servant from the Mayor of Tarraco's household reacting to Junius Silanus' story. Before daylight, the servant scaled the wall and hid under a bench. His stealth avoided the General's bodyguards and put him in a position to murder the man who threatened his Ilergetes relatives.

***

Cornelius stopped and leaned against the doorframe. Altars were always miraculous. Sunlight streamed in, and he could feel a breeze on his face. And while allowing a view of the blue sky above, it was enclosed on all sides, cutting off connections to the material world beyond. Further mesmerizing Cornelius, on the far end of the rustic shrine, a beautifully polished stone table drew his eyes to the purpose of the building.

"Jupiter, I've come seeking your blessing," he said before stepping completely into the shrine. "We've much to discuss before my Battle Commanders arrive."

He walked down the center aisle. At the front bench, Cornelius sat and lifted his face to the sky.

Two rows back, the servant drew his knife. Fittingly, as a gift from his uncle, it would be used to stop the mad Roman and end his plan to massacre Ilergetes spearmen and their families. Scooting sideways, the servant cleared the underside of the bench. But his grip on the hilt of his Ilergetes knife turned his knuckles white and sent tremors down his arm. With his heart racing, the servant paused to calm his nerves.

***

Sidia and the five infantry veterans saluted the gate NCO.

"If you're still drunk after a night in Tarraco," the Duty NCO warned, "I don't want trouble."

"No trouble, Optio," an infantryman scoffed, "much to the disappointment of my dry throat."

"But we did have a big beef breakfast," the hungry Legionary boasted.

While the five went to their barracks, Sidia rode to the General's quarters.

"He's not here Optio Decimia," an aid told him. "He went to the shrines."

"How many bodyguards did he take, sir?"

"Two from First Century."

"Just two? Not a squad?"

Before the junior officer answered, Sidia jerked the horse around and kicked it in the flanks. A moment later, the horse, much to the gate NCO's ire, galloped back through the opening. Outside the fort, Sidia guided the horse off the road and up the hill towards the four shrines.

Sidia had no reason to believe General Scipio was in danger.

However, as Aristotle stated, *excellence was not an act, but a habit. And a habit was an acquired disposition to perform certain types of actions.*

Having countless times performed actions to protect General Scipio, Sidia let habit drive him and the horse to the shrine of Jupiter.

Dismounting while the horse was still in motion, Sidia demanded, "Where's the General?"

"Optio, he doesn't want to be disturbed," one of the Legionaries informed him.

The other pointed at the entrance to the shrine.

***

With the Ilergetes blade held forward at waist level, the servant aimed the tip at the Roman's neck. Creeping silently forward, he held his breath. Then from the sky overhead, a high-pitched piping noise reached into the shrine. And his target turned.

Cornelius rotated his head, searching the sky for the eagle. But then he saw the assassin rushing forward and the tribal blade filling his vision. Falling backwards, he used an arm to deflect the blade. Blood flowed, his head hit the bench, and the General of Legions fell to the stone floor. With his vision blurred, Cornelius could only hold up his empty hands to fend off the coming slashes.

For a heartbeat, the murderer stood over Cornelius. Then he sailed through the air and collided with the altar. Bent over the edge for a moment, the killer sprang back and swung his blade at the assailant.

"Spare him," Cornelius mumbled, his voice hoarse from shock and surprise.

But the War Chief of the Hirpini was beyond hearing. His blood boiling from almost failing in his duty, Sidia Decimia wielded the gladius as if it was a fine skinning knife.

The results weren't pretty. And just before the servant dropped from the deep gashes, Sidia kicked him onto the altar.

"For Jupiter," he growled. Then with a look of horror on his face, he knelt beside Cornelius. "Sir, besides the arm, are their other cuts?"

"No Sidia, you arrived just in time," Cornelius answered. With the bodyguard's help, he got to his feet and looked at the assassin. "I did want to question him before the crucifixion. But a sacrifice to Jupiter and his eagle will have to suffice."

Act 8

Chapter 22 - Third Spear of Carthage

Anxiety filled the Legion commanders. All they knew was General Scipio had been attacked but they had no report on how bad, or why, or by whom. The eight of them, their aids, and servants occupied the General's dining hall. For men accustomed to directing maneuvers under combat conditions, idling away the afternoon without intelligence or a plan made the large room feel like a cage.

"Perhaps we should go to the medical tent," Colonel Nabars of Trumpet Legion suggested, "and see for ourselves."

The Battle Commander for Bolt Legion thought so little of the idea, he shook his head no, but didn't speak.

"What's wrong Marcius," the Colonel from Gold Cat Legion teased, "don't like the sight of blood."

In a quick turn, the Battle Commander of Winds of Nortus faced the joker.

"I don't think anyone here is afraid of the sight of blood," he snapped.

Gaius Laelius from Eagle Legion laughed, "I don't think he was being serious."

Although they each served Cornelius Scipio, the eight men lived and worked with their Legions. Rarely did the Battle Commanders of the Iberian Legions socialize.

"Senior Tribune Zeno are you sure you want this job?" the Colonel from the War Chariot of Deimos asked.

"Commanding a Legion has been a lifelong ambition," Zeno replied. "Steed of Aeneas is ready to die for General Scipio."

"That's really not the goal," Jace Kasia commented. "I believe our purpose is to make the other guy die for his General."

"Save your Greek philosophy for your artillerymen," Winds' Colonel remarked to Jace. "Wings Legion doesn't even have heavy infantrymen."

"Maybe not. But Wings of Nortus has a Colonel who will stomp you into the dirt."

"Gentlemen. This is not a pub serving Legionaries on payday," Lucius Marcius warned. "Control yourselves."

"Tell that to the Greek," Winds' Battle Commander deflected. Adding as he walked away. "Kasia started with the threats."

Jace dipped a finger in his berry flavored water, lifted it out, and stuck it in his mouth. Then the archer hooked the finger on the inside of his cheek and snapped it out, making a loud, "Pop."

The offended Colonel turned back.

"Keep walking Winds," Jace told him. "Your heavy infantry has been living off intelligence delivered by the blood and sweat of my Legion for months. Let me give you one piece of advice. Don't start a fight you can't finish."

The door opened. Cornelius Scipio, with a bandage on his right forearm and blood stains on his robe, walked in followed by Senior Tribune of Legions Silanus, and Optio Decimia.

"What did I miss?" Cornelius inquired.

"Colonel Kasia was explaining the finer points of combat theory for the benefit of Winds Legion," Gaius Laelius replied.

"I assume he didn't get far into the lecture," Cornelius submitted, "as I don't see blood on anyone but me."

Junius Silanus moved to the dining table and laid a knife on the corner.

"Anybody know the origin of this?" he asked. "The blade was used in the attempted murder of our General."

Blank stares were the only reply until Jace walked to the table. He bent, studied the carved handle, tapped the blade with a fingernail, and declared, "A fine example of the skills of an Ilergetes knifemaker. Good steel. And the handle is beautiful."

"Ilergetes. I've reached the end of my patience with Indibilis and Mandonius. We will," Cornelius growled then stopped. Looking around at all the extra people in the hall, he ordered. "Everyone except my Battle Commanders, clear the room."

***

Red faced in anger with his eyes squeezed tight, Cornelius waited for the room to empty. Once he was alone with his commanders, General Scipio told them, "I want the Ilergetes crippled. The brothers nailed to beams and hoisted up on crosses. And I don't want them to know we're coming."

His zeal brought out 'Rahs' from seven of his commanders. Only one refrained from cheering.

"Colonel Kasia, I don't see enthusiasm for my plan on your face," Cornelius pointed out. "Is there a flaw in my strategy. Perhaps you feel my vengeance isn't justified?"

"Retribution is historically the right of the offended," Jace proposed. "And sir, you certainly were offended. But the Ilergetes are a static enemy. They'll be there when you decide to attack. In the meanwhile, you have a mobile enemy that won't wait."

"You're talking about the Carthaginian Generals," Cornelius remarked. "Aren't they wintering at Ilipa, north of Seville? The last time I checked, we lacked the Legions to attack three entrenched armies. Or do we?"

"Hasdrubal Barca has moved away from his brother Margo and Hasdrubal Gisco," Jace reported. "He's dug in at Baecula on the upper reaches of the Guadalquivir river."

"Why would he leave a fortified position?" Laelius from Eagle questioned.

"The only thing my scouts and I can come up with is he's recruiting for a mission," Jace answered. "Either he plans to take back New Carthage or he's heading for the Republic to join Hannibal."

Forgetting his injury, Cornelius Scipio rammed a fist into the palm of his other hand. Pain gripped his right forearm, and he doubled over. Still leaning forward, he paused.

Sidia reached out to support him, but Cornelius shrugged off the assistance.

"Do you know what's more painful than a cut on the arm?" he asked.

Sensing a rhetorical question, none of the Legion commanders replied.

Cornelius straightened his back, tapped his coin purse, and answered his own question, "The cost of paying, feeding, and housing an army while waiting for an attack."

"The expenses are enormous," Silanus agreed. "But what does that have to do with current events, General?"

"Call the aids and servants back in," Cornelius announced. He paced for a few moments to allow them to be summoned. "We're going to march on the Ilergetes. We'll burn their farms, butcher their livestock, and kill their spearmen wherever we find them."

The servants and aids flowing in heard Cornelius Scipio's version of revenge.

"And the third spear of Carthage?" Jace inquired.

"I'm afraid if we attack Baecula, Mago and Gisco will come in and hit us from behind," Cornelius told him. "We'll have to settle for getting rich from selling the Ilergetes into slavery. And doubling the defenses at New Carthage. It's the best we can do with what we have."

"Yes, sir," Jace acknowledged.

***

Late the next morning, ten miles west of Tarraco, five wagons, two Centuries of Legionaries, and a mounted escort reached a clearing. Wooden pegs identified it as their destination.

"Those are the engineer's stakes," a teamster shouted to a cavalry officer.

"Give me patrols on our perimeter," the Centurion instructed his riders. "I don't want us surprised by a war band while we build the supply station."

The infantrymen stacked their shields and spears, then dropped their armor.

As a pair of Legionaries pulled a stockade log from a transport, one mentioned, "there's something I don't understand."

"And that's different today as opposed to yesterday?" his squad mate inquired while lifting the opposite end.

Holding the log, they stopped and looked at each other.

"No, really," the first insisted. "Rumor has it, the General wants to assault the Ilergetes as quickly as possible. But here we are building stockades for supply stations. Won't that give the Ilergetes days, or even weeks, to gather spearmen on their border?"

Their Optio walked up, lifted a leg, and placed his foot on the wall log.

"I heard from a First Century Legionary," the NCO said while pressing down, and increasing the weight of the log, "the General hates long and slow lines of supply wagons. And I can appreciate the emotion. You see, I hate it when Legionaries stand around playing staff officers. Now get this log to the stockade wall."

While they carried the beam to the assembly team, two grain wagons arrived in the clearing.

"What are they?" the infantryman asked.

"Supplies for the supply stockade."

"I still don't understand how this is faster than a wagon caravan."

***

It took an entire day and the work of four clothmakers, but on the second day after the meeting of the Colonels, eight banners were delivered to the headquarters of the Iberian Legions.

"They are impressive, sir," Sidia observed.

Next to him, Centurion Elche, from Trumpet's First Century replied, "They'll make the General a target on the battlefield. I don't like them. Besides, each Legions banner is carried by a man who has earned the privilege to bear the standard. Who has Kasia drafted for the duty of carrying the copies?"

"I think tall was his prerequisite," Sidia answered.

Elche sniffed as if he smelled something bad.

Waving in the midmorning breeze, the Eagle, Lightning Bolt, Trumpet, Steed, Golden Cat, War Chariot, Winds, and Wings standards created a magnificent display at the building. Cornelius and Jace walked out and perused the standards.

"Colonel Kasia, are you sure this will work?" Cornelius asked.

"We only need a few days," Jace told him. "Besides General Scipio, you'll look like a King with that many standards following you."

The reference caused Cornelius to flinch.

"Rather than a ruler," he complained, "I'll look more like a self-important *kafchisiáris.*"

"No one who knows you, sir, would ever accuse you of being a braggart," Jace assured him. "But your use of the Greek word was excellent."

"It's part of my studies to relate to different mercenary units," Cornelius admitted.

Around the Legion camp, the Legionaries, Velites, cavalrymen, teamsters, livestock handlers, craftsmen, and a handful of Ilergetes spies paused. They gawked at the display of banners. Rarely had any of them seen a collection of the Iberian Legion standards in one place.

"Bring on the standard bearers and let's get this over with," Cornelius instructed.

"It's only twenty miles and two supply stockades," Jace confirmed. "We'll be back before dark."

"And you're sure the Ilergetes will see us?"

"Their scouts have been snooping around since the first supply depot went up," Jace answered. "They have maybe ten thousand spearmen gathered on the border. Between your inspection tour, and the delivery of the fish wagons, the assassin's knife, and your letter, Mandonius will be forced to double the count."

After General Scipio and Optio Sidia mounted, Jace and eight tall riders came with the banners. A moment later, Centurion Elche and thirty veteran Legionaries trotted their horses forward and formed files behind the standard bearers.

In columns trailing Cornelius, the parade worthy entourage trotted through the gates, turned west, and headed for the first supply depot. The banners flapped majestically overhead as they rode away from the fort at Marçà.

***

On a grass knoll to the south, an Ilergetes scout watched the group exit the fort and vanish between the hills. He didn't know who was in the cluster, but eight Legion banners identified that someone important was out for a ride. On the backside of the hill, he untied his horse. Then with an urgency driven by what he witnessed, the scout mounted and galloped westward.

Three miles farther west, another Ilergetes scout spotted the assembly of standards. He remained in his perch long enough to count the number of riders. Then he climbed out of the tree, untied his horse, mounted it, and galloped away.

Two miles south of the second Legion supply depot, and just out of range of the Legion patrols, a Lieutenant of Ilergetes began his midday meal. He had taken a couple of bites from a sausage when a rider came into camp.

"No rest," he complained. After stuffing the spiced meat back in his pack, he walked to the scout. "This better be good."

"Riders with eight banners displayed, sir, and what looked like a General leading a Legion patrol," he reported.

"How many in the patrol?" the officer inquired.

"Aw, I didn't count them, sir," the scout admitted.

"Too many to count?" the Lieutenant encouraged.

"No sir. A small patrol."

"Why would a General be leading a small patrol?"

Flustered, the scout stammered. He was saved by the arrival of the second lookout.

"Forty-two Legionaries riding under eight banners," he reported. "And Lieutenant, I think their General Scipio is leading the patrol."

"No King goes pleasure riding towards an enemy with only forty-one cavalrymen," the officer said.

"Unless, sir, the General wants to check his supply lines before the invasion."

Once written, the message about an imminent attack on the Ilergetes Tribe by the Legions went out. Four of the fastest scouts left to carry the important news to the War Chief.

***

Fifty miles later, the couriers reached the forward lines of spearmen. The sun rested low in the sky, announcing the coming of night.

"We have a message for War Chief Mandonius," one reported.

Waved forward, the scouts were allowed to enter the tent of the tribe's War Chief.

"Why do you bother my husband at his evening meal?" Ama demanded.

"Lady Ama, we have reason to believe the Legion is on the march," a scout replied.

Another courier handed over the letter. After reading it, Ama took it to her husband.

"Read this," she encouraged.

Mandonius put aside his feast and read the Lieutenant's message. Then he started a note to his brother.

"Indibilis won't like it," the War Chief commented to his wife. "Because of the constraints from our last treaty with Scipio, the tribe's treasury is down. Maintaining what we have is costing us. And now, asking for another ten thousand spearmen and cavalry will empty the coffers."

"King Indibilis will like it less when General Scipio arrives at his doorstep for breakfast," Ama suggested.

"Coming to breakfast is not Scipio's style. He's more the annihilation of everything living type of enemy."

Mandonius finished the letter that would put the Ilergetes Tribe in debt for the next twenty years. Giving it to four other messengers, he told them to hurry. Darkness fell as they rode from the War Chief's compound, heading for Lleida.

***

At Marçà, the sun set on thirty-one riders accompanying the eight banners. The patrol rode through the gates and directly to the headquarters building of the Iberian Legion. There, the eight banners were anchored and displayed to let everyone know General Scipio was in residence.

The handful of Ilergetes spies took note of the standards. Over the next week, they would report that the banners remained in front of the building. Meaning General Scipio was still in the Legion fort and not leading an attack force on the Ilergetes tribe.

***

Five mile south of Marçà, three riders walked their horses onto a beach.

"General Scipio, we're ready to row out at daybreak," a ship's Centurion greeted the riders.

"Excellent," Cornelius replied. He dismounted, walked to a campfire, and inquired. "Did my Battle Commanders get out?"

"Colonel Kasia and I are the last, sir," Gaius Laelius told him. "Senior Tribune Silanus and the others left Tarraco during the day in separate warships. No one seemed to notice."

"Jace, what do you think?" Cornelius questioned.

"Sir, I think while the Ilergetes are buying grain to feed their army," Jace answered, "Hasdrubal Barca and his Carthaginian army are in for a rough patch."

Chapter 23 – Tiers of Pain & Sorrow

At twenty-six, General Scipio marched away from New Carthage with five full Legions and a sixth composed of light infantry and heavy cavalry. Adding to the uncertainty of the unwieldy masses, the General had no experience commanding a force of its size, nor practice in deploying multiple Legions in combat.

Colonel Laelius rode to Scipio's command position at the thirty-three-mile marker.

"Sir, typically we end the day's march at thirty miles," he advised. "It allows us to set up marching camps and rest the men."

Cornelius lifted his chin, not in a dismissive gesture, but to look at the sky. A moment later, he focused on the Battle Commander.

"Colonel Laelius, when Hannibal was in Taranto trying to break the Republic's hold on the citadel, Consuls Appius Claudius and Fulvius Flaccus decided it was the right time to recapture Capua," Cornelius lectured. "It should have been a successful siege. Except, Hannibal showed up four days later. He'd marched his entire army one hundred and seventy miles in four days. And no one saw him coming."

"Sir, I understand," Laelius remarked. "If Hannibal can do it, so can you."

"You don't understand," Cornelius corrected. "There are two armies one hundred and seventy miles southwest of Baecula. If they march from Seville, immediately, they'll catch us in a pincher movement. I plan on destroying Hasdrubal Barca and his army, and being away, before his brother can come to his rescue."

"Now I understand, General Scipio," the Battle Commander confirmed. "We'll push on until you call for a rest period."

Laelius saluted, turned his horse, and rode back to Eagle Legion. He carried with him a new appreciation for Cornelius Scipio.

***

Including teamsters, animal handlers, servants, and craftsmen, Cornelius Scipio forced marched forty thousand men, one hundred and sixty miles, to the Cazorla River. When scouts alerted him that the enemy was camped seven miles upstream, where the Cazorla met the wide Guadalquivir River, he called a halt.

Maps were drawn and given to the General. After studying the land and the enemy's location on high ground accessible only by climbing levels, Cornelius sat alone on a rock, looked at the sky, and thought. Finally, he stood and called for Colonel Kasia.

***

"I want the entrances to the area sealed," he directed as soon as Jace dismounted. "Use the heavy cavalry. From here, no one gets in or out. Over where the Guadalquivir flows out of the hills, I want the same barrier."

"We can do that," Jace told him. "But, General, that's not going to win the battle."

"Do you remember Lake Trasimene?" Cornelius asked.

"Yes, sir. Hannibal set up a false camp, then sent his warriors through the hills at night to come in behind the Legions. And General Gaius Flaminius marched us right into the ambush. What has that got to do with Baecula, sir?"

"Gaius marched us into the trap because Hannibal dangled an undefended campsite in front of him."

"Yes, sir," Jace agreed. "But Hasdrubal is in a fixed and easily defended location. He won't be tempted to come down and walk into a trap."

"I can filter my Legionaries through the forest overnight and get them close to the flanks of the plateau. Once in position, it's a quick climb up the slopes. However, it'll only work if we can get close before he notices our infantry," Cornelius explained. "I need Hasdrubal Barca to focus on something. Something he doesn't fear."

Jace took a deep breath and blinked his eyes as if trying to clear his vision. Finally, he offered, "Maybe if he faced a head on attack by a couple thousand light infantrymen."

"And excellent idea," Cornelius allowed. "But we want him comfortable and almost entertained. Make it twelve Centuries. And take your standard bearer with you. It'll help with the show."

"We'll have to do more than stand around looking pretty," Jace informed him. "And although I haven't checked, I don't think I have any jugglers in Wings for entertainment."

"I'll flag you through the trees," Cornelius described. "When you get the signal, attack up the slope. Then, Colonel Laelius and I will close in from the sides."

Jace began to ask what the fee was for suicide. But decided against it. Rather he asked, "When do we start, sir?"

"You'll move into position in the morning," Cornelius replied. "May your God of War, Ares, guide and protect you through the fight."

Jace started to inform Cornelius that in Sparta they had the statue of Ares bound in chains. It signified the horrors unleashed and the unpredictability on the world when the God of War was set free. Instead, he saluted and rode off to send out the blocking forces.

***

Shields lining the third tier created a barrier at the very top. Jace Kasia knew what waited behind the shields of the Carthaginian heavy infantrymen. On the bottom tier, tribal skirmishers waited. When his light infantry started to climb out of the valley, the spears of the skirmishers would disrupt his forward progress. But once breached, the first tier offered no real challenge to his Velites. It was the second tier where the concerns started.

"There's a comfort in that," First Centurion Turibas commented.

"A comfort would be if General Scipio let us set up ten onagers and gave us two days to drop a granite quarry on their heads," Jace protested. "But allow me, First Centurion, to think like our Prorogatio of Iberia for a moment. And I ask this diplomatically. Where in Hades is there any comfort in this mess?"

"Well sir, the slope from the second tier to the top is too steep for heavy infantry," Turibas proposed. "They may throw things at us, spit, scream profanities, call down curses from the Gods, but Colonel Kasia, they can't climb down and join the party."

"And why would they?" Jace pointed out. "Hasdrubal Barca has packed the second tier with all his light infantrymen while General Scipio limits our Velites to twelve Centuries."

"Nine hundred and sixty light infantrymen aren't very many," Turibas agreed.

***

The standard bearer, as he had done since they formed, strutted back and forth in front of the ranks. He provided a focus for the Legion light infantryman while they waited. And they had been waiting since early morning. And all the while, he had been silent, but in constant motion.

Then, accompanied by exaggerated gestures, the standard bearer shouted, "Wings Legion."

From the ranks of the bored and distracted Velites, came a weak response, "Wings Legion."

"I said Wings Legion," he repeated.

Waving the pole with the rolled-up standard in one hand, and pumping the other arm in the air, he kicked imaginary enemies with his legs while hopping from one foot to the other.

"Wings Legion!"

This time, "Wings Legion," exploded from the ranks.

The response carried across the valley floor, and up the slopes. It hit the Carthaginian skirmishers on the first tier, before reaching the forward ranks of their light infantrymen on the second level.

Warriors on both sides shouted insults, although the distance was too great for the words to have any impact. During the useless demonstration, the Senior Centurion of Wings Legion rode to Jace and dismounted.

Ceradin saluted and pointed at their Centuries light infantrymen, their officers, and NCOs.

"The natives are getting restless," he cautioned. "We can't hold them back much longer before they start fighting in the ranks. And if tribes that are hostile to each other draw blades, the Carthaginians can relax, we'll defeat ourselves."

"It's not just ours," Jace pointed out. "The Carthaginian infantrymen are just as bored as our Velites."

"Colonel, we need to begin this fight," Ceradin suggested, "or stand them down."

The bitterness Jace expressed in conversation with Turibas earlier vanished.

"We have orders, and we will follow them," Jace snapped. "If we standdown, it'll look like we're waiting for instructions."

"Sir, that is what we're doing," the Legion's senior combat officer reminded Jace.

Ceradin dropped to his knees, reached over, and pointed at a map spread on the ground. After waving a hand over the parchment, the Senior Centurion indicated Messina on the map of Sicilia.

"Have you ever been there?" Turibas asked. "I hear the fish stew is delicious."

"Before Iberia, I've never been farther south than Naples," the Senior Centurion admitted. "How long are we going to act like we're reading a map of the Baecula Valley?"

"Senior Centurion, I know standing around with the men in ranks makes us look like I am undecided. And that's the point. If we break out the pots and light cookfires, the Carthaginians will know we're waiting for something else to develop."

***

The sun hung in a portion of the sky between the horizon and the pinnacle of its morning journey. Across the ranks, Velites complained and fidgeted as they became more agitated. In keeping with the subterfuge, none of the senior officers approached the formation. To give a rousing speech when they wanted to appear ready, but hesitant, prevented Jace or the Senior Centurion from interacting with their infantrymen. And that caused more dissatisfaction.

"Standard bearer," Jace called out in a voice that made every head turn in his direction. "If you have a moment."

Centurion Usico jogged to the group of officers.

"Are we stepping off, Colonel, or standing down?" the standard bearer inquired.

"You've done a good job of maintaining order," Jace complimented him. "I expect you'll need to do it a little longer."

"Yes, sir," Usico stated.

He about-faced. But, as Usico walked towards the head of the ranks, Jace looked at the forest, nodded at what he saw, and called to the standard bearer.

"Centurion Usico, hold up. I'm coming with you."

Jace sprinted to him, and they marched to the head of the formation together. Turning to the light infantrymen, Jace broke the silence.

"You didn't see it, but I just saw a signal flag from the woods," Jace explained to the ranks of Velites. "We've been idling here until other Centuries got into position."

Grumbling accompanied the announcement. Most infantrymen, when doing unpleasant duty, assumed other Centuries had it easier. Probably eating honey cakes, drinking sweet wine, and swimming in the river all morning while the Wings maniple sweated in the sun.

"I don't blame you," Jace admitted. "But the wait is over. We're running across this field, climbing that slope, and cutting through the skirmishers like a skinning knife through a rabbit pelt."

When Jace drew his gladius, First Centurion Turibas and five veteran Legionaries ran to him.

"Colonel, your place is with the command staff," Turibas reminded Jace.

"When was the last time, First Centurion, you got your blade wet?"

"Not since New Carthage, sir."

"Me neither," Jace confirmed. Then from the side of his mouth he ordered. "Standard bearer, forward Wings Legion."

Usico stripped the tie off the banner and allowed the material to unroll.

"Wings Legion," he bellowed while waving the standard overhead.

"Wings Legion," the Velites replied.

"Forward."

***

Lulled into a false sense of confidence, the Carthaginian skirmishers found other things to occupy themselves. Sharpening blades, taking naps, playing games of chance, they participated in anything except watching the men standing in the valley.

"They are moving," a skirmisher alerted his squad.

"Really, after wasting all morning?" another mentioned.

Then a Sergeant noticed the nine hundred Velites in full stride. That was a concern. But a bigger worry were the two officers, five veteran infantrymen, and their Standard Bearer who had already started up the slope.

"Spearmen, defend the hill," the Sergeant yelled. But it was too late.

The skirmishers job consisted of sprinting at an enemy formation. Throwing spears into the forward rank, doing melee with skirmishers from the other side, then running back behind their infantry. To complete their task, they wore light animal fur instead of armor. Carried knives rather than swords. And used small shields if any at all. On a battlefield, compared to both light and heavy infantrymen, skirmishers might as well be naked.

Battle Commander Kasia's words about skinning knives and pelts proved too real for the Carthaginian skirmishers. Jace and his forward element reached the first tier and began butchering the slower Iberians.

Slashing viciously to both sides, Jace left wounded and dead skirmishers in his wake. Not slowing, he raced for the foot of the next slope. In the chaos, he found himself in a herd of running Iberians. With the red horsehair crest on his helmet, marking him as a Legion officer, he should have been stabbed in the back and sides multiple times.

The Fates often delivered surprising paradoxes in battle. In the case of Colonel Kasia, the comb on his helmet drew spears from the second tier. While none struck him, the presence of steel tips and shafts raining down around him drove the Skirmishers away from the Legion officer. Putting them out of stabbing range and allowing Jace to run free and dodge the thrown spears.

Using the footspeed of a Cretan Archer placed Jace far ahead of his maniple. And while he wanted to get up the slope and lessen the crowding on that level, he realized he couldn't do it on his own. Turning right, he cut into a line of fleeing skirmishers. And while he fended off knives, at least, the spears stopped falling from above.

"Are you touched?" Turibas ranted, while shoving a bloody shield into Jace's hand. Then, he added. "If you're going to act like an infantryman and not an officer, carry a shield."

"Who did this belong to?" Jace inquired as he strapped the light infantry shield to his arm.

"He held his shield too low and ate a spear," First Centurion Turibas replied. "Don't make the same mistake, sir."

With the five Legionary shields of the veterans protecting him from spears and his light infantry shield held overhead, Jace took stock of the status of his infantrymen. Some were down, most wounded by quickly thrown shafts from expert spearmen. The rest were dead from the same weapon. In the middle of the line and driving the final bunch of skirmishers from the first tier, Centurion Usico waved the standard.

"Seeing as I have a shield," Jace instructed the First Centurion, "put three shields on the standard. No matter what happens at the top, I want the Wings banner to survive for the rest of the Legion."

"Consider it done," Turibas swore. He used his bloody gladius to direct three veterans over to care for Usico and the standard. "I don't suppose, Battle Commander Kasia, that I can talk you into returning to the command staff."

"Not a chance, First Centurion," Jace replied to him while adjusting the straps on the borrowed shield.

"In that case, Colonel Kasia, there's only one thing left to do."

"Get to the next tier and inflict pain and terror on the Carthaginian spearmen," Jace stated. The Standard Bearer reached their position just as Kasia announced. "I'm going to the top. Anyone care to join me?"

Centurion Usico belted out a hardy, "To the top, sir. Rah."

The moving line of Velites roared, "To the top. Rah."

"Usico, forward the Legion," Jace ordered as he pushed through the screen of shields.

Colonel Kasia and his pair of veterans started up the slope.

Behind them, the orders were delivered, "Wings Legion, forward."

***

Under the canopy beneath the first tier, Colonel Laelius caught sight of the movement. The flag flashed the signal again to be sure he saw it.

"We don't stop. We break heads and crush dreams all the way to the top," he instructed. "Centurion Digitius, free our banner and display the Eagle. Senior Tribune, pass the word to forward the Legion."

"Eagle Legion forward," the Standard Bearer and the Senior Tribune bellowed.

Responding to the order, almost three thousand heavy infantrymen pushed out from under leaves, shook foliage from their shields, and leveled their spears. Behind Eagle, Legionaries from War Chariot Legion emerged from concealment and started forward.

In ten steps, the first of Eagle's infantrymen materialized from the trees. Prepared to absorb spears with their shields, they moved timidly. But to their relief, the Carthaginians, three tiers up, didn't respond.

***

Slightly ahead of the right flank, and behind Wings Legion in the center, Cornelius Scipio stepped off with the first maniple from Golden Cat Legion.

"Sir, we can't protect you up here," the Centurion of First Century cautioned. "Please fall back to the command staff. General, please."

"None of this should be possible," Cornelius declared as he continued to shuffle forward. "Not the Legions secretly in positions before daybreak. Not an enemy this close but unaware. Not me, and not six Legions of the finest infantrymen in the world, under my command."

Fearing the General had lost his mind, the Centurion considered physically restraining him. Prorogatio of Iberia or not, for his own good, General Scipio needed to be pulled back.

But the three ranks of Legionaries on either side of Cornelius responded to his speech. They closed ranks around Scipio, protecting their General, as they roared, Rah.

The veteran combat officer knew he would have to battle his own first maniple if he dared touch the General. Signaling his squads, they moved forward and out of the trees with the attack line.

Just as with Eagle Legion on the right flank, Golden Cat climbed the first tier unmolested by thrown spears. Something was drawing the attention of Hasdrubal

Barca's army away from the flanks. The diversion and the easy assault, unfortunately, wouldn't last.

Chapter 24 – Please Goddess Até

The grade of the slope required high stepping. Plus, each stride towards the second tier carried Jace Kasia closer to a line of shields held by Carthaginian spearmen. And while the giant steps helped him dodge spears and catch arrows in his shield, the pace was far from favorable for attacking uphill into the shield wall.

"This is going to get ugly," he remarked to the Legionary beside him.

"At least they're entertained," the veteran sneered.

Worried about breaking through the wall, Jace hadn't considered the presence of spectators. Yet, high above, Carthaginian heavy infantrymen crowded forward to the edge of the cliff. It appeared as if they were seeking a better view of a sporting event.

"This could be the biggest mistake of my career," Jace ventured before ordering his bodyguards. "Stay with me. I need to speak with Centurion Usico."

Fifteen feet on level ground was an easy trot, but not while navigating a steep slope and evading projectiles.

When Jace reached the Standard Bearer, Usico looked puzzled.

"In training, a target is pulled by a chariot across our front. It helps our Velites improve their javelin throws," Usico advised. His eyes shifted to where Jace had been and back to the Battle Commander. "Sir, are you trying to improve the Carthaginian's aim?"

The comment might have been viewed as lighthearted if not for two reasons. Usico wasn't known for his levity. And the presence of the red comb on the Colonel's helmet, and the Legion's banner at the same location, drew salvos of spears and arrows.

"I want you to fall back to the base of the hill," Jace instructed. "Use our rear ranks to form a defensive line. But make it look chaotic."

"What are we doing, Colonel?" the Standard Bearer inquired.

"We're trying to entertain their heavies while pulling their spearmen off the hill."

"Is this a fight or a show?" Usico demanded.

A spear arched across the sky, dipped overhead, and fell, directly at the Standard Bearer. Jace swung his shield up, caught the spear tip with the face of the shield, and deflected the steel point. Flipping horizontal, the shaft bounced off Usico's helmet.

In combat, a man who saved your life got the benefit of instant trust. Without further debate, Usico questioned, "Chaotic, you said, Colonel?"

"We need to hold the attention of the spectators, so the messier, the better," Jace confirmed. "But, when we retreat, I need your line to hold until we get organized."

"Yes, sir," Usico stated.

Stumbling sideways with his head wobbling, the Standard Bearer angled downhill and away from the attack element.

"Find me Senior Centurion Ceradin," Jace ordered his bodyguards.

***

After a quick consultation with the Senior Centurion, Jace rushed uphill behind the leading edge of Velites.

"Forward. Forward," he ordered. "Break their line. Break it."

Spears dueled, and a few shields clashed when brave men dodged their way into the forest of shafts. But none of Wings Legion came close to breaching the enemy's line.

From high above, a roar of approval encouraged the defenders. And to the delight of the Carthaginian army, the attack stalled. Then a few Velites stepped back and began moving downhill. In moments, a few more retreated. The breaking of the Legion attack caused the onlookers to scream louder. Just as if they were spectators at the Forum on race day.

Colonel Kasia screamed at his men. His helmet bucked back and forth with each yell, making the red horsehair comb wave in the air. It attracted the enemy's attention. Raising his arms, Jace shook the shield and his gladius at the fleeing men. Despite his antics, none paid attention to their Battle Commander. However, the heavy infantrymen on the upper level were delighted as the last Velites raced away.

***

For an eternity, Jace Kasia and two Legionaries stood alone on the slope. Bellows from on high encouraged the spearmen to break formation, run down, and kill the lightly defended Battle Commander.

"Sir, we really should go," one Legionary pleaded with Jace.

"Not yet," he replied. "Hold. Hold."

Several spearmen jumped forward but were pulled back by their officers. The movement brought the audience on top of the hill to a fevered pitch. It might have been the shouting from behind, their confidence after repelling the Legion light infantry, or the sight of the enemy commander exposed and vulnerable. In any case, as if it was a brick wall crumbling during an earthquake, the Carthaginian shield wall dissolved.

"Sir, they are coming for you," a Legionary warned.

"For us," Jace corrected. "Run. Now."

Jace in his war armor, his two bodyguards in their heavy infantry armor and big shields, would have difficulty sprinting uphill. Downhill, the weight and physical conditioning gave them the velocity of a rolling stone.

"Please Goddess Até," Jace shouted, "just a few more feet."

Although unfamiliar with Greek Goddesses, the Republic Legionaries echoed their Battle Commander.

"Please Goddess Até, just a few more feet."

***

Jace and the two Legionaries raced between the line of shields, lost their footing from too much momentum, and crashed to the ground.

"Here they come," Ceradin shouted. "Brace. Brace. Brace."

The commands of the Senior Centurion were picked up by his Legion combat officers. Up and down the defensive line, the Velites tucked shoulders in behind shields, dug their rear feet into the soil, and hardened their stance.

A hand reached down, gripped Jace's wrist, and helped him off the ground.

"You got them off the hill, sir," First Centurion Turibas remarked.

"What about our audience?" Jace asked.

Although the curses were muffled by distance, the gestures accompanying the sentiments relayed the feelings of the Carthaginian heavy infantry.

"I'd say disappointed describes them best, Colonel," Turibas answered.

In a reversal of fortune, the Carthaginian spearmen found themselves attacking a shield wall. Behind the Wings' assault line, the third rank prepared to throw a flight of javelins.

The pair of Legionaries who waited with Jace inquired, "Sir, who is the Goddess Até. And why did we pray to her for a few more feet?"

"Até is the Greek Goddess of mischief, ruin, and folly," Jace informed them. "I figured I was worshiping her with my plan. The least I could do was ask her for help in not getting a spear in the back as we ran down the hill."

"We'll sacrifice to her when this is over," they promised.

Jace glanced at the top of the plateau. The cliff top was empty. The heavy infantrymen gone, no doubt to defend against the Legionaries attacking from the flanks.

"I'll join you in the sacrifice," Jace told the Legionaries. "For now, let's get into this fight."

***

On the right side of the plateau, Standard Bearer Sextus Digitius and the assault line climbed to the first level. A spear, thrown from above, impacted the ground in front of the Centurion's hobnailed boot. Instead of circling the shaft, Digitius kicked it out of his way.

"We are Eagle Legion," he shouted while waving the Legion's banner. "We laugh at danger. We shrug off arrowheads. We rise to every challenge. And we have only scorn for their shields and spears. Rah!"

"Rah," the Legionaries near him answered.

"We laugh at danger," Digitius chanted.

Spears, arrows, and stones struck shields held overhead. The Legionaries felt all three differently. They stumbled from the heavy shafts while flinching at each rap when an arrowhead embedded itself in their shields. But the stones, they ignored. A few spears deflected from the shields and pierced the flesh of neighbors. And several arrows slipped between the barriers, burying their arrowheads in arms, legs, or feet. The stones simply bounced off.

"We laugh at danger," the Legionaries on the assault line answered.

Legionaries in the second rank shifted forward and filled in empty spots to maintain the integrity of the attack line.

"We shrug off arrowheads," the Standard Bearer proclaimed.

The ground grew steeper, and the projectiles transitioned from falling downward, to hugging the grade. Now, the spears, arrows, and stones from slingers came directly at the faces of the Legionaries.

"We shrug off arrowheads," the Legion infantrymen repeated.

The sounds of the impacts on the shields grew louder. And almost as if planks left out at the start of a rainstorm, the missile noises went from tap, tap, tap, to a continuous, repetitive thunder.

To be heard over the storm of incoming steel tips and stones, Standard Bearer Digitius roared, "We rise to every challenge."

At segments of the assault line, facing powerful spearmen or accurate slingers, bleeding Legionaries dropped to their knees. Scooting around their wounded comrades, other Legionaries moved ahead to fill in the gaps.

Relentlessly, the forward element of Eagle Legion continued up the slope.

And despite the hail of shafts and rocks, they sang out, "We rise to every challenge."

As they approached the top of the hill, the Standard Bearer exclaimed, "We have only scorn for their shields and spears."

Six paces from the crest, the onslaught of shafts and stones ended. Carthaginian shields appeared in the holes used by the archers, slingers, and spear throwers.

In the face of a solid shield wall, the Legionaries echoed, "We have only scorn for their shields and spears."

Standard Bearer Sextus Digitius finished his chant by hollering, "We are Eagle Legion, halt."

"Eagle Legion, halt," the Legionaries replied.

***

Just out of range from a jab with a spear, the assault line waited for instructions. Several feet separated the shields and men could see the eyes of their adversaries. But, where the trained Legion ranks stood stoically, the ranks of Carthaginian mercenaries yelled to keep up their courage and to hide nerves.

His job done, the Standard Bearer planted the pole and leaned it forward, allowing the banner to hang free.

"First maniple, stand by to advance," the maniple Tribunes alerted the attack line.

Only ten Centurions of the original twelve combat officers repeated the orders. But two Optios replaced the dead Centurions, and they repeated the instructions for their Centuries.

"Advance, advance, advance," the staff officers ordered.

***

On the left side of the plateau, Cornelius Scipio paced behind the assault line of Golden Cat Legion. Halted at spear's length from the Carthaginian shield wall, the first maniple breathed hard from the climb. Or, possibly from the shower of spears, arrows, and stones that accompanied their trek up the hill.

"Congratulations, General," the First Centurion told Cornelius. "You've done it."

"Only because we were halfway up the slope before their infantry realized we were here," Cornelius added.

On each side of the attack line, Tribunes of the maniple instructed, "Centuries. Standby to advance."

Their words were relayed to the Legionaries by eight Centurions, an Optio, and three Tesserarii. The climb up the hill had cost first maniple, Golden Cat Legion, four combat officers and three senior NCOs.

"Advance," the pair of staff officers bellowed.

A heartbeat later, three hundred and twenty Legion shields hammered forward. But there were no opposing shields. Most pushed air, but a few caught spearmen unaware and broke the shafts of overextended spears. Equally useless, the gladius strikes of the first advance cut nothing but sunbeams. Then the assault line stepped forward.

"Advance."

Again, the shields plowed air and the gladii cut sunlight. Then the Legion attack line stepped forward to meet the enemy's stagnant shield wall.

"Advance."

As any practitioner of Apollo's sport would attest, getting into a rhythm was the key to overwhelming an opponent's defenses. And just as a boxer during a fist fight, the next advance maintained the quick one-two, one-two punch.

The hammering shields shoved a number of soldiers out of line. With holes in the shield wall, the gladius strikes found flesh, widening the gaps. And while the step was halted at a half pace by the remnants of the shield wall, the wounded Carthaginian infantrymen were stomped as the assault line moved up.

Once again, the maniple Tribunes ordered, "Advance."

And just as a winning fighter in Apollo's sport might pummel his opponent in the face, the shields of the attack line pulverized the shield wall. Then three hundred and twenty gladii slashed out. Almost as one blade, the steel cut down infantrymen. And when the line stepped forward, the Legionaries walked on a blanket of bodies.

"First line, rotate back," the staff officers instructed. "Second line, move forward and hold."

The assault line of Golden Cat halted, not from exhaustion, they had fresh arms and legs on the front line. They stopped because there were no infantrymen close enough for an advance attack.

"Shield wall," the Tribunes warned.

A horde of Carthaginian mercenaries ran at the Legion lines in an attempt to drive the Legionaries off the plateau. But months of shield training and drills held the Carthaginians. Next, with the enemy in close proximity, the tactic changed again.

"Advance," the Tribunes shouted above the war cries.

"Advance," the combat officers repeated.

***

At the center of the plateau, Jace Kasia stepped through the last of the melees. On either side, his Velites in a concentrated assault sent the spearmen fleeing. Victorious, Wings Legion raced to the top unopposed.

"It reminds me of my father's farm after a storm," Ceradin mentioned. He indicated the Legionaries appearing over the right and left edges. "We'd dig a trench to siphon off the trapped rainwater. Leaves, twigs, and mud flowed into a funnel shape as it poured out of the pond."

The funnel shape on the plateau consisted of the Carthaginian army running towards the rear of the mound. Streaming in from both sides, Legionaries chased them down the grade.

"Orders, sir?" the Senior Centurion inquired.

"Walk our Velites behind the heavy infantry," Jace told him. "But don't get caught up in the fighting. We've done our part to break the Carthaginians."

"Yes, sir," Senior Centurion Ceradin responded. "Centurions of Wings Legion, at a walk, forward."

First Centurion Turibas fell in beside Jace. They hiked several steps before he addressed the Battle Commander.

"You survived another fight, Colonel," he mentioned. "How many more before you fail?"

"What do you mean, First Centurion?"

"Just what I said," the combat officer insisted. "Since you arrived in Iberia, you've risked your life for General Scipio, for Rome, and before that General Nero. How long can you temp Cossus, before he withdraws his protection."

"Cossus?" Jace asked.

"The Iberian God of Warriors," Turibas said. "He's helpful, but eventually, every brave fighter reaches a bad end."

"Have you seen signs?" Jace asked.

"No, sir, but I do see a man consistently on campaigns of war. Most men are fighting for something. Take me for instance, I'm Iberian. Someday, when my land is no longer a battleground between Rome and Carthage, I'll buy a farm. That's why I fight. Why do you fight, sir?"

Jace started to say every Cretan Archer was charged with earning a profit and staying with a client until the contract was fulfilled. But in the midst of the blood and gore, it sounded hollow in his mind. He couldn't imagine how it would come across if spoken aloud. Then, the thought fled his mind.

"Bounty," a group of Legionaries shouted. "The Carthaginians left their camp. Everyone is raiding it. The fighting is over."

"Should it be?" Jace questioned.

Act 9

Chapter 25 – An Unfinished Battle

As if unattended market stalls, rows of neatly spaced tents sprawled across the rear of the plateau. Although the shelters lacked vendors, there wasn't a shortage of consumers. But they weren't shopping. Rather, the Legionaries were pillaging the camp of the Carthaginian army.

A muscle at the side of Cornelius' jaw twitched. To mask the annoyance, he rubbed his cheek to hide the sign of irritation.

"Congratulations on a great victory, General Scipio," Jace said, acknowledging the success.

He and Senior Centurion Ceradin braced and saluted.

"But why didn't we pursue Hasdrubal, General?" Ceradin inquired.

Cornelius lifted his face and gazed at the blue sky. In the distance, clouds gathered, threatening rain.

"Colonel Kasia, my Legionaries decided that plunder was more important than chasing down a fleeing enemy," Cornelius mentioned. He maintained his inspection of the heavens as if reluctant to look at Jace. "I wonder where they got the idea that looting a camp was more important than fighting?"

"Plunder is one of the benefits of being victorious, sir," Jace replied. "We used the promise of riches to keep the recruits committed to the training. And it worked.

Against an enemy on high ground, they fought their way to the top and routed their adversaries."

"But then they stopped to fill their coin purses and stuff their bundles," Cornelius growled. Lowering his chin, he locked eyes with Jace, "while allowing the enemy to escape. Maybe you should rethink your training methods."

"Yes sir, it appears so," Jace affirmed.

Sidia Decimia looked at Jace from the other side of General Scipio. He scrunched up his face in sympathy at the scolding. But the insult aimed at his cousin didn't end with the dig at Jace's skills as an infantry instructor.

"Ceradin, I want to know where Hasdrubal Barca is headed," Cornelius ordered the Senior Centurion. "And the state of Mago Barca's army. Have they broken camp?"

Going around the Battle Commander of Wings Legion, and issuing orders directly to his second in command, emphasized the General's displeasure with Colonel Kasia.

"Yes, sir, I'll send patrols right away," Ceradin vowed.

He started to turn when Jace restrained him with a hand on his arm.

"Let the patrols know, Senior Centurion," Jace advised, "in the morning, we're marching north to Marçà."

"Just a moment," Cornelius snapped. "When did you, Colonel Kasia, take over as my planning and strategy staff?"

A Century of Legionaries, herding a bull, passed by and the Centurion saluted.

"It's a great victory," Cornelius gushed.

"Rah to General Scipio," the combat officer yelled.

Seventy-four dirty and bloodied Legionaries responded, "Rah."

"I owe a great debt to my infantry," Cornelius boasted. "Salute to my Legionaries. But, may I inquire, where are you going with the beast?"

"We're taking the bull to the priests," the Centurion informed him. "I lost six good men today, sir. And I want them honored."

"Be sure they butcher the meat into small pieces," Cornelius suggested. "You'll need the excess cooked and cooled for packing by morning."

"We're leaving, sir?" the Centurion asked.

"That's what I've been told," Cornelius remarked. General Scipio waited until the Century was away before turning to Jace. "Why are we marching north in the morning?"

"Sir, you left the Ilergetes on high alert and bunched up on their border," Jace answered. "If Hasdrubal Barca joins the remnants of his army with the spearmen of King Indibilis, they'll march over Març a in a half day. And take Tarraco the next afternoon."

"And supplement their spearmen's rations with the grains I staged," Cornelius pointed out. "Like a trail of seeds leading to a bird trap, they'll follow them to my ruin."

"Not if we march at dawn, sir," Jace proposed.

***

As hard as Cornelius pushed the Legions on the way to Baecula, he added extra miles on the way to Març a.

"We can rest when we're in position to defend our fort," he advised any officer who questioned the rough march.

But General Scipio didn't cloister himself with his staff. During the long days, he and Sidia rode to different Centuries. They dismounted and hiked alongside the Legionaries. At first, his presence would intimidate. But the longer he marched with the Century, the more relaxed the infantrymen became.

"This is brutal," Cornelius complained after a couple of miles. "Whose idea was this?"

"Ah, General Scipio, you're in charge," infantrymen would reply. "Sir, it was you're idea."

"Somebody should wish blisters on the feet of any commander requiring his beloved Legionaries to march fifty miles in a day."

"We can do it, sir," the infantrymen assured him. "We'll do it for you."

Although General Scipio left after a short visit to the ranks, his presence lingered.

Six days and three hundred miles later, the Legions arrived at Marçà. Yet Cornelius, as weary as anyone, sat on his mount. He watched as every infantryman and cavalry rider passed in review. Under the eyes of Cornelius Scipio, the ranks straightened, and with each step, the hobnailed boots came clear of the ground. No one wanted to show weakness in front of their General.

"Sir, you've been here all morning," Sidia commented. The parade of exhausted Centuries flowed by in a never-ending stream of men and weapons. "You need to rest."

"On the banks of the Trebia River, Hannibal unleased his barbarians on the Legions of Consul Longus," Cornelius replied while saluting the next Century in the procession. "Not once during the battle did the Carthaginian General leave his station. Even when his concealed cavalry struck our Legions from the side, Hannibal sat his mount so every one of his warriors could see their General."

"Do you think it makes a difference, sir?" Sidia inquired.

Cornelius pounded his fist in the air and shouted, "Steed Legion."

Throats dry from eating dust, stomachs empty from the long hike, and muscles exhausted from carrying equipment should have dampened the enthusiasm of the infantrymen.

Yet, they responded in full voice to Cornelius' cry and bellowed back, "Steed Legion."

"I guess it does," Sidia uttered.

***

The rapid movement of the Legions outpaced both the patrol heading south and the one chasing Hasdrubal Barca. On the third morning after arriving at the fort, the patrols reported in.

Cornelius had the cavalrymen fed while he waited for his Battle Commanders. Once they gathered, he called in the NCOs of the patrols.

"The Ilergetes are an unfinished battle, as are the soldiers of Hasdrubal Barca," Cornelius said. He indicated the map table and instructed. "Let's start with the northern patrol."

"Sir, we followed the Carthaginians to the Pyrenees," the cavalry Optio explained. "By the time they reached the mountain, they had moved far to the west. The last we saw of them their columns had started up the pass."

Lucius Marcius cleared his throat and asked, "Any chance of them turning around and coming at us?"

"Sir, there's always a chance a wounded animal will turn and attack," the patrol leader advised. "But they moved with purpose as if under orders. I didn't get the feeling they were unserious about leaving Iberia."

"Senior Centurion Thiphilia," Cornelius instructed, "take Steed Legion and retrieve the grain, then dismantle the supply depots."

"Are you pulling back the threat from the Ilergetes, sir?" Nabars asked.

"They aren't my biggest worry right now," Cornelius informed the Battle Commanders. "Now that we know the tribe isn't getting reinforced, we can focus on Mago Barca and his army."

Sidia stepped forward and passed a few coins to the patrol leader.

"From the General as a token of thanks for a job well done," he whispered.

***

Once the cavalry NCO left the headquarters building, Sidia waved the southern patrol leader forward.

"We received good news from the northern patrol," Cornelius informed the NCO. "Hopefully, your report will be as equally pleasing."

"General Scipio, my report is anything but pleasing and mostly unattractive," the cavalry Optio admitted.

"Show me," Cornelius ordered. He waved a hand over the map table, encompassing the south-central region of Iberia.

Using his thumb, the patrol leader covered a circle next to a line marked as the Guadalaviar River.

"At Carmona, General Barca has been joined by forces commanded by Lieutenant/General Hanno," the cavalry NCO informed the group. He pulled a piece of parchment from a pouch and handed it to Cornelius. "We captured a courier and took this off him."

Cornelius unrolled the parchment and handed it to Jace.

"Can you translate that, Colonel Kasia?"

Jace studied the document for a moment before stating, "Hanno arrived from the west with reinforcements for Mago Barca. It appears that Mago sent an earlier letter to Hasdrubal Gisco demanding he bring his army to Carmona. But Gisco hasn't responded and Mago is upset."

"Mago needs to die," Sidia growled.

"Do you have something to add, Optio Decimia?" Cornelius questioned.

"Mago Barca needs to die, sir," Sidia replied. "He ambushed the Legions of Consul Gracchus. He needs to die, sir."

"Wasn't he guided into the trap by Hirpini scouts?" Cornelius inquired.

Both Sidia and Jace shrunk a little at the truth. Hirpini tribesmen had guided the Legion and Consul Gracchus into the mountain trap.

Realizing the discussion had gotten off course, Cornelius suggested, "With Mago and Hanno in one location, we can march on Carmona."

"Not so easily, sir," the cavalry scout interjected. "Hasdrubal Gisco has moved his army to Fuentes de Andalucía. That's only seventeen miles from Carmona."

"Two armies, that close together, is unattractive," Cornelius projected. "If we attack one, the other will fall on us while we're occupied."

"It gets worse, General," the cavalryman told him. He lifted his thumb to reveal the symbol for a large city. "Both Fuentes de Andalucía, and Carmona are near Seville. If we linger too long, or offend the Turdetani Tribes, we'll have to deal with their mercenaries."

Sidia handed the NCO a few coins, told him the General appreciated the report, and walked the cavalry NCO to the exit. Once the man left, Cornelius held out his arms in resignation.

"Comments or thoughts, gentlemen," Cornelius proclaimed. "I'm fresh out of ideas."

Jace stepped forward and held out his left arm.

"Cretan Archers wear a small shield on their left wrist," he described. "It's not large enough to stop a spear or an arrow. It's used for hand-to-hand combat. Even then, it's best deployed as a distraction before stabbing an opponent with a knife."

"But I've seen you smash a head or two with the small shield," Sidia added.

"It wouldn't be much of a distraction if it was made of feathers," Jace advised.

Cornelius walked around the map table.

"Too often, we've seen divided Legions fail," he proposed. "My father and uncle split their Legions hoping to catch the Carthaginians by surprise. It resulted in tragedy. But keeping with the left arm and right arm analogy, we might be able to attack one fortification while holding the other in position."

"Which one do we hold, and which one do we hit?" Thiphilia, Steed's Senior Centurion, inquired.

Cornelius stared at Jace for a moment before Jace nodded.

"I'll have the information for you before you reach Fuentes de Andalucía and Carmona," he stated.

"What's this going to cost me?" Cornelius inquired.

"Nothing extra General Scipio," Jace informed him. "But sir, you're going to need a new Battle Commander for Wings Legion. After this mission, I'm resigning."

Chapter 26 – Legion Tritons

Sinebe, Centurion of Horse, twenty cavalrymen, and Jace Kasia watched from the foredeck as the warship entered the harbor at New Carthage. Traveling light, they left their warhorses, armor, and lances at Marçà. The mission required speed and stealth more than equipment for a cavalry charge.

"We'll pick up horses, provisions, and leave immediately," Jace told the Centurion. "I'd rather not have spies tailing us all the way to Carmona."

"Why Carmona?" Sinebe inquired. "On the map, Fuentes de Andalucía looks like an easier approach."

"It's the approach to Andalucía that worries me," Jace told him. "Why camp your army on flatland dotted with farms and drainage ditches and streams? That leaves us channels to attack Gisco and limits his lines of retreat. We're missing something."

"Maybe we'll see why when we get closer," the Centurion offered.

The warship u-turned and backstroked to the shoreline. Once the keel was high and dry, Jace and the cavalrymen marched down the ramp to the beach.

"Five of you secure horses. Five of you get waterskins and dried meat," Sinebe instructed. "And five of you collect bread and vegetables."

"What about us?" a cavalryman in the last group asked.

He and the four unassigned riders stood in a line looking dejected.

"Let me think," Sinebe murmured. "What else would a mounted patrol need?"

"Grain for the horses," a cavalryman suggested. "If we need to run and don't have time to graze, the mounts will need feed."

"You may be officer material," Sinebe teased. The Centurion dismissed the last five cavalrymen and addressed Jace. "Colonel, do you really believe we can find a weakness in the defenses of two Carthaginian armies?"

"We're not probing for weaknesses," Jace explained. "Look at Andalucía, we've already identified the weaknesses. But it doesn't help General Scipio."

"Because we don't know why Gisco picked the location," Sinebe mentioned. "If not weaknesses, sir, what are we looking for?"

"A way in, Centurion," Jace revealed. "Get behind their walls and open their gates. An open gate is the weakest area of any defense."

"And that's why we start with Carmona," the Centurion concluded. "It's the one with multiple gates."

"And now you know what I know," Jace told him. "So, let's go find a way in."

They strolled towards the five cavalrymen coming from the Legion stables, leading twenty-two horses.

***

Ten days later, Sinebe and a cavalryman sat on branches in a tree on top of a cliff. To their left, the plain of Andalusia stretched into the distance. Three days ago, dark clouds rolled in, and rain drenched the area. The clouds cleared off and yesterday they saw the roofs of Fuentes de Andalucía. Even from the heights, they were too far away to make out any of Gisco's army. Today, neither was looking to their left but to the south. At another part of the cliff, a far-off stone wall dominated the lower plain, and closer in, a wooden bridge spanned a shallow stream. In the center of the defensive wall, a gate of iron and oak secured the northern exit from the city of Carmona.

According to early reports, part of the Carthaginian army, mostly high-ranking officers, and guard units, were camped in the city. The rest of Mago and Hanno's army bivouacked on the far side of Carmona.

"You attack up that road," the cavalryman offered, indicating the wagon trail that twisted and turned up a flattened part of the cliff, "and your warhorse will die alone."

"How can the horse die alone if you're riding it?"

"Well, sir, halfway up the road, you'd be dead from a spear thrown by a defender," the cavalryman told him. "But a good warhorse will continue to charge up the road with the squadron."

The Centurion of Horse worked with the man because his stories irritated the other cavalrymen. And while Colonel Kasia and five men rode around the Andalusia plain trying to untangle the mystery of Gisco's defensive posture, and the rest of the cavalrymen probed the walls and army camps around Carmona, Sinebe had to listen to irrational tales.

"It's going to rain hard this afternoon," the storyteller announced.

Sinebe searched the sky. Except for a few clouds on the horizon to the south, it was blue. He didn't want to fall for the bait. Yet, curiosity compelled him to ask, "How do you know it's going to rain hard?"

The Centurion expected another simplistic answer. But the cavalryman pointed at a spot to the right of the city gate.

"They've opened the flood channel, sir," he answered.

Although Sinebe searched, without a stream of water coming from the opening, he couldn't locate the hole.

"Explain that," Sinebe ordered.

"The other day, I saw water gushing out of the wall and figured it was a clay pipe. But a moment ago, something, possibly a sliding door, was removed, and I saw light through the stone wall. And, sir, it's bigger than a drainpipe."

"Big enough for a man to crawl through?" the Centurion questioned.

"Yes sir, but it's only opened when it rains," the cavalryman reminded the Centurion. "He'd need to be part fish to swim upstream through that."

***

At dusk, Jace and his patrol rode into a grove of trees and dismounted. After handing the reins of his horse to a cavalryman, he headed towards their camp. An exuberant Centurion of Horse met him halfway.

"We've found our way in," Sinebe boasted. "But there is a problem."

"A problem, I can deal with. Unfortunately, we've discovered why Gisco's heavy infantrymen are camped on the plain," Jace reported. "They have couriers riding between fortified towns. If General Scipio bypasses Andalucía and attacks Carmona, Gisco's army will come together and counterattack."

"And if we attack Andalucía?" Sinebe asked.

"Gisco will retreat to his forts," Jace answered. "And while General Scipio besieges them, Mago and Hanno will come out of Carmona and attack our rear."

"Then we'll take Mago and Hanno off the battlefield," Sinebe offered.

"How, in the name of the Gods, can we do that?" Jace questioned.

"Not Gods, sir, just one," the Centurion informed him. "The God Triton."

"Triton, the Greek God of the deep sea," Jace pointed out. "He's half man with the tail of a fish. How can he help?"

***

Cornelius pushed the Legions. Not because he was in a rush to fight. General Scipio hoped to arrive before the

Carthaginians had a chance to prepare. In his mind, they were lax and partially off guard while in winter quarters.

The grind had taken its toll on men, animals, and transports. Left in the wake of the Legions were hobbled Legionaries, lame horses, crippled mules, and broken axles. Yet, General Scipio kept the rest periods short and the day's marches long.

Weary and stiff jointed, the Legions plowed onward, their minds numbed by the continuous movement. When, Bolt Legion's standard bearer bellowed, it startled First Century, and the staff officers.

"Riders coming forward, General."

Quintus Trebellius' rough voice rattled the Tribunes and servants. A few jerked their horses away from the officer in charge of the Legion's banner. Cornelius, as usual, maintained an air of dignity. Behind him, Sidia had half drawn his gladius before realizing the battle roar had been a simple announcement.

"Riders coming forward, sir," Quintus Trebellius proclaimed again.

"I heard you, Centurion Trebellius," Cornelius assured him. "Thank you."

Five riders appeared at the vanguard. In moments, they reached the staff officers. But First Century tightened the security band around the General, stopping Centurion Sinebe.

"General, greetings from Wings Legion," the cavalry officer declared. "And welcome to Andalusia."

"I expected Colonel Kasia to be here," Cornelius mentioned.

"Sir, he's been detained," Sinebe informed him.

"How long will he be detained?"

Sinebe glanced at the sky, searched a few clouds on the horizon, and answered, "At least three days, sir. But he sent me to show you where you'll set up the marching camps."

"He did? Suppose my planning and strategy staff takes affront to the suggestion?"

"Then, General Scipio, to quote Colonel Kasia, you'll ruin the surprise," Sinebe divulged. The Centurion of Horse produced a scroll from a fold in his shirt. He passed it forward and advised. "If you don't follow the plan, sir, you'll end up fighting on two fronts."

***

Late in the afternoon, Cornelius sat on his horse gazing across farmland at the walled town of Fuentes de Andalucía. A slight shift to the north, and he scanned the fortified city of Écija.

"My backside is exposed, and this isn't a public bath," he complained. "We're setting up our marching camps ten miles from two walled towns surrounded by elements of Gisco's army. What's to keep them from coming forward and converging on us?"

None of the staff officers had an answer. Cornelius twisted and pointed southwest. Far in the distance, rain clouds gathered on the horizon.

"And if I understand it right, Hanno and Mago's armies are camped twenty-two miles from here at Carmona. What's stopping them from riding over, joining Gisco, and annihilating us?"

Again, nobody spoke up. How could they? Only Centurion Sinebe had firsthand knowledge of Colonel Kasia's strategy. Thus, the General focused on him.

"Sinebe. Can you shed light on why I'm positioning my Legions between armies of my enemies?" Cornelius asked the Centurion of Horse. "What am I supposed to do besides stay up all night pacing the floor of my pavilion?"

"Sir, I only know you're supposed to wait for it to rain," Sinebe replied.

"Then get wet, I know," Cornelius scoffed. "Sidia. Is your cousin mad, or am I for following his directions?"

"General, Jace is mildly touched," the bodyguard allowed. "But tactically, he sees things most people miss. Of course, he has been known to be wrong on occasion, sir."

"Is that a diplomatic way of dodging the question?"

"Would I do that, General Scipio?" the bodyguard inquired.

"Every time," Cornelius stated. "There is one consolation, you'll be with me in the rain. What do you think Colonel Kasia will be doing when it starts pouring?"

"Truthfully sir, I have no idea," Sidia ventured. "But considering his history, he'll probably be getting just as wet as us."

The statement wasn't exactly accurate.

***

At the eighth turning of the camp's sandglass, the duty Optio in the General's pavilion heard the first drops. It put him in a quandary. If the rain stopped, he'd look like a fool for sounding the alarm. If the drops were a precursor to a storm, his hesitation to wake the General, and the camp in the middle of the night, could ruin his career.

From the back of the tent, a voice asked, "Is it just passing through?"

Jumping up from the campstool, the veteran NCO saluted.

"General Scipio, I didn't see you."

"Rain, Optio. Is it coming or not?"

Before the NCO could answer, the tapping on the goatskin tent increased until the downpour resembled the pounding of fists on the material.

"Never mind, we have our answer," Cornelius proposed. "Roll the infantry out of their tents. And order the cavalry and Velites to their assembly point."

Drums were useless in rain, but not trumpets. Brass had no problem with moisture. Although the men, awakened by the horns in the middle of the night and ordered by their officers to dress in their combat gear, certainly did.

And while the Legionaries complained and grumbled out loud, twenty-two miles to the south, a small detachment didn't have the luxury of protesting their situation. As a matter of fact, in a perverse way, they appreciated the arrival of the bad weather.

***

On dry days, the stream flowing under the wooden bridge was barely visible through the tall grass. Closer to the base of the slope, the course remained a single ribbon of wet. Then, the stream split into several channels that snaked up the grade, giving the appearance of muddy trails between the tall weeds.

From the top of the defensive wall of Carmona, the drainage ditches resembled brown scars on the earth. As a result, none of the sentries paid attention to the slope below the wall. Consequently, the officers thought nothing of it, when on stormy nights, their guards took shelter. The rain and the darkness, after all, cut the view from the top of the wall to nothing. Unwatched and invisible from above, the drainage ditches began to swell with water.

To the right of the gate and partway down the grade, the water washed a layer of mud and handfuls of weeds off a woolen shirt. The shirt shifted allowing water to flow around Jace Kasia's face. Stifling a cough, he reached ahead and tapped on a buried cavalry boot. From behind, a hand tapped the sole of Colonel Kasia's boot.

Dirty, hungry, wet, and chilled to the bone, six men rose from the mud. As if spirits secretly leaving their graves, they remained stooped. After two days of being under a layer of damp soil, none of them wanted to stand erect. They feared losing the little warmth provided by their chests and bellies.

Jace slipped a coil of rope off his shoulder and rinsed it in the ditch. Then he bent, placed his hands in the rushing water, and began climbing uphill against the current. The five cavalrymen followed his example, staying midchannel so the downpour would wash away any signs of their passing.

The rainfall increased and all across Carmona water from roofs and streets rushed to gutters. A fair number of the gutters collected in the trench that flowed to a large drainage culvert. From a steady stream, the water leaving the city bubbled up in a pond as it passed through the defensive wall.

Outside, the six Legion Tritons fought against the flood and prayed for the blessings of the God Triton. Not just for the ascent, but for their passage through the port and the wall of water.

Chapter 27 – Remember, I Love You

Huddled against the defensive wall beside a violent churning pond, Jace and his five-man team watched the rise and fall of the surface and the flow out and down the hill. From a spillway to a writhing and agitated pool, the drainage culvert had become a nearly impassable obstacle.

"It can't be done, sir," a cavalryman volunteered. "I swam in angry seas, and on raging rivers where I dodged boulders. But nothing like this. You might as well try swimming up a waterfall."

"We have one advantage over a waterfall," Jace remarked. "We don't have to swim upward."

"Just upstream, sir. And that's not very inviting. Who's the first drowning victim?"

"I'm going first," Jace informed the group. "Once I'm through, I'll anchor the rope and send it back."

"Colonel, how will we know if you've made it or not?" a cavalryman inquired.

"We'll know when his body bobs to the surface and washes down the hill," one offered. "Or when the end of the rope comes through."

Jace lifted his jerkin and rapped on his chest.

"Haven't you ever been sledding?" he challenged. "I'm going to sled right through the water."

"I don't think it works that way, sir," one of the raiders stated.

Jace pulled his wrist shield from behind his back.

"I'll need help getting in," he informed them. "Lift my body and two men push me down against the current."

The Cretan Archer put the strap for the wrist shield between his teeth. Partially armored at his face, he allowed himself to be lifted and aimed at the boiling surface as if he was a battering ram. His face and the small shield bounced off the water several times before he lowered his head and plunged under.

For a moment, the only things holding him in the current were the cavalrymen pushing on his boots. In a mighty effort, Jace extended his arms and located fissures on the sides of the culvert. While pulling against the current, his shirt and trousers ripped off. They washed away and the strong current began scouring his naked flesh. Water forced itself into his nostrils and Jace heaved. Then his mind took flight, fleeing from the horror of the watery grave.

***

From the confines of the drainage port, Jace was transported to a fateful day in Eleutherna. His last happy day with Neysa Kasia and Master Archer Zarek Mikolas.

"Zarek. Zarek," Jace called as he ran towards the archer and Neysa.

He carried two war bows and a pair of quivers.

"What's the matter?" Neysa asked. "Is Dryas ill?"

"No, ma'am, Uncle Dryas is fine," he answered. Shifting to face Zarek, Jace told him. "There's a barrel seller on the back row. Uncle Dryas said he recognizes Bettina."

"It's fine, the family is allowed to sell their product at the market," Zarek remarked. "I'm sure it has no connection to the demise of the Rhodian soldiers."

Jace leaned closer to the archer's ear, "It's just that Iphis, Bettina's father, isn't with his family. Another vendor told me a group of soldiers were here at dawn. They helped Iphis unload his wagon of barrels. Then they escorted him into the city."

"Two questions," Zarek remarked. He reached out, took the quiver, and tied it around his waist before grabbing the bow. "Was he escorted or arrested? And who were the soldiers?"

"According to the vendor, Iphis was guided into the city by several soldiers from Rhodes."

Crowd noises caused them to look around.

"Should I string the bow?" Jace asked.

"No," Neysa replied. "There's no threat."

"Do it," Zarek told him.

The Master Archer looped the string around the bow tip then placed that end of his bow behind his left leg. Flexing the bow around his right thigh, Zarek hooked the loop of the bowstring into the opposite bow tip. Jace did the same.

A flatbed wagon backed up to block the road. Once the horse stopped moving, Magistrate Timarchus and a man dressed in the tunic of a Rhodian Admiral climbed onto the bed.

"The citizens of Knossus and Polyrrhenia have formed a partnership and they want every citizen of Crete to join them," Magistrate Timarchus exclaimed. "I want to hear the pros and cons of joining with our sister cities. But first a word…"

Only because Zarek and Jace were searching did they identify the spearmen. Although not in the uniform of the

Rhodian Navy, their stiff postures, and the outline of their spears, making depressions in the grass, gave them away.

"I have four spearmen on my side," Jace whispered.

"Four more on my side blocking access to the path up the hill," Zarek reported while untying the cap on his quiver.

"Five more coming from the city," Neysa added.

"…please give a warm welcome to Admiral Polemocles."

The naval commander nodded to the crowd and turned to Timarchus.

"I'm afraid I lied to you, Magistrate," Polemocles declared. "Although I have been hired by Polyrrhenia to blockade the colony of Lyttos, I wasn't authorized to visit your city."

"If you don't represent the alliance, why are you here?" the Magistrate demanded.

His words reached the crowd, and they made menacing sounds, but none moved.

"I'm here to arrest a rogue bowman and his associate," Polemocles replied. He glanced around and spied his soldiers coming down the hill. As they closed with the flatbed, it was obvious their formation escorted a civilian. "There is a witness."

"Jace. What's the color of Bettina's hair?" Zarek inquired.

"Dryas said it's dark brown," he answered.

From the wagon, the Admiral continued, "But I learned last night the name of the murderers. Will someone kindly point out Zarek Mikolas and his student to me? There is a reward."

"Just a second, Admiral," Timarchus complained, "I didn't agree to a manhunt."

"No, you didn't," Polemocles replied. The knife came out of its sheath, and in a smooth arc, it rose to the Magistrate's chest and plunged into his heart. "But I didn't ask your permission."

Horrified at the murder of their Magistrate, the crowd and council stood in silence. In a moment, they would have rushed the flatbed wagon. But a voice rose up before the mob surged forward.

"There they are," a familiar voice shouted.

Jace and Zarek spun to face Dryas Kasia. The Uncle, the brother-in-law, the family trader stood with an arm extended and a finger pointing at Jace and Zarek. Behind him, a pretty girl with dark brown hair waited with a smile on her face.

"Those two," Dryas said doubling down on his accusation, "are the murders of the Rhodian patrol."

People moved away from the three forming a circle. Shocked by the betrayal, neither Jace, Zarek, nor Neysa moved.

"Kill them," Admiral Polemocles ordered from the wagon bed.

Spearmen snatched their weapons from the grass and four threw.

"No," Zarek screamed as he tackled Neysa, landing on her upper body.

Seeing the woman who raised him only partially protected from the spears, Jace leaped onto her legs and her lower body.

Every animal, when struck a fatal blow by an arrow or a spear, exhales. Not a sigh or a quick expulsion of air, but an outbreath that comes from deep in the lungs. Hunters knew the sound. It signaled that the hunt was over, and the animal would run no farther.

Tears came to Jace's eyes when he heard Zarek utter his final breath. Then a voice came to him. From under the archer's carcass, the voice that sang him to sleep at night when he was four years old and having a nightmare about a raging sea.

"Run, Jace," Neysa ordered. "Get to the cabin, gather a long pack, and get to Phalasarna. From there, sail away from Crete. And remember, I love you. Now run!"

The nightmare of being slung about by a raging sea, unable to draw a breath, and being overpowered by towering waves returned. Fear gripped Jace's heart just as it had when he was a four-year-old orphan.

Then Neysa Kasia's comforting voice cooed in his ears.

"And remember, I love you. Now swim."

***

Running hills gave Cretan Archers deep lungs, and water training, the confidence to hold their breath underwater. Jace squeezed his eyes shut tight and tried to recall the sound of Neysa' voice. But all he could hear was the gurgling of water rushing by with the force of a gale. And it made him angry.

Pulling with his powerful shoulders, Jace moved forward. After locating another set of handholds, he braced and pulled again. Then his face came out of the water. Still in the torrent, and within the confines of the drainage culvert, he hung to a side, while looking up at a short waterfall.

"Thank you, Neysa," he said.

Then Jace scrambled to street level. Standing for a moment, he allowed the rain to wash his flesh and rinse away his anger.

***

The third cavalryman to emerge from the culvert, climbed to street level, and embraced Jace.

"For getting me out of that pit, sir," he coughed up rainwater as he spoke, "I love you."

"There's a lot of that going around," Jace assured him. "Now get up the street and keep watch. We need to haul in the rest before the city comes to close the port. We don't want to get caught."

"Naked, sir?"

"What?" Jace asked as he tossed the wrist shield and rope into the culvert.

"Caught naked," the cavalryman said.

"I don't get it," Jace admitted.

While Jace fed the rope out, the cavalryman headed to the end of the block. A few moments later, another head emerged.

"The next time you have a special mission, Colonel," the dripping wet man advised. "Count me out."

"Get up the street and keep watch," Jace instructed. "We'll be moving soon."

***

The hammering rain changed to a slow drumbeat and streaks of weak light lit the clouds. High above the five crouching men, the roof of the abandoned building leaked rain and let in the pale light. With those clues, the state of the storm and the new day weren't in question.

"What's the plan, sir?" a cavalryman inquired.

"If General Scipio follows through with the tactics," Jace explained, "we should hear the Carthaginian army call up their infantry and head for a gate."

"And what do we do?"

"Once it starts, we're going to capture the southern gate," Jace answered. "Our goal is to keep the portal open for the Legions."

"With just the five of us and no armor, and you naked, sir?"

"When you put it like that," Jace commented, "it sounds bad. But we can do it."

From the street outside the building, they heard voices issuing orders, boots scraping on pavers, and male voices grumbling. For a heartbeat, Jace and his four men braced, preparing for a fight. But the soldiers passed by. Shortly afterwards, the sixth cavalryman in the patrol slipped into the building.

He went to Jace and handed him a folded bundle of cloth.

"It's the only thing I could find, Colonel," the rider apologized. "The streets are filled with mercenary spearmen, and you said not to get caught."

"General Scipio has arrived," a couple of cavalrymen offered.

"Not exactly," Jace corrected. He took the bundle, unfolded it, and shook out a large rectangle of cloth. "This will do."

As Jace wrapped the material around his waist and expertly tucked an edge into a fold, one of his men pointed out, "That's not a toga, sir. It's too small."

"This is a himation," Jace explained as he shifted the material. Soon, it wrapped his body from chest down to shin level, and draped over his left shoulder, while leaving his right shoulder bare. "On Crete and in other Greek cities, it's considered fashionable. And you're right, it's not as voluminous as a toga."

"You said, it's not exactly General Scipio," a cavalryman reminded Jace. "If not the General, sir, who is attacking Carmona?"

"It should be Senior Tribune Silanus outside the walls, assaulting the Carthaginian camp," Jace answered. "General Scipio, hopefully, is at Fuentes de Andalucía. Probably making evil faces at Gisco's army and cursing me, if everything is going according to plan."

Act 10

Chapter 28 – When Out is In

A sad fact for Legionaries, leather straps, iron and steel equipment, padding, helmets, gladii, shields, and spears attracted moisture. And while infantrymen didn't mind getting wet, it happened whenever it rained, they absolutely detested the following day. For it meant drying, sanding, shining, and oiling every piece of equipment they owned.

"This is a travesty," an infantryman announced.

Another Legionary seconded the notion by saying, "It's a violation of everything holy."

"Oh rejoice," their Centurion exclaimed. Rainwater ran off the red horsehair comb on his new helmet, streaking the sides with pale red dye and carrying the stain down the sides of his neck. The combat officer ignored the discomfort and declared. "We have a legal scholar and a warrior priest in our ranks. Truly, I have the most talented Century in all of Bolt Legion."

The sarcastic comment brought laughter from the ranks, marking it as the first happy incident of the morning. One that started before the pale light of a rainy day washed away the night and found Legionaries standing in ranks under a sky that continued to pour down on them.

"If we're not going to assault," an infantryman suggested, "we could have kept our waterproof covers on our shields and wraps over our armor."

"And a philosopher," the Centurion bellowed. "How did I get so lucky?"

***

The Legionaries of Bolt Legion weren't alone in their misery. Four Legions of heavy infantrymen stood in ranks, getting soaked. And while enemy spearmen waited just a half mile away, the Battle Commanders of the Legions had not ordered their maniples forward.

"You were right, sir," Sidia said.

"I'm so rarely wrong," Cornelius replied, "remind me of the specific instance."

The General's aids, staff officers, senior Centurions, and infantrymen of First Century sat their mounts in silence, bearing the storm without protest. They had no choice, General Scipio exposed himself to the weather and remained silent about it. But his remark pulled at the corners of their mouths, and in their sodden despair, the entire headquarters staff grinned.

"As you promised, sir, we are getting wet," the bodyguard stated the obvious. "But sir, do you think Gisco has figured it out?"

Cornelius smiled at the question. Glancing to his right for a moment, then to his left, the youthful Prorogatio of Iberia pondered the question. The standard bearers of four Legions and their Battle Commanders held positions at the front of their heavy infantry. Behind Cornelius, four matching banners identified him as the General for those Legions.

"Eleven thousand Legionaries, plus their NCOs, and officers make a formidable war machine," Cornelius granted. "I believe what you're asking, Optio Decimia, does Gisco, or his advisers, realize our weakness?"

Sidia Decimia mimicked the General and peered right and left. The solid rows of wet infantrymen with naked shields and spears, stood in three lines, offering potential violence. But heavy infantrymen were all that composed the Legions. There were no cavalrymen to hold the flanks, nor skirmishers or Velites to disrupt the forward element of a charging enemy.

"I'm positive he hasn't caught on, General," Sidia declared.

"Why so sure?" Cornelius inquired.

"Because, General, Gisco's riders, spearmen, and soldiers are like us. They're standing in the rain and getting wet, instead of attacking."

***

Twenty-two miles to the south, there was no hesitation to engage.

"Forward the next wave," Junius Silanus ordered.

Using a Celtiberi trick, passed on by Prince Allucius, each cavalry horse towed two light infantrymen. Although the tactic slowed the cavalry charge, the configuration quickly inserted Velites into the heart of the Carthaginian camp.

"We've only twenty squadrons of horse remaining, and four thousand light infantry in reserve, sir," Captain Bekeres cautioned. "If you commit them, we'll have no forces left for an orderly retreat."

"And if we don't use what we have, we'll leave Mago and Hanno intact," Silanus pointed out. "Tomorrow, or the day after, they'll be at our backs when we face Gisco. What would Cornelius have me do?"

"You've been around him a long time, sir," the Celtiberi cavalry officer proposed. "I'm sure you know the answer."

"Cornelius Scipio has the ability to make rational men impulsive, daring, and slightly mad," Silanus admitted. "Forward the last wave. We will end this today, one way or the other."

Bekeres gestured the forward motion, and his signal corps sent the instructions to the waiting heavy cavalry and light infantry.

"Sir, the gate is opening," the cavalry officer announced. "Carmona is ripe for the taking."

"Or to puke out Carthaginian reinforcements and destroy us," Silanus growled.

From the portal, officers and their staff raced from the city.

"Not reinforcements," Bekeres stated.

"It's worse," Silanus asserted. "Their commanders are coming out to take charge."

"I'll get Captain Darsosin and we'll cut the camp in half with our Celtiberi," Bekeres proposed. "It'll give you a better sense of the momentum of the battle."

The Captain galloped away and Junius Silanus sat watching the fighting. There were only two orders he could give at that point. Attack through the gates or retreat. In a motion he'd seen Cornelius do a hundred times, the Senior Tribune of Iberia lifted his chin, raised his eyes to the sky, and prayed.

***

A smartly dressed Carthaginian officer and his staff galloped down a road in Carmona. As they raced towards the fighting, they passed a Greek and five laborers.

"He's so pretty, he must be important," one of the laborers offered. "If I had my lance, he'd be one dead Carthaginian."

"Keep your voice down," Jace warned the cavalryman. "When we get to the gate guards, keep your eyes downcast and your mouths closed."

"Yes, Colonel," they mumbled in response.

A block from the south gate, a second Carthaginian noble and his staff trotted by.

"Do you suppose one of them is Hanno and the other Mago?" a cavalryman whispered to Jace.

"Now I want a lance," Jace grunted. "Mago owes me for a Legion."

"Do you know him, sir?"

"Never met the General," Jace admitted. "Doesn't stop me from wanting him dead."

***

Moments later, they rounded a corner, and encountered a courtyard. On the far side of the plaza, the six approached the southern gate.

"Where are you going?" a Sergeant of the city guard challenged.

A Turdetani tribesman with public responsibilities needed to be proficient in Iberian and Phoenician. Additionally, an NCO at an entrance to the city would also be familiar with Greek and Numidian, the other trading tongues. Plus, he would be alert for Latin, the dialect of his enemy.

"The Carthaginian ordered me to help secure the gate," Jace said in perfect Greek.

As his native language, the Hellenic speech contained no hint of Latin. Jace hoped, between the Greek and his reference to a mythical Carthaginian, the Sergeant would allow his cavalrymen to remain at the gate.

The NCO cocked his head to the side, concentrated on translating the words, then pointed out, "You look Latian."

"My hometown on Crete is better than any Roman city, Lochías," Jace shot back as if the Latin remark was an insult.

"What's a Lochías?" the Sergeant demanded.

Talks with traders and merchants rarely involved a discussion of positions in a phalanx formation. The unfamiliar word made the Sergeant curious if he'd been insulted. And as Jace intended, the NCO's question about the new word moved him further from his initial challenge.

"A position of importance in a fighting formation," Jace answered. He indicated the seven city guards at the gate. "A Lochías is a commander of a rank. It identifies you as the leader of the noble defenders of this city."

The NCO puffed up his chest before inquiring, "why are you here?"

"I'm a Greek tradesman traveling with General Hanno," Jace lied. "Because my apprentices, and myself, are not trained with shields and spears, he sent us to handle the gate. That frees up your warriors to do the fighting, if the Latians get too close."

A long, worrisome pause followed the fib.

Master Archer Mikolas often warned, *"Be judicious with your compliments. Accolades can make a situation better or cause the target to become suspicious."*

Jace waited for the results of his flattery.

"Watch the gate, Greek," the Sergeant ordered. "We'll guard the approach."

The NCO and his seven gate guards marched through the portal and formed a semicircle in front of the entrance.

"He was dying to get out there and watch the fighting, sir," a cavalryman whispered.

"They all were," Jace agreed. "When I give the word, arm yourselves and prepare to defend the gate. I'm going to have a look."

Jace pointed at a pair of spears and shields resting beside the open gate. The implication was clear, three of the cavalrymen would have to disarm guards to secure weapons. Then he climbed a ladder and peered over the wall at the battle raging south of the city.

***

The battlefield was divided in two. Far from the walls of Carmona, one Carthaginian General attempted to rally his forces. But the Velites and the Legion light horsemen smashed their defensive formations before they solidified. Islands of soldiers in armor with infantry shields fought back-to-back. Yet, they were unable to shuffle to join other clusters of their comrades. And preventing the upper field of conflict from moving north and joining with the other General was a broad no man's land.

North of the empty ground, the second Carthaginian General managed to collect a fighting force. In one melee after another, he fought his infantry around his half of the battlefield and claimed dominance over one section after another. Although he brought together soldiers and spearmen, he didn't move to help the Carthaginian General to his south. Mostly because the walls of

Carmona were adjacent to the northern field of battle. And to aid the other Carthaginian, required him to abandon the security of the walled sanctuary. Not to mention crossing the strip of death that separated the two conflicts.

Mercenaries attempted to flee the southern zone and reach Carmona through the northern fighting. But each died on lances or under the hooves of charging horses. In a rotating loop of murder, Captain Bekeres moved his heavy cavalrymen in one direction while Captain Darsosin charged in the other. And as surely as a wide, deep river would, Princes Allucius' gift to Cornelius Scipio divided the battlefield.

***

On the walls of Carmona, spearmen shouted suggestions at the Carthaginian armies and their Generals. Unheard by the combatants due to the distance, the ruckus came down muddled to the gate guards. For Jace Kasia, the noise presented an opportunity.

A lesson from archer training came to Jace, *"A man with a plan and a vision could do many things in the midst of chaos: escape, attack, hide, or turn the tide of a battle."*

"Many things," Jace pondered. "But what, Master Mikolas?"

While Jace considered his choices, one of the Celtiberi cavalry officers turned his mount to the north. He reined in and signaled for a wedge. A moment later, five hundred heavy cavalrymen lowered their lances and charged the Carthaginian General's position.

And Jace realized, his original plan to hold the gate open was the reverse of what was needed. After climbing down the ladder to the courtyard, he ran to the center of the gateway.

"Lochías. Pull in your file, the Latians are charging," Jace shouted to the gate Sergeant. From the walls, the clammer gave the NCO no way to confirm the information. He called for his guards to move back. Meanwhile, Jace rushed to his five Legion cavalrymen. "After the Carthaginian General comes through, start closing the gate. Before it shuts, slip out and run. But stay close to the walls."

"I thought we were going to hold the gate open," one mentioned.

"The other Carthaginian General is far outside of the city. I don't want him to get in."

"When out is in, right, sir?" the cavalryman who liked creating phrases offered.

"Don't get caught inside."

Then, to Jace's delight, the tribesmen on the walls began throwing spears. At what he wasn't sure. There were no Legion units close enough to hit. But the action served to confirm that the Legion was attacking the gate.

Moments later, the Carthaginian General and his staff raced through the portal. Lagging far behind the riders, his infantrymen tried to keep up.

"Close the gate," Jace bellowed. "Close the gate."

The five Legion cavalrymen pushed the giant oak and iron door. As it swung, first one ducked out of the opening. Then another, and finally, the last three hopped through as the edge of the gate and the frame touched.

"You ungrateful rats," Jace shouted at the closed gateway. "I fed you, clothed you, and taught you a trade. And when I need you, you desert me."

"Step aside, Greek," the Sergeant instructed. "We'll set the bar."

Jace backed away and watched four of the gate guards lift a log and drop it into brackets. With the gateway sealed, he drifted across the courtyard and vanished into a back street of Carmona.

Chapter 29 – You're Out of Uniform

One Carthaginian General made it into Carmona. Then, miraculously, the gate closed, trapping the second General in the southern battle area.

Junius Silanus grabbed a mounted signalman by the arm, almost pulling the young man off his horse.

"Send every free squadron after the Carthaginian," he shouted. "Send them now. Now."

A series of flags issued instructions, while junior tribunes with messages rode to Centurions. Long after they began, according to Silanus' accounting, Captain Bekeres drew his heavy cavalry out of the no man's land. From the back-and-forth track, the Celtiberi officer drove his mount towards the fighting around the Carthaginian General.

A deficiency of a light attack force, Legion Velites got hung up on the shields of heavy infantrymen. Spears and shields, blood and courage, wounds and death passed back and forth between the shield walls. Despite a valiant try, the Legion light infantrymen couldn't break the protective wall around the General. Then Captain Bekeres and the leading riders of his heavy cavalry peeled off the outer layer of Carthaginian heavy infantry. Behind the first squadron, a second set of ten lances sluffed off another layer of soldiers.

In a massive push, the Velites plowed into the formation. Four of them pulled the General off his mount.

"Your name, sir," a Centurion inquired.

"General Hanno of Carthage," the man replied. "I wish to speak with your General."

"And I believe, sir, he wants to talk with you."

With the fall of the last senior commander, the remaining soldiers and light infantry from Mago and Hanno's armies scattered. Scouts reported most headed home. They'd had enough of the campaign season.

***

Junius Silanus beamed all the way back. When he walked his victorious light infantrymen and cavalrymen to the marching camps, he was surprised to see the rows and rows of damp and sodden Legionaries in the distance. After signaling the Centurions to head for the stockades, he rode to General Scipio.

"Senior Tribune, tell me this was worth it," Cornelius said in greeting.

"We broke both armies, and captured their General Hanno," Silanus reported. "What's left is right in front of you, sir."

Cornelius glanced at the sun, then to his left and right.

"Let's see what Gisco is made of," he stated. "Senior Centurion forward the Legions."

Trumpets blared, and a roar came from the ranks. Angry about standing in the rain since before sunup, the Legionaries were spoiling for a fight.

"Legions, forward," came the order from the four Battle Commanders.

Eleven thousand heavy infantrymen stepped off to the cadence of left-stomp-left-stomp-left-stomp. And General Scipio nudged his horse.

It was a little less than half a mile between combatants when the Carthaginians moved. But rather than attack the Legions, they broke left and right. Not long afterwards, Gisco's army fled from the field of battle.

Some vanished behind the walls of Fuentes de Andalucía and others entered the defensive walls of Écija.

"I believe he doesn't want a fight, sir," Sidia proposed.

"And I don't want to spend the winter besieging a series of fortified towns," Cornelius proclaimed. "Senior Centurion. Turn the Legions around and march them home."

***

Getting out of Carmona proved easy. Once the Legions marched away, stretcher bearers, grave details, and NCOs rushed out to take stock of their losses. In the mass of spearmen, Jace Kasia, in a stolen cloak, left the city. He headed south, soon settling into a comfortable jog.

***

The officers' mess was a glorious affair. For the cavalry officers and the officers of the Velites, it was a chance to regale heavy infantry officers with their exploits. Cornelius listened with pleasure at the retelling of the battle of Carmona. But when he stood, the pavilion fell silent.

"You all did your part today. And I am proud of every Century and squadron. But I have to ask, has anyone seen Colonel Kasia?"

"Sir, we located his five raiders. Although, for some strange reason, they prefer to be called Tritons," Silanus explained. "The last time they saw Jace, he ordered them to flee through the closing gate of Carmona."

"I want to speak with them in the morning," Cornelius announced. "I've known Colonel Kasia for over a decade. I am confident that he will show up."

A noise at the entrance drew everyone's attention. A moment later, Jace strolled into the tent dressed in what could only be described as a light toga.

"Colonel Kasia, you're out of uniform," Cornelius scolded.

Jace held up both arms and brushed the fabric of the himation with his hands.

"No, General Scipio, I am not out of uniform," Jace informed Cornelius. "Because sir, I resign my position in the Legions of the Republic and the Iberian Legions specifically."

"Well, well, well. Kasia, this is a military banquet," Cornelius stated. "And the only way for you to stay is to be my guest of honor. Do you accept?"

"General Scipio, indeed, I do."

Chapter 30 – Welcome Home

Jace Kasia braced as the merchant ship approached the dock. Workers caught and pulled lines, drawing the vessel against the pier. In the hustle of securing the trader, Jace breathed softly, absorbing the familiar atmosphere of Crete.

"First time visiting Phalasarna?" a man called to Jace from the dock. "My cousin is an excellent guide."

From the scruffy dress and smashed nose, Jace judged the only thing excellent about the man would be his unreliability.

"Not my first time," Jace assured him.

Bending, Jace slipped a strap over his shoulder. Standing upright, he lifted a heavy wooden box from the deck. All the earnings from his years with the Legion filled the container.

"Phalasarna is not a safe city for visitors. There are pickpockets and rogues on every corner," the disheveled man warned. Although he stayed on the dock, the man shuffled closer to the rails of the ship as if to intimidate Jace. "You had best take advantage of my generous nature. For your own good."

Ignoring him, Jace scooped a pack from the deck. At the sight of two bow cases and two quivers strapped to a long pack, the ruffian stepped away from the gunwale. He wasn't sure if a Latian could become a Cretan Archer, but he wasn't going to chance it. Backing away, the man apologized, "Sorry to have bothered you, Archer."

Not long after leaving the boat, Jace took the path upward from the harbor and entered the city.

***

The tree lined street hadn't changed nor had the long brick wall of the archer school. An older student from a Troop stood sentry at the gateway. As Jace approached, the teen shifted and blocked the entrance.

"The Agoge is not open to the public," he sneered.

"Are you capable in a fighting circle?" Jace inquired. Taken aback by the question, the teen hesitated while Jace advised. "Because, Troop, challenging a File Leader will land you in a hand-to-hand combat class you aren't ready for."

"Your name, Archer?"

"Jace Kasia, File Leader for Lieutenant Gergely's company. Where is the Herd today?"

The youth blinked as if confused by the description. Finally, he swallowed, stepped aside, and pointed towards the armory.

"Thank you," Jace said.

Without fond memories, he crossed the parade ground. His stay at the Agoge hadn't been as a student, but as a bower. And a not too popular one at that. After weaving between a few buildings, Jace saw the archery range and a bitter memory washed over him. Then he noticed a bunch of little boys in front of the armory and a pleasant thought replaced the ill. He'd enjoyed teaching the rudiments of bow-and-arrow making to the youngest students in the agoge.

***

The Herd were sitting in a semicircle listening to a lecture by an instructor. As the Master Archer spoke, he lifted his arms in the air. Jace stopped. Rather than a hand on his right arm, the man displayed a scarred stump.

"I need someone to watch my long pack," Jace announced after a moment of gawking.

Slowly, Acis Gergely lowered his arms and turned to face a ghost from his past.

"File Leader Kasia, you are about eleven years late reporting in," the former Lieutenant of Archers scolded Jace.

"Sir, it's been a profitable contract," Jace assured him. He jostled the box and coins rattled against the wooden sides. "Are these bowmen able to guard my pack? Do they know their dances?"

"File Leader Kasia, the Cretan Agoge welcomes you back," Gergely exclaimed. "This Herd is learning. But they have a long way to go before earning the title and taking their place in a File with Cretan Archers."

"I'd like to see a war-dance," Jace remarked.

Without pausing, Gergely barked, "Cretan counter-march firing. Set the beat."

The boys, a mixture of ages eight and nine, jumped to their feet. Several started a chant, "Mártios, mártios, step left, step right, mártios."

The call of march-step was soon repeated as the fourteen formed two single files. Then the first two in each column positioned their arms as if holding bows. And while they were still, the chanting and marching in place continued behind them.

"Your target is a hundred feet away. Release five and rotate," Gergely instructed. While the boys ran the drill, the Lieutenant marched to Jace and hugged him. "There's been no reports of an active Cretan Archer in the Republic. We figured you were dead."

"Close, a couple of times," Jace admitted. "But Zarek Mikolas taught me survival skills that carried me through tough times. I need to see the Archon and pay him a share of the mercenary contract. It should be enough to clear Mikolas' name of any disgrace and to give you credit for the completion of the contract."

Gergely grabbed the strap and tested the weight of the box.

"I'm going with you," he insisted. "As you pointed out, it was my contract that took you to the Romans. Plus, you'll need me to vouch for your credentials as a Master Cretan Archer from the respected Agoge of Zarek Mikolas."

***

Morning fog hung over the hills behind the farmhouse. In the garden, as she did every day during harvest season, the woman stooped and plucked vegetables from neatly arranged rows.

"If you taste a carrot once in a while," Jace said from the side of the garden plot, "it'll help you appreciate the hard work that went into growing the crop."

Neysa Kasia straightened her back, brushed loose strands of gray hair off her face, and glared at the tall, broad-shouldered man.

"Is it beneath the dignity of an archer to help with the harvest?" she asked. "There's an extra basket near the shed."

Jace hiked to the porch of the farmhouse and rested his long pack next to the door. Then he went towards the shed. As he approached it, memories of learning to construct hunting and war bows flashed before his eyes. Next, he remembered smelting iron for arrowheads, shaving arrow shafts, and splitting feathers for fletching. And, he recalled the hundreds of lessons taught by Zarek Mikolas as they worked in the shed. Lessons that had kept him alive during war for over a decade.

After several moments of reflection, he snatched a basket from a stack of containers. But as he began to turn, a pair of strong arms encircled his waist.

"Are you hurt, hunted, or just exhausted?" Neysa inquired. "Don't answer. Cretan Archers are always one or the other. It doesn't matter, as long as you're here."

"I've seen Sicily, Rome, their Republic, the coast of Africa, and too much of Iberia," Jace informed her. "But no matter where I've gone, nothing felt as comfortable as this farm. Or filled my heart as much as seeing you."

"Then I've done my job as your stepmother," Neysa whispered. "Are you hungry? Cretan archers usually are."

"I can eat," Jace told her.

"Then come inside and I'll fix you something to eat," Neysa Kasia proposed. Then she released his waist, grabbed one of his hands in hers, and offered. "Welcome home, Jace Kasia."

The End

A sample chapter from *A Legion Archer* series

Book #7: *From Dawn to Death*

Chapter 00 – Payment in Promises

King Syphax's compound consisted of several buildings built around a central park. His personal residence, with a balcony overlooking the garden, took up one side of the green space. A building with offices for magistrates and the barracks for his personal guards occupied the opposite side. On one end of the park, a cluster of isolated cottages for visiting dignitaries filled a half-acre of ground.

The location of the cottages forced dignitaries to stroll through the park to reach the other end. They always arrived refreshed from a walk through the trees and flowers. At the other end, they entered the King's reception hall and banquet room.

At the seven entrances to the King's park, Numidian infantrymen stood sentry. Trained by Legion officers and NCOs, the guards were as deadly as any foot soldiers in the region. The one drawback to their effectiveness came from their placement. Because the King mandated privacy for himself and his guests, the sentry posts were designed to keep undesirables out and not to maintain vigil on the interior of the park.

On the night of the feast, a million stars dotted the sky. Their combined light created pale shadows in the park. Along the walkways, between the trees, trellises, grape arbors, and flower beds shapes were simply lighter versions of the same background. For predators and eyes trained to identify movement, the phase of the night held few secrets. Yet at moonrise, the brighter illumination would generate contrast. Dark recesses standing apart from solid objects produced deep shadows appropriate for hiding assassins.

***

Inside the banquet hall, a servant filled a glass. He crossed in front of adjacent couches to the next table. While the servant filled a glass there, Hasdrubal Gisco lifted his. He took a sip, beamed a smile in the direction of the King, and saluted him. By deliberately excluding the occupant on the neighboring couch, he demonstrated his dislike for Cornelius.

"King Syphax, you are to be congratulated on your choice of wines," Hasdrubal Gisco purred.

"You should appreciate them," Syphax told him. "They're from Carthage."

"Aha, no wonder it's so refreshing," the Carthaginian acknowledged, "it's a taste of home."

"Have you been away long?" Syphax inquired.

"Six long months," the Carthaginian answered.

"And you, General Scipio," Syphax questioned, "how long have you been away from home?"

Cornelius took a sip from the glass and made a face.

"My preference is for a full-bodied red. This wine, while tasty, is very sweet," Cornelius observed. "As far as home, it's been three years since I've seen my wife and children. But there were matters in Iberia that required my attention."

Gisco flinched at the meaning of the remark. He'd enjoyed the wine during dinner, and the distance from the Roman. But afterwards, out of some sick sense of humiliation, King Syphax had placed the General from Carthage and the General from Rome on adjoining couches. For Gisco, the wine had gone from a source of enjoyment to a way of drowning his discomfort.

"At least we aren't sharing a table," Gisco thought.

"What was that Hasdrubal?" Syphax inquired.

Realizing he'd spoken out loud, Gisco tried but his tongue refused to form a lie. Then the first thing that came to mind, came out, "Why do you Romans care about Iberia?"

***

Cornelius rested the glass on the table, stretched his neck, and gazed at the ceiling.

"Why do we Romans care about Iberia?" he repeated. "Let me start with the obvious. Twelve years ago, your Hannibal Barca crossed the Alps and invaded our northern territories. He brought spearmen, cavalry, and livestock from Iberia. At the Trebbia River, his light and heavy horsemen routed our Legion cavalry and almost captured a Consul of Rome."

"I've never heard that," Gisco admitted. "All we were told was the Legion riders fled in fear."

"We did not flee in fear," Cornelius insisted. "It was an orderly retreat."

"You sound as if you were there," Syphax pointed out.

"I was in the battle," Cornelius said.

"What I should have asked earlier, General Scipio," the King of Western Numidia proposed, "how long have you been at war?"

"Almost half my life," Cornelius answered. "But we were talking about Iberia, not my chosen profession. Iberia, like my Roman Republic, represents opportunity."

"In that vein, Scipio, Carthage represents opportunity," Gisco challenged, "as well as east and west Numidia, and the Greek states."

"That General is where you're wrong," countered Cornelius. "My test for an opportunity is what countries will flock to your banner, fight alongside of you, and accept payment in promises."

"That could be said of any country," King Syphax insisted.

"Hannibal Barca is in my Republic commanding mercenaries from other regions," Cornelius proclaimed. "And in Iberia, I gathered fighters from local tribes as well as from Greece, Numidia, and Macedon. And why did they come? For payment in promises because Iberia is an opportunity for taking land and building settlements. Carthage and Numidia aren't. If I took my Legions to Carthage, few if any foreign units would join me."

"Because Carthage is strong," Gisco boasted. "And we always find a way to win."

A moment after the statement, Sidia stepped close to the couch and touched Cornelius' shoulder. Silent communications passed between them.

"Optio Decimia. We're going to be awhile," Cornelius told his bodyguard. "Go stretch your legs."

"Yes, sir," Sidia confirmed before marching to the exit.

"Carthage is like an island. A wealthy, well defended island, but one just the same," Cornelius described. "After picking through the bones of the city, there's not enough land to settle nor metals to dig up to pay off mercenaries."

"That's an insult," Gisco protested. "It's like saying my wife is ugly."

"Is she?" Cornelius asked. Gisco flexed as if to come at Cornelius. But after a moment, he settled back, and smirked. Cornelius offered. "It's a good thing you remained on the couch. Or we'd have had a replay of the battle at Ilipa."

"Generals please," King Syphax urged, "we're here for a social evening. Not a knife fight. Let's talk of other, less arousing, subjects."

***

In the park, Sidia drifted down a side path. While inhaling the fragrance of the vegetation and enjoying the fresh night air, he stretched his back and swung his arms. A little ways down the garden path, he reached under his chest armor and opened the left side buckles. As he turned around to head back to the banquet, he dropped his helmet and the armor on the side of the path. On the next step, the armored skirt and his under tunic fell to the dirt. Yawning loudly enough to be heard down the center of the garden, he strolled towards the door to the King's hall. But the Legion bodyguard never reached the threshold. Somewhere between the edge of the park and the doorway, Sidia Decimia vanished.

***

The grape arbor over the central walkway offered good concealment. Between the climbing vines on the tall structure, the narrowing of the path as it passed under the trellis, and the deep shadows, the two assassins felt confident of a quick kill.

In robes with hoods to break up their silhouettes, the pair stood in the shadows next to a wall of grapes. Their unsheathed sicas held at their sides. To complete their assignment, they required only the Latian victim and his bodyguard.

A twig snapped and both killers braced while looking around. When nothing followed the sound, they relaxed. Then, a thud on the other side of them caused tension to grip their bodies. But no other noises followed, and their muscles loosened. A twig snapped farther away and one of the killers leaned forward. Either he was attempting to find movement in the dark or to hear better. In either case he didn't catch sight or sound of a potential foe.

But while the killer didn't, Sidia did. And two heartbeats later, a man-beast rushed through the park. As primitive as a mountain cat and bearing the marks of the Goddess Mefitis, the War Chief slashed the throat of one and hammered the other to the ground.

"The Hirpini people have hunted in mountain forests for a thousand years," he whispered to the dazed assassin. "The rustling of trees and the crunching of leaves are but ways to track our prey."

Reaching down with both hands, he twisted the killer's neck. Not until the head faced the wrong way and the bones in the neck snapped, did the War Chief release the dead man's head.

From around the garden, footsteps disturbed dirt as they converged on the grape arbor. Sidia sheathed his Legion dagger and picked up one of the long-curved knives.

"Good weapon," he acknowledged before fading back among the trees and the trellises.

End of sample from book #7 in *A Legion Archer* series *From Dawn to Death*

A Note from J. Clifton Slater

Congratulations on finishing *Unlawful Kingdom*. Together, we've journeyed into the 2nd Punic War through 6 books. The welding of an historical figure, Cornelius Scipio, and a fictional character, Jace Kasia, has been a challenge and an honor. Your support of my storytelling gave me the confidence to continue when the research got too deep and the tale too convoluted. Thank you for reading the books.

Now, let's separate fact from fiction with notes on history.

The Passion of Cornelius

It's recorded by some writers that Cornelius Scipio had a reputation for taking lovers. But seeing as he had as many enemies as friends, I wondered if maybe the reports were erroneous. For instance, when Cornelius seized New Carthage, modern day Cartagena in Spain, two events took place.

Among the Carthaginian hostages he freed was the wife of Mandonius and the daughters of Indibilis. They were the two war chiefs who took part in the battle where his father died. If he had trouble with women, you'd expect him to have abused the hostages.

At the same time, a beautiful bride and her bridal party were brought to Cornelius. And seeing as her betrothed was a Prince of the Celtiberi, the tribe that deserted his uncle's Legions, he had good reason to mistreat her. Yet, as history reported, he treated her well and even returned the ransom as a bridal gift.

Hopefully, you enjoyed the stories of the hostages caught up in the New Carthage situation. For me, it was fun to write the scenes about Cornelius Scipio and the women.

Algerri, Spain

The Ilergetes Tribe were an Iberian people who dwelled in the plains area of Lleida along the banks of the river Segre. From foothills in the north, their lands extended south to where the Segre and Cinca rivers joined the Ebro river.

For the story, I needed a likely location for a fortified city or a fort. After scouring the Ilergetes region, I settled on the town of Algerri, Spain. On the hills above Algerri are the ruins of a fort, the Castell d'Algerri. Also in the hills around the ancient fortifications are three locations marked Els Trullets - basically holes carved in the rocks, some with brick borders at the openings. And here my skills as a researcher failed me. I couldn't uncover any information on what Els Trullets were or who built and occupied Castell d'Algerri. If you have any knowledge about the history of Algerri or the surrounding area, please email me.

Using the Ilergetes Tribe

The Ilergetes Tribe famously had dealings with Cornelius Scipio, and before him, with his father and uncle. The history between them started not with the battle that killed Publius Scipio, but a few years earlier when Indibilis was captured by the Roman governor and freed after negotiations. The personal interactions continued when Cornelius discovered, among the hostages in New Carthage, Mandonius' wife, and the daughters of Indibilis.

Greek Historian Polybius wrote, "The poverty of some regions, as well as the reigning oligarchy of their populations, drove them (Iberian men) to seek resources in richer areas, both by mercenary work and banditry, which generated a convulsed national environment where fighting was the main way of living. Hispanic indigenous are described as men who loved war, who preferred death before capitulation, and who professed a strong loyalty to whomever they perceived as their war leaders."

We know that it wasn't until years after Cornelius Scipio that Rome managed to pacify the tribes in the Iberian peninsula. For this book, I focused on the Ilergetes Tribe. But there were other tribes just as desperate and unafraid to wage war with their neighbors, with Carthage, and against the Republic Legions stationed in Iberia.

Women in Ancient Iberia

Typically, I don't have a lot of women in my novels. Mostly because the Legions didn't enlist women and my books are centered around Roman military history. However, when dealing with Iberia, my research hinted at female warriors, at least to defend the homestead. Considering the poverty and unemployment that comes from a society of aristocrats, it makes sense for women to take up arms to defend their homes from marauders. And possibly to take part in battles. Although, I didn't uncover any warrior women, as has been recorded in ancient Britain.

There are hints that point to strong women in ancient Iberia. In *The Image of Women in Ancient Iberian Culture* (6th - 1st Century B.C.), Archaeology Gender Europe (dot)

Org described the necropolis at Baza, Spain. It appears the entire ancient cemetery was centered around the tomb of a young woman who was buried with armor among other earthly items. From the same Iberian period, archaeology finds pointed to cults of women. Considering most ancient cults or sects were for males, I can only guess that women held a high place in the society of ancient Iberia. And of course, I had to use a secret cult of women in the story.

To reinforce the conclusion that women were valued in ancient Iberia, when Cornelius Scipio captured New Carthage, he discovered a number of women hostages from different Iberian Tribes. In order to be valuable as hostages, the women would need to be important to their tribes and the tribal leaders. From Cornelius' negotiations and actions, we saw the benefits for him and his Iberian Legions when he returned the women.

Albarracín, Spain

Albarracín, Spain, while not an ancient fortress, is located beyond what was Oretani Tribe's territory. And, a couple of miles inside the Celtiberi land of antiquity. Meaning, Celtiberi spearmen would have been stationed there to guard the mountain route against invaders.

The Historian Polybius doesn't say where the wedding between the beautiful former hostage and Allucius, the Celtiberi Prince, took place. Only that Cornelius freed the bride. And next gave the ransom, her father had paid for her freedom, to the bride and groom as a wedding present. In return for his generosity and fair treatment of the bride, Allucius gifted Cornelius 1,500 Celtiberi cavalrymen for the Iberian Legions.

To help the story, I choose the mountain village of Albarracín as the sight for the nuptials. Although the story never made it into the town. As with all historical fiction writers, we find cool places but can't always fit them into the story. If you have a chance, look up Albarracín, Spain on earth maps. The town is spectacular. Surrounded by red limestone walls and stone battlements, with picturesque streets and shops, I really wanted to use the location for the wedding.

Numbering Within a Legion

The Republic didn't number their Legions until after the Marian reforms in 107 B.C. Before then, they took the name of their General and he distinguished each of his 2 legions by placing a specific God or animal on the Legion's standard. This also changed during the reform when Marian declared the eagle would represent every Legion. While the Legions during the 2nd Punic War weren't numbered within a Legion, they did have a numbering system. But like the ancient quinquereme warships, the actual maneuvering of the maniples, or the corvus boarding ramp, the system and designs were lost to antiquity.

I've explained my understanding of the Roman Legion maniple formation before. I think in a *Clay Warrior Stories* book. If you have read this already, I apologize.

Greek historian Polybius (200 B.C. - 117 B.C.), "The order of battle used by the Roman army (Legion) is very difficult to break through - since it allows every man to fight both individually and collectively. The effect is to offer a formation that can present a front in any direction. The maniples that are nearest to the point where danger threatens can wheel (pivot) in order to meet the threat."

Each Legion at its core had three maniples, or three triple lines of combat infantrymen. The first maniple was composed of unbloodied Legionaries. Next, the second contained the experienced Legionaries, and the third maniple was reserved for veterans. Up through the First Punic War, the Legionaries brought their own armor and weapons. This was reflected in the composition of the maniples. By the 2nd Punic War, with the addition of landless recruits, the requirement was relaxed but not official until the Marian reforms.

Now we get into my research and understanding. Often when I don't have facts or a written description, such as Polybius' dissertation on the warfighting benefits of the maniple, I reverse engineer the topic.

The 1st Century of a Legion was oversized with 120 veterans. They formed the core of a Roman General and his staff's guards. This we know from records. Beyond that, no one thought to write down what number the rest of the maniples used. To write historical adventure, I needed a numbering system to keep track of a Century's location in a combat line, which maniple, and their level of experience. Here are the numbers of the 36 Centuries of Legionaries in a Legion, and their location in a battle formation.

First Maniple, inexperienced Legionaries: left side Centuries #2 thru #7, right side Centuries #8 thru #13.

Second Maniple, experienced Legionaries: left side #14–#19, right side #20-#25.

Third Maniple, veteran Legionaries: left side #26-#31, right side #32-#37.

Because none of the other units in a Legion were as regimented, I don't have specific numbers for any units beyond the heavy infantry. The number of Centuries of Velites (light infantry & skirmishers), archers, bolt thrower crews, and cavalry changed with each campaign. But the heavy infantry was consistent. Each Century had 80 Legionaries, a Centurion, an Optio, and a Tesserarius.

In my books, I used this convention to maintain order during battles and to select Centuries for assignments. Just as I used the Twenty-fifth Century to guard the bridal wagon in *Unlawful Kingdom*. I trust, you can see the reasoning behind my system of numbering within a Legion.

Lleida on the Segre River

We don't know the details of the release of Indibilis' daughters or the wife of Mandonius. However, one of the results of returning the hostages can be inferred from a report by Livy. A few years after the return of the hostages, there were rumors that Cornelius Scipio had taken ill and died. Upon hearing the news, Indibilis and Mandonius revolted against Roman authority. Cornelius recovered, returned to Iberia, and defeated the brothers in battle.

Surprisingly, they had honored the agreement while Cornelius Scipio lived. But promptly broke the treaty when they thought they were beyond the reach of the General. We can only surmise that Cornelius demonstrated his vengeance as a warning to the brothers before he allowed the hostages to go free. I chose Lleida on the Segre River as the site where Cornelius possibly showed Indibilis and Mandonius the consequences of breaking a treaty with him. And, as you can tell, I changed the timing of the rumor about Cornelius' health for *Unlawful Kingdom*.

Aemilia Tertia Paullus

Cornelius Scipio's wife, Aemilia Tertia, was the daughter of Consul Lucius Aemilius Paullus, who died at the Battle of Cannae. Historian Polybius noted Aemilia enjoyed displaying her wealth and using her connections. These ostentatious displays of wealth reflected high levels of status among the female members of the elite class in the middle Roman Republic. Aemilia was known to travel with a large entourage when she attended events, and she traveled in a gold and silver adorned carriage.

Being a competent political wife, Aemilia covered for Cornelius in instances of scandal and maintained the family's status by organizing prestigious marriages and holding public gatherings. Aemilia and Cornelius had four children, two sons and two daughters. Neither son followed in their father or grandfather's footsteps as a General of the Republic.

The Myth of an Eagle's Scream

For such a big bird of prey, the majestic eagle emits a surprisingly weak-sounding call. Typically described as a series of high-pitched whistling or piping noises. The piercing screech we associate with the eagle in films is actually the call of a red-tailed hawk. Years ago, filmmakers created the myth of an eagle's scream by inserting the hawk's call for effect.

Baecula (Santo Tomé, Spain)

With Hasdrubal Gisco at Ilipa, and Mango Barca camped at Carmona, just north of Seville, Cornelius feared an attack on his rear if he hesitated. Hurriedly, Cornelius ordered an attack on Hasdrubal Barca's army at Baecula. He started the assault at the center of the plateau on a lower tier. Cornelius made it look like a skirmish by using his light infantrymen against Iberian spearmen placed there. During the fighting, Cornelius Scipio on one side, and Gaius Laelius on the other, snuck their heavy infantry into positions to advance uphill on the flanks. And, as described in the book, he won the battle.

Cornelius, however, failed to totally defeat Hasdrubal's army. During the rout, his forces stopped and plundered Hasdrubal Barca's abandoned camp. This allowed two thirds of the enemy to escape. As happened often, the Senate of Rome blamed Cornelius Scipio for allowing Hasdrubal and his army to escape from Baecula.

History reported that Hasdrubal Barca's army crossed the Pyrenees, and later the Alps. In Italy, just south of San Marino on the Metauro River, Marcus Livius and Gaius Claudius Nero defeated the Carthaginian General. Hasdrubal was beheaded and his head carried in a sack to Hannibal's camp. To show the victory of the Romans over Hannibal's brother, the head was thrown over the wall. The delivery of the head seemed appropriate considering the treatment of Latin prisoners by Hannibal after earlier battles.

The Battle of Carmona

Historically, Cornelius faced a dilemma. Hanno and Mago Barca set up camp on the heights of Carmona while Hasdrubal Gisco camped not far away. No town was given for the second camp, so I used Fuentes de Andalucía. Fearing a fight on two fronts, Cornelius sent Junius Silanus to attack Carmona. Why he chose the more heavily fortified location for his second in command isn't known. After the Legions ran off Mago and captured Hanno, Cornelius directed the attack on Hasdrubal Gisco's camp. In an inconclusive battle, Gisco separated his army and sent them to cities with defensive walls around the area. Unable to lay siege at multiple locations, Cornelius withdrew his Legions.

Rhodian Admiral Polemocles

In 220 B.C., two powerful cities had forced every city on Crete to swear allegiance to them. But, the Spartan colony of Lyttos refused. To aid in bringing Lyttos into the alliance, the cities enlisted Polemocles, an Admiral from the Island of Rhodes. He arrived with six ships and began visiting the cities on Crete.

On a tour of Eleutherna, the Admiral was accused of assassinating a citizen named Timarchus. I positioned the Kasia farm near Eleutherna and made Timarchus the Magistrate. His death became part of an emotional episode for Jace.

We began *Unlawful Kingdom* in 209 B.C. and closed it out in late 207 B.C. Here's hoping you enjoyed the story and the notes.

***

I appreciate emails and reading your comments. If you enjoyed *Unlawful Kingdom*, consider leaving a written review on Amazon or Goodreads. Every review helps other readers find the stories.

If you have comments e-mail me.

E-mail: GalacticCouncilRealm@gmail.com

To get the latest information about my books, visit my website. There you can sign up for my monthly author report and read blogs about ancient history.

Website: www.JCliftonSlater.com

Facebook: Tales from Ancient Rome

I am J. Clifton Slater and I write historical military adventures.

Other books by J. Clifton Slater:

Historical Adventure of the 2nd Punic War
A Legion Archer series
#1 Journey from Exile
#2 Pity the Rebellious
#3 Heritage of Threat
#4 A Legion Archer
#5 Authority of Rome
#6 Unlawful Kingdom
#7 From Dawn to Death (Next in series)

Historical Adventure of the 1st Punic War
Clay Warrior Stories series
#1 Clay Legionary
#2 Spilled Blood
#3 Bloody Water
#4 Reluctant Siege
#5 Brutal Diplomacy
#6 Fortune Reigns
#7 Fatal Obligation
#8 Infinite Courage
#9 Deceptive Valor
#10 Neptune's Fury
#11 Unjust Sacrifice
#12 Muted Implications
#13 Death Caller
#14 Rome's Tribune
#15 Deranged Sovereignty
#16 Uncertain Honor
#17 Tribune's Oath
#18 Savage Birthright
#19 Abject Authority

Printed in Great Britain
by Amazon